Superior Moon

Walker James

Chapter One

Footsteps crunched in the leaves outside her tent. Raccoon, maybe, or more likely a mouse. Everything gains a magnitude of size in the woods at night: chipmunks sound like bears, possums like sasquatch.

The young woman lay still, listening to the forest. On her hike in alone during daylight it had been quiet, but now owls called to their prey in the darkness, saying run, simply run and it will be over soon. Porcupines grunted and screamed during careful copulation. Twice she heard deer follow the streambed past her camp. One had to be a buck—it snorted a challenge at her tent when the nylon billowed in a gust of wind. She shifted position on the thin foam pad. Her shoulders ached from carrying the backpack.

Northern Michigan University had been her first choice because it lay in one of the few large wilderness areas left in the East—the Upper Peninsula, known to locals as the U.P. The area also held a deep trove of folklore for her graduate studies, populated by the ghosts of cultures that had washed over its shores through the centuries seeking copper, fur, timber, iron. It was a place where humans felt small, and they told stories to push back the shadows.

She hung one foot outside the sleeping bag to feel the chill of the autumn night. One nagging quandary from the real world had stuck in her head: that undergrad she'd allowed to seduce her at the intersection of cheap wine and good prose. If only he wasn't her student. Teaching a couple sections of English Comp paid the graduate stipend she needed until her thesis was complete. If only he was a good student . . . although in place of brains or maturity he did have other redeeming qualities like manual dexterity and a truly artistic attention to detail. And muscles. She slipped one finger between her thighs, falling into that tiny circular motion as she pictured the rhythm of his broad shoulders above her. Definitely needed to leave him alone, at least until next semester when he'd be out of her class and back to being another lovely part of the student body. Like so many of the others he didn't believe in the intrinsic power of what she taught, the immediacy of sharing a story with another soul. Fairy tales were not all pleasant, and somewhere back in time at the birth of the narrative there lurked a bloody and dangerous truth waiting to be uncovered.

Pounding hooves broke her reverie. The deer that had earlier walked downstream spooked now, wheeling and thrashing through her camp. She sat up and listened, wondering if a bear had set off their flight. Black bears were nocturnal and shy, closer to over-sized raccoons than fearsome predators. In years spent hiking she had seen exactly one, and only his furry butt disappearing over a hill at top speed.

She felt for her digital camera in the pocket of her pack, then found the zipper on the tent. The animal sounds of the night had ceased. Something walked out there that struck fear into the small and tasty creatures. The zipper buzzed under her fingertips as she slowly split the door open far enough to stick her head out. October clouds slid across the face of the enormous low moon. Her eyes tried to make sense of the shadows under the trees. She slipped out the door and stood, the wind touching her bare skin, dry pine needles pricking her feet. The girl faced toward the lake, shivering in the chill, and held the camera out in front of her like a talisman. Clouds fell away to reveal one particular shadow, blacker than the night and hunkered in muscular rounds reminiscent of her lover, crouched beneath the high branch where she'd hung her bag of food.

"Smile, Mr. Bear."

She triggered the camera.

Chapter Two

The landmass is a strange empty peninsula three hundred miles long, ancient rock shot through with veins of metal. It is the head of a wolf in profile, a predator's skull looking due east as if deciding whether to take a bite out of Ontario. Water cages the beast, vicious gray Lake Superior above the ears and muzzle, the calmer silver of Lake Michigan below the lean throat. The Upper Peninsula seen from high above.

Dive through the thin night air toward the wolf's eye. The multitudinous forests are black, almost unbroken darkness hiding the swamps, the arterial rivers. Pinpricks of light mark towns huddled along spindly roads. The area above the eye glows brighter, a crescent of electricity marking one small city perched on the inland sea that is Superior. The luminescence resolves into individual lights: houses, the docks, the single lit runway of the airport. Close enough to see trucks crawling the roads, separate trees, finally the sign at the southern edge of a bridge marking this as Marquette, population 20,401. Beyond it, a full parking lot and the neon haze of beer signs.

Inside, the Walleye Tavern has steel implements nailed to the walls among the deer heads: single-handled crosscut saws nine feet long for sawing blocks of ice from frozen lakes, axes of all shapes, even the thin curved picks that taxidermists used to scramble and pluck the brains from trophy skulls. The crowd in the Walleye used an older, liquid method of pruning gray matter, and for the most part they seemed to be enjoying it. They moved in the easy flow of people who'd known each other most of their lives: bumping elbows, using first names, nicknames, the wrong name misheard twenty years ago that was adopted out of politeness, asking after the health of favorite dogs, horses, snowmobiles and spouses.

At least half the crowd had been delivered by the retired doctor at the bar nursing a ginger and rye. He attempted to ignore both the taut shapeliness of the young ladies he had brought into the world and the stuffed beaver on the stool next to him, the constant companion and drinking buddy of the dentist. In a larger city the dentist's eccentricities might have cost him business, but in the north woods it was hard to find one of any stripe. Beside the scarcity there was the fact that the dentist had a gentle touch. He also let the beaver set his prices and the animal couldn't count very high. For seventeen-dollar cleanings, the people of Marquette were willing to let more than a few things go unremarked upon.

Two people didn't fit into the ebb and tide of the locals.

The man at the bar was broad-shouldered, square-jawed. He wore a blazer over a tailored polo shirt, and unlike most looked as though he may have played the game. Blue eyes over a cruel mouth, immaculate dirty-blonde hair with a few steel streaks that looked placed by an artist. The women watched him out of the corners of their eyes. The doctor sighed and turned back to the beaver.

The other outsider sat alone in a booth reading a paperback, his feet up on the bench opposite. He was lithe, with dark hair and skin, a smooth forehead and high cheekbones that might be Ojibwa, but if he turned his head at the right angle it suddenly seemed unlikely. The nose. Something about the nose was too long. It made him seem like he was eternally leaning forward a few degrees. The remains of a perch dinner lay on the plate he'd shoved away. A teenage waitress stopped at his elbow and rested her tray on the edge of the table, which also sat level with the hem of her denim skirt. She bobbed her head as she asked him a question. He flipped the book over to show the cover. Nabokov. *Lolita*. She pinked before fleeing.

The crack of a punch brought conversation to a halt. The handsome stranger at the bar snatched his hand from beneath the skirt of the angry petite blonde who'd slugged him. He turned away as she wound up again, only to get a hook to the jaw from her carbon copy to his right. Angry twins. He jerked to his feet, arms raised to protect his face. The first girl gave him a roundhouse knee to the ribs. As he twisted in pain he caught hold of her pony tail to yank her head back. A hand locked onto his wrist and applied pressure in the bundle of nerves below the palm.

"Let go," the Nabokov fan said. He stood between the man and the girl whose hair he still clutched.

"Eat shit," the handsome one got out through gritted teeth. The fingers cutting into his wrist dug deeper, found a tendon that seemed to vibrate and bore down causing pain like a knife.

"Allow me to rephrase the request. Let go of the nineteen year old girl you just groped in front of two dozen witnesses."

The only movement in the place was the bartender slowly sliding the girls' drinks into the sink.

"I don't know what you do for a living," the dark man continued calmly, as if he wasn't killing nerves with his hold, "but being on the sex offender registry doesn't advance many careers. Not a great idea in divorce proceedings either."

They both let go, her hair first then his wrist.

4

Polo guy slid off his expensive blazer and squared his shoulders. The dark man was tall, a hair under six feet, but Polo still had a few inches on him.

"How about if I make one less witness?"

The smaller man showed his teeth in something that wasn't quite a smile. "Let's start over," he said. "I'm Alain—"

"You a fucking Indian?"

"No one's really sure," Alain said. He considered his opponent. "Is this one of those scenes where you keep needling until we fight?"

"What?" Polo was off his prepared script.

"Big guy versus the little guy, lots of talk and then a brawl. You've seen it in the movies a hundred times, right?" Alain asked.

"Movies?" Polo's train of thought seemed as though it had not completed final boarding.

"Who wins? In the movies, who always wins those fights? Is it the big guy?" Alain unfolded a few bills and tented them on the bar. "I don't think it is. So maybe this is a sign that it's time for both of us to leave. No winners, no losers—"

"Pussy," Polo said.

"Of course," Alain continued as if the man had not interrupted, "there is one more solid indicator that the night is over for you."

"What's that?"

"Your jacket is on fire."

Alain strolled out into the gravel parking lot with adrenaline singing in his blood, glad to gain the high without the consequences of a fight. The asshole made a lot of noise after the sisters had helped his blazer live up to its name, but the real bluster had gone out of him like a leaky balloon.

Alain unlocked his Ford F-150 pick-up, climbed in, powered the windows down and sat for a moment, enjoying the rush and the night. October felt perfect for driving with the windows open: the moon full and powerful, the wind off Lake Superior like an animal. The leaves had done their one brilliant-colored trick but fewer than half had fallen. The trees trembled and swayed in the grip of the breeze. Alain felt the desire, too, to run, to hunt. Autumn stirred him with a wonderful unease.

The roar of a cannon cut the night.

Alain cocked his head to listen. Echoes of the blast rolled off the dunes to the west, a sharp crack even on the rebound. That meant a rifle, the loudest he'd ever heard.

Another shot rang out. The percussive thunder rolled down the highway. Wherever it came from, that barrel aimed in this general direction. Detective Alain Logan of the Michigan State Police cranked the truck to life and tore out of the parking lot heading south, toward the gunfire.

He clawed his handheld radio from the dash mount.

"Base, 3-17," he said, running the speedometer up to seventy-five.

"3-17, this is Base," dispatch came back.

"Shots fired on Highway 28, south of the Walleye," Alain said. He added the number off a mile marker as it cut past the headlights and dropped his radio onto the seat. Dispatch put out the general call for assistance. Responses trickled in as he sped down the road. The one local unit was tied up in a domestic dispute involving a hammer; they couldn't disengage. A trooper on patrol called in with a signal so broken and full of static he must be at least forty miles away. A sheriff's deputy was rolling up 28 from farther south, perfect, but twenty minutes out. Alain was on his own for now.

He drummed his fingers on the wheel. Rifle shots in the UP weren't out of the norm. Every home had a deer rifle, but this didn't sound like any normal weapon and that season didn't start for three weeks. He let off the gas, allowed the truck to slow to fifty and then flipped off the headlights. The world inverted: the white tunnel of the road lined with neatly spaced reflectors became a dull trail crowded by leaning shadows. Nailing a deer even at this speed would ruin his night, not to mention the deer's. The full moon reflecting off pavement gave him enough light to stay on the road. His heart pounded. He took a deep breath and tried to relax, allowed his peripheral vision to sharpen. He'd learned to navigate the forest this way, using his oblique sight.

Taillights came into view, a vehicle skewed across the centerline. A beam of light from one of those obscenely powerful handheld spotlights wagged through the ditch and up into the trees. It hung in the air, a solid white bar connecting the vehicle to the forest, to the whitetail deer pinned by the light. Alain knew what came next. He still jumped at the blast when a tongue of flame erupted from the vehicle.

The buck folded in half. It collapsed before the gunshot echoed off the hillside. Good-sized deer taking a direct hit in the heart and lungs usually had the strength for one last leap, but this weapon dropped the animal like cutting the strings on a marionette. The spotlight went out. Two figures climbed from the vehicle. They ran to the carcass.

He stopped his truck fifty yards from the scene, idling quietly. If he got any closer he might be spotted, although between the wind and their whooping and shouting they might not notice a full cavalry charge. He radioed in an update. The deputy was hauling ass but still ten minutes out—too long. The poachers would be loaded and gone before reinforcements arrived.

Alain allowed the truck to roll forward at an idle. He felt along the dash and located the switches for his lights and siren. It was his personal truck, but he'd mounted a small red and blue flasher on the dash, a siren behind the grill and wig-wags: devices that flashed the headlights in a pattern of high-low, left-right. He kept his eyes on the scene, trying to discern if another man had remained in the truck, and it would be fair to say that the exact location of that monster rifle was also on his mind. Every pine branch hung sharply outlined by moonlight. The smell of cordite filled in the air.

Two figures struggled out of the woods dragging the deer carcass behind them. They reached the rear of the vehicle and were lit by the red of their taillights. They would have their hands full while lifting the deer. He waited until the figures bent and hoisted before hitting every switch on the dash.

The lights and siren exploded to life, destroying his night vision and probably deafening his quarry, both hefty men, soft-looking and pale, clad in expensive shooting clothes of leather and, God help them, tweed. They froze with blank expressions, the animal held at waist height. They looked just like deer caught in the headlights. The cop and the poachers stared at each other for a bare second in the strobes of red, white and blue. Alain could see the fist-sized crater in the deer's shoulder where it had been shot. He expected them to drop it.

The two men threw the deer into the bed of their expensive four-by-four truck and ran for the cab, one grabbing his lower back as he crabbed along. The other one, the fatter one, flipped Alain off. The Chevy rocketed up the highway, then swerved off the highway to a side road heading away from the shore.

Alain felt for his radio handset in the dark. The sheriff's deputy should be on the scene any minute. He'd only worked this territory for six months but drove the back roads every day trying to memorize them. The driver of the Chevy took turns at random, climbing higher into the hills. They fell onto a long straightaway, and the poacher gunned his truck up to seventy. The ride smoothed out as the tires began to float over the washboard ridges in the dirt. Alain knew something the driver of the Chevy didn't: this straight stretch of road ended in a sharp blind turn. Brake lights burned in the night. The poacher's truck slid wide, tail in the pines on one side of the road, headlights painting crazy beams on the opposite side.

Alain hurled his truck into the turn. His rear wheels broke loose on the gravel and he slid it through, the palm of one hand balanced on the center of the wheel, firm pressure on the gas until the truck swung back in line. The Chevy didn't make it. The front wheels lost their grip, and the shiny new four-by-four shuddered once before being snatched by the trees. It cartwheeled through the ditch, crushing small jack pines and brush before coming to rest with the wheels toward the night sky. The carcass of the deer catapulted clear of the wreck, a broken shape arcing through Alain's strobing lights and into the night.

Alain braked to a stop. He radioed for rescue, slid out of his truck. In one motion he drew his pistol and a small flashlight as he ran toward the wreck. Two men rolled and groaned on what had been the ceiling of the truck. Cans of beer geysered their contents over both of them.

He holstered his pistol, reached into the wreck and slid out the gun they'd used to shoot the deer. Alain didn't mind the loss of the animal, although from the expensive truck and their hunting clothes they weren't poaching to put food on the table. The U.P. had a few million whitetails to spare, outnumbering the human population a half dozen to one. Firing a weapon from a paved road, however, was a special edition of stupid. The gun he pulled out of the truck looked like a thick-bodied shotgun. Cartridges fat as cigars lay scattered on the ground.

The driver rolled over and stared into Alain's light. He blinked and shaded his eyes.

"I've sure learned my lesson, orifice," he got out before breaking into giggles. His partner joined him, alternately snorting with laughter and moaning in pain. Judging by the beer can-sized ring imprinted deeply into the lower half of his face, he'd been swigging when he'd hit the dashboard.

Alain removed them from the wreck, gave them a quick pat-down for weapons and wounds, and cuffed them face-down on the ground before they regained their belligerence. It came back soon enough, and they bellowed threats about lawyers and various political connections into the duff of the forest floor until long after the volunteer firemen rolled up.

He radioed for a tow truck and a local officer to supervise the scene, snapped a few photos of the wreck with the digital camera from his glove box, then began looking for the deer. Alain swept the woods with his flashlight, expecting to find it crumpled within a few feet. Nothing. He ducked into the underbrush and promptly took the end of a branch in the eye. He retrieved shooting glasses from his truck, swearing, and tried again. The deer couldn't have walked off; the carcass he'd seen looked like it had been shot with a bazooka.

Headlight beams filtered through the trees, casting jagged shadows as he searched.

"Logan?" a voice called from the wreck site, "What're you doing out there?"

"Getting in touch with my manhood," he called back.

"That's a short task," Leon Gilhall said as he emerged from the brush. He was a Marquette county sheriff's deputy, long and bony, with a penchant for shadow-boxing that most people found amusing. He looked like a pissed-off windmill, but no one laughed after he landed a punch. Alain had only sparred with him once without headgear, and his ears had rung for three days.

"My evidence walked away." Alain explained the jacklighting and the rollover crash.

"Can't have gone far," Leon answered. "Did it get stuck up in a tree?"

They circled like trailing dogs off a scent, flashlights poking the night, but found no trace of the dead deer within a hundred foot circle of the wreck.

"I had no idea you state boys dealt in raising the dead. I'm impressed." Leon said as they walked back to the wreck, ducking branches along the way.

"We learn it in the academy," Alain said. "It's right after lunch and before the class on coping with hick deputies."

"What kind of grade did you get in lunch?" Leon asked. "Is that where they taught you how to prosecute poaching with no deer?"

9

Alain stopped at his truck to kill the lights. The clearing already shone bright from the collected vehicles and the full moon. He slid a notebook out of his jacket and began to jot details of the chase and arrest. The idiot twins would still go down on unlawful use of a firearm, reckless endangerment, speeding, resisting arrest and a few other things, but there would be no poaching case without the missing carcass. The local judge was a sportsman himself who had hunted these woods for fifty years. There was nothing he hated more than a poacher, and he had a tendency to revoke hunting licenses for a decade. Alain continued to write, composing his report in outline form. It looked to be a long night.

Chapter Three

Dirt under his hands and knees, not loose but earth packed by the weight of generations. The darkness pressed down on him, filled his eyes, ears, his lungs. Smells, too, powerful as physical contact: wet fur, milk, hints of carrion and an undertone of old blood. He wanted to plunge his hands into the dark, find the walls of this place and locate a way out. The growling froze him. It echoed thick and low off the walls of the . . . cave? Den? He could feel the vibrations in his chest. Some live thing was in here with him. Some angry animal. He clenched impotent fists and waited for the teeth in the dark.

The slam of waves on the beach woke Alain. Lake Superior had to be upset for him to hear it from his bedroom, almost a quarter-mile from the shore. October was a bad time to trust the water no matter the weather. When the breakers came in hard it formed a vicious undertow, not that many people swam in fifty-degree water even when it was calm.

He reached for the clock on the night stand without prying his eyes open. It wasn't there. No clock, no nightstand. His outstretched arm found only a hard level surface even with the bed, which, now that he swam closer to consciousness, also felt firmer than usual and cold to the touch. Alain opened his eyes to a steep drop-off of wooden steps. He lay curled at the top of the broad staircase in his house with no bedclothes, no clothes at all. He scrambled back from the edge on hands and knees.

A quick inventory told him nothing hurt, but his breath came short and sharp.

Shaking his skull from side to side, blinking to be sure he was awake, Alain attempted to play back the end of last night in his head. He'd gotten in at three after the chase with the poachers and remembered dropping into bed like a falling tree. The sheets had had a musky odor. He distinctly recalled thinking about changing them and deciding to wait until morning. No booze or meds. How had he made it out here? The hall clock read eleven a.m., almost five hours past the time he normally rose. The only thing he could grasp was a splinter of a dream where he'd been kneeling in darkness on a dirt floor.

Alain slowly pulled on yesterday's jeans and a sweatshirt before shuffling down the steep back servants' stairs to the kitchen. His house was what was known in the Upper Peninsula as a "lumber pile." One of the robber barons who'd scalped the U.P. of timber late in the nineteenth century had built it in a grandiose style that would have stuck out even in Chicago with the rest of the gilded breed: wedding cake eaves below a widow's walk, turrets and gables sprouting off at every angle. Among the shacks, cabins and mobile homes of the north woods it stood gray and sagging now after a hundred brutal winters with grand bones propping it up. The place needed work, but it still should have been far out of his price range. When he'd wandered into the county auction the day he'd been assigned to his new post no one else among the cluster of retirees and amateur real estate flippers had even tried to bid on it. They'd sat and silently watched him take it for back taxes and half the assessment. In the months since he'd found the time to bust exactly one hole in a damp and sagging wall at the base of the front stairs, but he'd uncovered pieces of the town's past in the attic: furniture, playbills for the opera house, stacks and stacks of an odd local newspaper from the late 1800s and he'd barely scratched the surface.

What he couldn't find in the kitchen was the scoop for the coffee grounds. He dumped too much into the pot. While the black mess brewed he shook the can to see if the scoop had simply sunk out of sight. It had to be in there somewhere. Alain had been losing a lot of things around the house and combined with his new sleepwalking trick it made him uneasy.

"Thirty-three," he gravely told his coffee mug, "and senility just around the corner."

A yellowed newspaper lay on the table, one of a handful he'd gathered to read during his latest trip to the time machine that was the attic. *The Palladium Superior* was quite a title for what seemed to be the early twentieth century equivalent of a supermarket tabloid.

Farmers in the area of the lower Peshekee River report incursions of the lutin are much worse than last season. These miniature hobgoblins take the best horses from the barn at night and ride them hard, leaving them lathered and worn for the morning's work. Skeptics are invited to view the tangled manes where tiny hands steered the poor pounding drays.

"Who bought this stuff back then?" Alain asked aloud.
The phone rang before he got a reply.
"Logan," he answered.

"Alain, out of bed so soon? I can imagine you staying there all day." There was a teasing note in Janet DeMott's voice. She was dark-haired and married, but not firmly.

"You're thinking about me in bed?" All the men at the small state police post in Marquette had a collective crush on their day dispatcher.

"I have a body for you," she said.

"Yes, you do," was his automatic reply, but the excitement he felt wasn't from her flirting. He sat forward in his chair and reached for a pen.

"Accident?" he asked.

The Upper Peninsula was by most measures a peaceful place. Drunks crashed their cars, ATVs and snowmobiles with regularity, usually into innocent pines. The murderous Great Lakes took more than their share of unwary boaters and swimmers, and overdoses and suicides spiked during the long winter, but actual homicides were rare. Enough empty space existed for everyone to get away from those who drove them to the edge.

Janet paused before answering.

"I don't know. Things are sort of excited out there. Bob Androtti called it in."

Alain knew Bob, a Department of Natural Resources state forest ranger. They'd worked a case trying to catch a poacher killing black bears. Bear paws and organs were worth a fortune in Asia. They'd had no luck finding the perpetrators, but the deaths had simply halted one day.

"Bob's as excitable as a fence post, Janet," he said.

"Well he's wired today," she answered.

She rattled off GPS coordinates and road names which he scrawled in a notebook. While she gave him a short background and promised to contact the coroner on duty, Alain pulled on a Gore-Tex jacket, grabbed his keys from the table and liberated his Sig-Sauer pistol from its hiding place in the grandfather clock that stood in the front hall.

"Alain," Janet said before he hung up.

"Something else?"

"It's a body. It'll wait for you. Try to keep your speed under ninety."

Only fifty miles of expressway exist in the entire U.P., and that lay far to the east of Marquette, closer to Sault Ste. Marie and the reservation where he'd grown up. Alain took his truck up the state highway northwest for thirty miles, paralleling the Lake Superior shoreline. Pines crowded the shoulder and the rhythmic pounding of the waves carried over their tops.

He blew past an RV. The highway, at least until he got far out of town, had the blend of poverty and wealth that's only found on the waterfront. Expensive cottages lined the lake side, if you could call a five thousand square foot house a "cottage," most owned by people from the Lower Peninsula or from Chicago who used them a few weekends a year. Across the pavement sat the weather-beaten homes of the locals: utilitarian boxes one third the size but full year-round.

North of the ghost town of Buckroe he followed a paved fork west away from the lake and untangled the web of paths using the GPS coordinates Janet had given him. The pavement ended miles short of the location. Dirt logging roads led him to a trailhead where he found a DNR truck, a sheriff's cruiser and a beat-to-hell little Subaru pulled to one side.

His GPS indicated that the site lay a bit over a mile away in a straight line. Alain tucked it into his shirt pocket, pulled his daypack from the back of the cab and followed the path under the pines.

Millions of years ago the Huron Mountains had stood high and jagged, teeth of crystalline rock that had been part of the earliest land mass in North America. Assaults from mile-thick glaciers had ground them down. Now they rolled like thousand-foot waves at the edge of Lake Superior.

Alain broke into a run. For a brief time he floated on the surface of the wilderness, leaping a small stream, reveling in the smells of the woods enveloping him: musky beaver scent from the streambed, the exhalation of the loam under his footfalls, twenty years of pine needles slowly returning to sand. The age of the land made it feel solid, immutable. No matter what happened here today it would remain unchanged in his lifetime. Alain had grown up outdoors, preferring to sleep in the woods behind his various uncles' shacks, cabins and trailers rather than inside them. In the woods he belonged. He had a dozen bolt-holes scattered throughout the reservation and state forest land that abutted their property, including a hollow tree that he could only use in three seasons because it housed a bear in winter. Reclining inside that den, breathing the old musk left behind by the cold weather tenant, Alain could feel his heartbeat slow. It wound down to an older rhythm. Solemn, quiet, dignified. Live trees swayed around his hole, but dead trees no longer compromise with the wind and his stood unmoved by its environment. The year he turned fourteen the old bear did not return to den in the dead tree, and Alain could no longer feel the rhythm in that place. He never went back to see if it still stood.

A glimpse of yellow through the trees brought him back, not birch leaves but a slice of crime scene tape.

Bob stood in a huddle with two deputies at the point where the trail entered a small clearing. His shoulders slumped forward, his head down.

"Took you long enough," Bob said as he stepped forward. He was in his sixties now. The lines around his eyes ran deeper than Alain remembered.

"What've you got?" Alain asked. He felt guilty about enjoying the hike.

"College girl. Just the one. She's . . . ah . . . it's bad." Bob's voice quavered, and his Adam's apple bobbed up and down as he swallowed.

"Who found her?" Alain asked.

"I did." Bob spoke almost too low to hear. "Got some kids on dirt bikes that tear up this section. Thought I'd come out and see if I could catch them at it. I saw the mess and then her."

Alain remembered that Bob himself was close to retirement but he had two college-age daughters. Twins, in fact, who could each throw a mean punch. Alain would not have mentioned seeing the girls the night before at the bar if he'd been staked to an anthill.

"How many months have you got to go?" Alain asked. He caught the eye of a deputy he vaguely knew over Bob's shoulder and gave him a curt nod.

"Seven," Bob said. "The girls graduate . . ." He trailed off.

The deputy stepped forward. His name was S . . . something.

"Deputy Saunders?" Alain guessed.

Saunders seemed pleased to be remembered.

"Why don't you and Officer Androtti start getting some notes down, go over it a few times. Up the hill a bit."

The deputy pulled the shaken forest ranger out of sight of the clearing. Alain stalked along the tape. The other deputy stood in the way, hands in pockets. His nametag read H. Burke.

"I'm Alain Logan, with the state," Alain said.

Burke looked young, maybe a recent hire. Short, with the thick frame of a weightlifter, he had a bristling haircut and wore wraparound shooting glasses despite the overcast sky. They couldn't quite conceal the nasty bruising that ran under his right eye.

"Burke." The young man rocked on his heels, ducked his head. Nervous.

"You all right, Deputy?" Alain asked.

"Harold," the boy said. He licked his lips. "This is my first ever. My first call."

"I'm going in. Harold." Alain stepped past him, dismissing the young man's bad luck. Hell of a draw for popping his cherry.

15

The clearing spanned less than thirty feet and was bordered by a creek to the east. The ground was strewn with what looked like trash, but on closer examination was destroyed hiking gear, torn nylon and bent aluminum poles and what appeared to be part of a backpack frame hanging askew on a pine branch. Deep parallel scratches crisscrossed the hard earth as if something had clawed it or tried to dig. The end of a sleeping bag protruded from a mound of loose dirt and leaves, the only place in the clearing large enough to hide a body.

Alain found the spot where Bob had entered the circle, his boot tracks clear against the disturbed ground. He stepped from one print to the next carefully, avoiding further contamination of the scene. A rank stinging scent hung in the air. He fished a pair of latex gloves from his pocket and pulled them on before folding back the purple nylon shell of the sleeping bag.

She lay on her side. The exposed jaw made it look as if she smiled. Her face had been torn and chewed, the neck ripped open from side to side. Blood had congealed in her blonde hair and in the pine needles beneath her head. He slid the bag far enough aside to note that her upper torso was bare and also missing flesh, notably most of the left breast and what he could see of the midriff. He laid the sleeping bag carefully back into place and straightened up.

"You going to hurl?" Harold asked. He seemed genuinely concerned.

Alain turned to the young deputy.

"Get a video camera, a stretcher, at least four warm bodies and the coroner's ETA. Cordon off the Subaru at the trailhead. Now." He thought he said it in a calm tone, but Harold flinched before trotting his bulk back down the trail.

In less than an hour the scene buzzed with more officers. Volunteer firemen hung around the periphery. Bob had returned with his mouth set, determined to help. With Alain he cast away from the site in a large spiral, circling wider on each pass to find any tracks.

Saunders shouted Alain's name. He cradled a silver digital camera in his gloved hands.

"Found it in the roots of that pine." He indicated a tree at the edge of the clearing. "It fell down the hole there. Saw it out of the corner of my eye." The case was cracked.

"Power it up," Alain said.

Scott slid the lens cover to one side, and the LED screen flickered to life accompanied by a grinding sound. The screen read "no photo".

"Blank," he said. "Maybe she didn't take any."

16

"Or someone erased them." Alain had taken off his gloves while looking for tracks. His hands itched to touch the camera. "Turn it over."

The deputy flipped the camera over, cradling it in his palm, and one of the assembled officers gave a low whistle. Dried blood covered the lens, with a partial print visible on the glass.

Alain could hear his pulse in his ears. A murder: time to hunt.

"Definitely somebody else here last night," Saunders offered.

"Big sonofabitch," stated a trooper.

"Thumb," said another deputy. "Still christly big, though."

Bob's voice rose from down near the lakeshore. Alain left Saunders to bag the evidence and ducked back into the woods, sliding down a slope covered with dead pine needles to reach the spot where Bob stretched a small fabric tape measure above a spot on the ground.

"Got a track?" Alain asked.

"Have I ever," Bob said. "Take a look at this."

Alain knelt next to him just short of the spot where the creek flowed into the small mountain lake. At first he couldn't make out the indicated track. Then he realized it wasn't a boot print.

"Is that coyote?" he asked the ranger.

"Coyotes don't get that big." Bob said it 'kai-yotes', a habit picked up from his yearly pilgrimages to the big parks out West. "It's a large dog."

"A dog made that?" Alain asked. The track was almost the size of his outstretched hand, maybe seven inches long and almost as wide. It had four toes with claws that had punched deep into the ground. It did resemble a dog print, but it was enormous.

"Well, maybe dog, or coy-dog, or . . ." Bob rubbed at his mostly-gray chin whiskers. "Or a wolf," he said. "It could be. Some folks claim they've been seeing them regular. Never heard of one doing anything like this, though, so I'm guessing big feral dog. Got this now, and the piss back at the site."

"The what?" Alain asked.

"That musky smell in the clearing. It's urine. Large predators do that sometimes when they can't eat a . . . a kill all at once." Bob cleared his throat. "They cover it up and mark all around it. It's a no-trespassing sign. Wolverines do it, cougars and grizzlies, too. Black bears like we got around here, not so much." He stood up from his squat, knees grinding like barn hinges, and settled his ranger hat on his head. "I guess I called you out here for nothing, Alain. Whatever attacked that sweet girl was definitely an animal."

Alain stared at the track in the wet sand.

Les Feu Follet, the will-o'-the-wisp, attempted to take Robert Deschamps this Thursday evening last as he made his way home afoot from L'Anse, by leading him into the swamps to steal his immortal soul. Only by the brave efforts of his wife was Robert rescued from the mire.

October 17, 1897. The Palladium Superior.

Chapter Four

The wipers slapped at the windshield as Alain pulled away from the trailhead. He swore. They'd covered the clearing with tarps before the rain, but any remaining tracks in the forest would be lost. Bob hadn't been able to pick up additional sign, which was odd. Even in the short time he'd been around, Alain had heard more than one person pass on tales of Bob's tracking abilities in hushed tones, half-joking about a possible deal with the devil. On the poaching case they'd worked the ranger had easily followed the trail of a wounded bear for miles, commenting on its weakening state as if he was actually watching it walk rather than interpreting scrape marks on the ground. He sighed and shook his head near the end, right before they rounded a boulder to find the bear slumped dead in the middle of the trail as if asleep. He should have been able to find more here. Animals don't walk carefully on rock to avoid leaving tracks unless led by a human. The body had definitely been bitten by something with large teeth. Bitten, hell, she'd been eaten. The missing flesh wasn't found anywhere around the site. Was it a meal for a predator or a killer's trophy? Did the fang marks cover knife wounds? Alain wanted to know if the bites were from post-mortem scavengers. If not, the animal was a possible murder weapon.

The coroner had finally arrived to pronounce her dead, which allowed them to prepare the body for shipment. Firemen working in teams would carry the body out by stretcher to the road. A state plane would take her to the medical lab down in Lansing.

They had a name, Aimee Henderson, from a tag inside the foot of the sleeping bag. Alain would be willing to bet that the owner of the thumb print on the camera had taken any other ID that may have been at the site. He had the deputies putting together a list of people with huge dogs in the area. Bob was adding those known to raise coy-dogs and wolf-dogs: cross-breeds of coyotes and wolves with domestic dogs.

Alain reached the paved road and gunned his truck south toward Marquette. There were two things to do in his territory when a young person showed up dead. First, ask the local deputies. If they didn't recognize the deceased, check the college. Not one of the officers at the site knew Miss Henderson, if that turned out to be the victim's correct name. He refused to set off a parent's worst nightmare due to a loaned piece of camping gear. He called Janet and asked her to alert the administration at Northern that he was on the way.

Trees blurred past the side windows, the speedometer hovered at eighty and the big V-8 roared. His fingers drummed on the steering wheel. Alain's eyes focused at a point beyond the road. The hunt was on, and this time his prey ran on both two and four legs.

The admin building at Northern Michigan was one pile of institutional red brick among many. The state must have gotten a great deal on brick back in the seventies because every school of that era looked the same. He swung his truck into a spot reserved for the President's office and slid out. Out of habit he patted his pockets before closing the door: knife, notebook, flashlight and phone. He could feel the weight of his pistol and spare magazine clipped at the small of his back and covered by his rain jacket.

He took one guilty look around for Marvin Keys. The chief campus cop never failed to stick his nose into cases whenever possible. Alain had to admit that if his job dealt with the possibility of writing a thousand public urination tickets he'd probably do the same.

Marvin had been a little miffed when the state police declined to raid a dorm room for him. He'd learned through the use of a "confidential informant"—a pissed-off roommate—that a "substantial amount" of marijuana was located inside. The photo of Marvin holding up a small baggie of weed made the front page of both the campus rag and the quirky Marquette paper, in the latter case below the fold, losing the headline to a story about strange lights spotted hovering over the water tower. Marvin sent a request to the DEA office in Detroit asking for cooperation. The agents had swamped the Marquette state police post with phone calls requesting extra copies of the newspaper. They enjoyed reading the article every time they had a bad day in Detroit, which meant most days.

Alain would still have to include him if the girl turned out to be a student. Despite taking his job too seriously Marvin had his uses.

The Provost's assistant had a Nordic complexion and a deep-cut green blouse. She tucked a strand of white-blonde hair behind her ear when he came through the office doors. Her husband ran a floating poker game somewhere in town every weekend night and dealt a little coke on the side. Alain had dropped by their house several times looking for him, and although he never found the husband, the wife always invited Alain to pass the time waiting with her. He'd politely refused thus far.

"Detective," she said.

"Violet."

The blessing of the Provost would supposedly open all doors on campus, but in reality Violet ran the place like a military camp while he hid from her in his office.

"Have you been working too much, Detective? You seem to be getting leaner."

Violet had an edge on her like jagged ice, and when she looked him up and down Alain had the feeling that she knew exactly how much money he made after taxes and when he'd last shaved. She smelled like something he couldn't place—a white, cold scent.

"No rest for the wicked," he said. It sounded stupid in his ears.

Her lips twisted in what may have been a grin, but he couldn't tell if she was laughing at him or not. She let him off the hook by tossing a file across the desk.

Alain caught it. Henderson, Aimee. He copied the local address down and noted the blank Emergency Contact area while Violet pulled up Aimee's student ID photo on the computer. A printer hummed and he had an eight by ten color copy.

It was her: whole, lovely. Not drop-dead model looks, but round and cute and alive. The eyes had that shine that looked like a joke was on the way. The tilt of her chin said dirty joke. She flirted with the man behind the camera. Or the woman. Now she lay on the forest floor, covered in dirt and the scent-mark of a predator.

Alain turned the photo so that it faced Violet.

"Where do I find the people who know her?" he asked.

Alain wondered why the English Department was located so far from the library. His own university days had been as a commuter, first to the three-room community college run by the tribal government, then to Lake Superior State twenty miles away. He'd won an academic scholarship to Western Michigan University down in Kalamazoo but had transferred home within two months. In the farm country of the Lower Peninsula he felt disconnected and loose, with wild bouts of homesickness that had escalated to nausea and migraines. After a night spent blinded by a crushing pain in his skull he'd packed his bags and transferred to the Criminology program at Lake Superior.

He passed the hockey arena, where the college's only real shots at athletic glory played every sold-out game, just like LSSU. English had been tucked into one of the original structures of the college, its red sandstone facade worn to the color of liver. History shared the place, time and words moldering together. Alain wandered the halls of the deserted third floor until he located the walnut door he sought. He'd barely knocked when the doorknob pulled from his hand.

"I told you I can't help you. You'll have to meet with the dean." The speaker didn't even look at him. Alain caught a glimpse of auburn hair pulled into a bun and a face buried in a book. The door swung shut.

He stood for a moment. Raised his hand to knock again. The door flew open.

"I hope you realize how insulting this is. Your grandmother dies every semester. How many do you have?" She had lowered the book, and he looked at large brown eyes behind glasses. "You're not him," she said.

"I don't think so. I don't have a grandma," Alain said.

"Did he leave?" She looked both directions down the hall but didn't wait for an answer. "Are you a student? You're not a student. A parent? God, I hope you're not a parent. I don't have any twelve year-old students. Come in. Come in." She turned on her heel and led the way into the office. The glasses and the hairdo helped, but she didn't look much older than a coed herself.

Books heaped every flat surface in the office. A chair-shaped pile proved to be hiding the real thing, and Alain sat, unconsciously adjusting his holster to keep the butt of his gun from digging into his kidney.

"Dr. Bourbonnais, I'm—" he began as he reached for his badge.

"Stephanie. With a P-H, Stephanie, and I'm twenty-nine. You were wondering. Everyone does. Sorry for the crack about twelve year-olds. This job will make you feel old in a hurry," she said, sitting down behind her desk.

"Stephanie," he said. He had been about to do something. "Did you have a student named Aimee Henderson?"

"Did I?" she asked. "Not do I? Oh no. You're a policeman."

Alain gave himself a mental kick. "Very perceptive."

"What happened?" The professor cradled her head in her hands and rested her elbows on the desk.

"I hoped you could help me figure that out." Alain forged ahead. He took out his pad and flipped it open to the notes he'd taken in the clearing. "How did you know her?"

"She's my advisee," Stephanie said. "Folklore is pretty much my domain here at glorious State U." She made a gesture that took in the yellowed blinds and fluorescent light fixture. "You haven't told me what happened. I'd say a car wreck but you're not in uniform."

Alain felt pinned in his chair. He was supposed to be the interviewer. He tried to get on top of the conversation again.

"Ms. Henderson—" he said.

"Aimee," she said.

"Aimee's body was discovered in the woods northwest of town. I need to speak with her family before releasing more detail."

"In the woods. That's . . . ironic, I suppose."

"Ironic?" Alain asked.

"The cosmic kind. Black humor of the gods. It's scholarly talk for a stupid coincidence," she said. "Aimee studied local folklore: the tales of the U.P., most of which deal with what in big bad woods might kill you and how to avoid it. Do you believe in coincidence?"

He shook his head.

"Me neither. What's your name?" she asked.

"Alain. Detective Alain Logan. State Police."

"Alain is French. Logan is . . . I don't know what Logan is," Stephanie said.

"That makes two of us," he said. "My uncle liked the sound of it." He bit back the rest of it: the man wasn't truly his uncle, and both names had been chosen from old tales he'd heard somewhere. Why was he telling her things? Alain felt like a dog trying to read a book. This woman changed directions like a summer storm and it knocked him off balance.

She stared at him as if deciding where to place him on the shelves.

"Aimee was one of the bright spots," Stephanie said. "She loved discovering new folklore, adding to the collective knowledge, all of that stuff that no one else gives a rat's ass about. Sorry. True, though. Sorry and true."

"You don't like your job?" Alain asked.

"I do. It's . . . not what I expected."

"Which was?"

She laughed. It wasn't friendly. "Who knows . . . students who want to learn, I suppose. Respect," she said. "Not being pigeon-holed by tenured old farts. Ah, that's not fair. I didn't expect to have any students die, how about that?"

Stephanie stood in the center of her office. She seemed to have run out of the steam that had driven her since the moment the door opened. Alain waited. He made an effort to gather himself. Now that the shock had passed he might get better answers out of her, something unguarded.

"Shit," she said quietly.

Professor Bourbonnais provided him with Aimee's background—a mildly well-to-do girl from Ohio, lost academically until she discovered story hunting. That's how the professor put it, the process of tracking down the threads of history pulled from an older generation.

"Anyone would talk to her," Stephanie said, "age, sex, race didn't matter. They all told their stories to Aimee. She knew how to listen and how to make them feel important."

"Do you know of anyone who might hold a grudge against her? Another student?" he asked.

Most witnesses would jump on this question and insist the deceased was perfect, an angel come down to Earth. Stephanie thought, toying with her glasses, then slowly shook her head.

"She really was a sweetheart," she said. "Aimee could be pushy on the trail of a story, but in general she made it warmer by entering a room."

"What about a romantic relationship?" he asked.

"No, and not getting laid either, as far as I know," she answered. She caught his carefully neutral expression. "We talked. Girls have to do something to pass the time up here in the frozen north."

"Family problems?"

"None to fight with. Her parents died in an accident when she was still an undergrad. No siblings or even extended family that she talked about."

Alain looked down at his notebook to be certain that his face didn't give anything away. An orphan. He remembered life with Waagosh, the man he'd called uncle, his own time running wild and alone in the woods for days on end. He'd been told he was too young to remember, but he recalled looking up at the ceiling in the cabin where he'd been found. Unable to move or even roll over. The rough-hewn planks did not fit tightly, and light sifted down with dust from the loft.

23

Stephanie stood, unconsciously adjusting her wool skirt. Alain rose with her.

"Raised properly, I see. Aimee would have liked that. We agreed about the death of chivalry," she said.

Alain dug a business card out of his wallet.

"If you think of anything else I should know, call me any time. Dispatch can usually find me, but my home number and cell are on the back," he said.

"Detective?" she asked. "I need to know how Aimee's story ends."

Alain considered her before answering. She seemed to have a greater stock in this than a simple friendship with a student would warrant. All the things that occurred to him to say seemed like movie quotes, a pithy line to drop before striding down the hall. He nodded to her by way of goodbye and didn't speak before leaving to find who had killed the girl with no parents.

It was at least an hour before he realized that he hadn't asked Dr. Bourbonnais where she had been the night before.

Mrs. Louie Pond of Ishpeming, invalid for weeks, recently expelled a live frog from her stomach. Both are expected to make a full recovery.

30 April, 1898. The Palladium Superior.

Chapter Five

A normal day might find three or four cars in the gravel parking lot of the state police post at six p.m. Today it held a dozen, including a pair of county cruisers. Alain swung by his tiny cubicle and picked up phone messages before entering the conference room. A huddle of cops surrounded one end of the table. Leon stood a head taller than the others, and he waved Alain over.

"Nice toy you brought in last night," Leon said.

The gun confiscated from the poachers rested on the table. The remnants of fingerprint powder on the thick stock told Alain that Janet had already gone over it. She doubled as their evidence technician in between calls.

"Why is this out?" Alain asked.

"While we wait for the Lieutenant we wanted to see how the upper crust hunts." Leon answered. "I always planned to get a gun like this for my wife, but no one wants to make the trade. I suppose it would help if she lost some weight."

Alain pulled on a pair of white gloves lying on the table and picked up the gun, amazed at its heft. He hadn't had time to examine it the night before, just tagged it and bagged it. At first glance it resembled a double-barreled shotgun, but on closer inspection it was a side-by-side hunting rifle, a modern reproduction of an old firearm. Silver inlay on the receiver was engraved with a scene showing men on safari, great white hunters followed by bearers and guides.

"Is this an elephant gun?" he asked.

"It's a guide gun, the kind you take into the brush after a wounded elephant or lion," Leon answered. "The hired help got to finish the deed when the big bwana no shootum straight."

Alain slid the selector lever to the center and broke open the receiver to expose the huge black holes of the twin barrels.

".600 Nitro Express," said Leon. "It'll stop a train, if you're into that sort of thing. Those Illinois boys had a hundred rounds in their truck, each one handmade. Run about forty bucks apiece. I figure they got drunk and read some Hemingway. They found an outfitter in Chicago and got loaded up, couldn't wait to get to Africa so they came up here to blast some of our ferocious native deer."

The gun snicked shut like oiled silk.

"How much?" he asked, knowing Leon would have the answer. Leon had gun magazines in every room of his house.

"Thirty thousand," Leon said.

One of the troopers whistled low and long; that was most of a year's salary for a hunting rifle.

Alain placed the gun carefully back on the table. "Let's get this back in the evidence room."

Janet stuck her head around the corner and gestured for him. "The Lieutenant can't make the meeting," she said through a false smile.

Ben Hinton had been a good leader until a shooting at an elementary school two years ago in the spring. The U.P. didn't have negotiators, only ranking officers. When Ben had heard the gunshots through the phone as the madman began to kill the children, something drained out of him. He still signed papers and wore his spotless uniform and sat behind his desk as if posing for a picture, but there was no weight to him. He seemed to be in that classroom, listening to a crackling phone line for some sort of message. He called in sick whenever anything happened.

"You're on deck," Janet patted his arm and left the room.

Alain looked around the room at the cops settling in, slouched against tables or crouched in chairs, watching him expectantly. He had the rank. It was his investigation.

"Listen up," he said. "We're going to be working closely with the sheriffs," he nodded at Leon, who winked, "and the greenies on this one." Greens were the state forest rangers, biologists and anyone else employed to keep plants and animals alive instead of people. "I guess I'm PR." A murmuring told him good luck and good riddance. "So, forward any questions or requests at me. We're going to release this as solely an animal attack, and keep everything else to ourselves. If I find anybody talking to the press solo you're off the case and can go back to chasing jet-ski thieves." The assembled cops kept their poker faces.

"We have one victim. No motive yet. No means—"

"Means, hell, it's a fucking wolf," a deputy with a bad mustache spoke up. "Maybe we ought to have a little hunting season."

Alain stopped. He let his gaze drift to the man slowly.

The deputy fidgeted in the hard chair, touched his gun. "That track, and the . . . heck, everybody knows they're stone killers."

Alain kept his face smooth. He leaned forward almost imperceptibly, and waited. No one else chimed in. The wall clock's minute hand leapt ahead with an electric snap.

The deputy dropped his eyes to the floor. There was a coolness in the room, a studied shifting of weight and attention.

"We have one, and a thumbprint found at the site that was not canine in origin," Alain finished. He didn't look at the deputy who'd spoken but every other officer did. "And we'll process the evidence we have and go from there. Leon will have assignments for you. It's knocking on doors, looking for witnesses and big dogs." They collected notebooks prepared by Janet and the admin staff containing the thin amount of evidence they had and filed out. Leon lingered.

"Boss-man ready to knock off for today?" he asked in a deep voice. He fished a pair of boxing gloves out of his bag and held them up. "Workout?"

Alain shook his head.

"What are you going to do?" Leon asked. "You can ride along with me tomorrow, but anything new coming in tonight will be from the patrols, the canvassing. Once we find the dog you will know where to effectively make use of your manly detective package."

Alain took one of the prepared notebooks for himself. He leafed through it. The binder held a bit of life and a great deal of death in ten pages: passport, license and transcript, then photos of a dead young girl. It seemed heavier that it should. Alain realized he was angry.

Leon could tell. "Spar with me. Fight it out. You'll feel better."

"Let's go downstairs," Alain said.

"That's right." Leon slapped him on the arm with the gloves. "You can toe up with Harold. You're in a bad mood, right?"

"Maybe," Alain answered. "Why? Have you got something against the new guy?"

"Nope, he's a good kid. I'm not allowed to fight him anymore because he's going to be my brother-in-law unless I can stop him." Leon started to loosen up as they headed for the door, sticking sharp jabs into mid-air.

"Brother-in-law?"

"Yup. He's marrying my wife's sister," Leon replied. "I never liked her. The sister, that is. Harold needs some backbone, maybe a brain transplant. Actually what he needs is a map out of town. That woman is fifteen years older than him and has given more free rides than a hotel shuttle. She's going to eat him alive unless he wises up."

Alain ran his shoulder into deputy, knocking him off-balance so Alain could get through the door to the stairs first.

"And he's marrying her because?"

Leon tried to trip Alain down the stairs but couldn't reach.

"I think the boy may have played football without a helmet," Leon said. "Maybe his momma huffed gasoline when she was carrying. Or he could just be an idiot. Don't matter. You tell him not to do something, he's going to do exactly that. Nice kid—trying to do the right thing, settle down, better himself, all that crap—but stubborn like those warts I've heard you got from animal relations."

"So, why aren't you allowed to spar with him anymore?"

"Who do you think gave him the black eye?" Leon asked with a tight and merry grin.

The basement of the post smelled of sweat and the metallic tang of gun oil. Boxes of files were stacked in one section while another held weight benches and racks of iron plates. Lockers lined a wall. The largest open area had a threadbare canvas judo mat stretched across the concrete and a heavy punching bag hanging from the rafters. Leon wrapped his arms around it and grunted as he lifted. Alain stretched up to unhook the chain. Leon dropped the heavy bag unceremoniously in the corner while Alain opened his locker and grabbed his workout gear.

Movement by the weight bench caught his attention. Harold racked plates onto the bench press bar. He had three on each side already and wasn't done. He stopped at three hundred and forty-five pounds. Alain sized him up, figured him to weigh one-ninety, two hundred at the most.

Harold lay back on the bench and grabbed the bar, flexed and powered the weight up off the support pegs. He pumped it rhythmically down to his broad chest and up six times. He slammed it back onto the pegs and sat up, catching Alain watching him.

"You want to try?" Harold asked. There was something about him that did seem a little boyish. Alain wondered how he'd passed the tests to become a deputy. They required a certain amount of grit.

"Leon offered to teach me a few things on the mat," Alain answered. "He'd get all jealous and cry if I tried to play with someone else."

Leon snorted. "Go on, Alain, I can wait. Show him how it's done." He knew as well as Alain that neither one of them could lift that much weight.

Alain pulled on his sweats. He strode across the cold concrete to the mat, dropped his pads and began to stretch.

Leon glanced at Alain's bare feet. He sighed.

"You're going to kick me, aren't you?" he asked.

Alain continued strapping on the sparring pads that covered his shin and instep.

"Might as well," Leon said. "Everybody else does. Unless, of course, you'd like to take a turn, Harold?" Leon snapped his fingers. "That's it! You need a nickname. Something to make you tougher. Harold . . . Hal . . . how about Hell? Hell Burke."

Harold shook his head and looked at the floor. He didn't seem to know if he was being mocked.

Leon turned to Alain. "Would you mind going a round or two with the dangerous Mr. Hell, here? Light contact, of course."

Alain shrugged and slid his hands into speed gloves as Harold took off his shoes. "Light contact" in the post basement meant no trips to the emergency room. They faced each other in the rough center of the mat. Despite his build, Harold's baby face made him look harmless. Alain dropped into a fighting stance, elbows tight, gloves high, and they began to circle.

Harold had a pained look. He tried a rush, clumsy and slow, and Alain slid to one side. He had a little reach on the man, although obviously not as much as Leon.

Another rush, faster this time, and Alain popped a roundhouse kick at Harold's ribs as he passed. He blocked with violent speed, almost catching Alain's foot. Quicker than he looked.

Alain feinted with his left, switched feet and drove forward with a low kick. When Harold dropped his guard to block, Alain spun and backfisted him to the side of the head. He pulled the blow, but it was still like hitting a piece of knotty oak even through the padding of the headgear. Harold shook his head and gave his shy smile again, exposing teeth in need of straightening, then came at him. Alain stood his ground this time, bringing his right knee almost up to his shoulder before driving the heel straight out in a push kick. Harold twisted, taking the impact on one side of his chest rather than in the solar plexus, and he caught hold of Alain's leg. He kept coming, using Alain's own leg as a lever to ride him back and to the ground. Alain rolled onto his back and drove his other leg straight up into Harold's midsection, flipping him up and over. Harold crashed to the concrete at the edge of the mat and groaned.

Leon leaned over him. "You dead yet, Hell?"

"Broke . . . he broke my arm," Hell said, cradling his wounded limb.

"Oh shit," Alain said. He felt like an ass.

Leon reached out for it, and Hell flinched away. "Let me see it, you big baby," Leon said, "and Alain didn't break anything. Gravity did this to you. You looked like a duck trying to take off." Hell reluctantly held out his left arm, and Leon slowly manipulated it back and forth. "Feel anything grinding?"

"No," replied Hell.

"I don't think it's broke. Could be a bad sprain. Of course, I'm not a doctor, but I do play one at home," Leon said. "Get yourself over and get an x-ray. Damn shame about you trying to catch a falling weight and hurting yourself like that." It might make the community nervous if they knew how often their law enforcement professionals beat each other up. "At least it's not your shooting hand. Or your relationship hand, if you know what I mean. You may need that. God, I hope so."

Hell grimaced. It could have been the arm. Or the needling.

Alain slipped off his right glove and held out his hand. "No hard feelings? We can get a re-match when you heal up."

Hell shook as best he could. "It's not a big deal, Mr. Logan." He headed for the stairs.

"I can see what your sister-in-law likes about him," Alain said. "He's a good kid."

Leon shook his head. "Not you, too. I do not know what he's thinking. She's mean as a snake with a backache and twice as ugly. We need to find him a nice hefty immigrant girl or a tranny hooker or something."

The intercom popped, and Janet's voice cut into their conversation. She could watch the goings-on in the basement on security monitors.

"If you boys are done playing, you might want to head over to Willow Lane. Patrol checked the girl's last known address, and it looks like the place has been broken into," she said. "Brett has it locked down. No rush."

Alain yanked off his gloves as he headed for his locker.

Chapter Six

Leon caught Alain's elbow as he was about to open the door. He gave Alain a fake smile and said, "Don't look outside."

Alain wanted to look. "Why?"

"Paul Maki," Leon said.

A reporter, likely the first of many. Paul covered the crime beat for the *Mining Journal*. He also handled obituaries, the community calendar, restaurant reviews, entertainment, living green, the church pages and a column entitled "Healthy Weight Choices."

"Get the truck," Leon said. "I've got this." He strode out the door, beaming ear to ear with his arms spread wide. "Paul, you old cock-knocker, I have been looking for you everywhere." He hugged the round little man and held on.

Alain headed for the parking lot. He didn't run. That would be undignified. He had important business he needed to attend to. He could hear Paul struggling in Leon's grip, calling his name. There may have been questions but they were muffled by Leon's jacket.

"I have the perfect human interest story for you," Leon said. He held the reporter by his elbows and shook him for emphasis. "You know as well as I do that my left testicle never dropped. Well, the other day the wife says to me something about a baby. Of course, she has the deformed ovary, so aren't we a pair . . ."

Alain thankfully closed the door to his truck before he could catch any more of the details of Leon's performance. He got the engine started and pulled up to the curb as Leon snatched Paul's keys from his hand and lobbed them onto the roof.

The deputy hopped in, calling back over his shoulder. "Sounds good. We'll do this again."

"You're cruel," Alain said, "but you bought me a few hours at least."

"What was wrong with that? Friends should be able to talk about these things. I have nothing to hide."

Dusk had fallen. Alain didn't use the flasher lights but pushed it hard through town, rolling stop signs and using the shoulder to cut around a slow-moving Buick.

"Stop," Leon yelled as they passed a laundromat.

Alain hit the brakes to slow the truck to a crawl. He didn't see any kids or cats running into the street. No traffic.

"What the hell?" he asked.

"I said stop, dammit. Swing around behind the Clean-O." Leon unbuckled his seat belt and readied himself to jump out.

31

Alain gunned the truck, took a hard right and swung into the dirt lot behind the grimy white building. His headlights illuminated a laundry cart abandoned on its side up against the cinder block wall. One rusted blue minivan with windows fogged over from the inside sat at the far end of the lot.

"We're stopping for a couple of teens discovering nature?" Alain asked.

Leon didn't answer. He popped his door and reached the side of the van before Alain could get the shifter into park. The lanky deputy's frame was tense, all angles and edges. Alain leapt out his side, put his hand on the butt of his gun.

Leon yanked at the handle on the minivan's slider, then the front passenger door. "Shit. Try your side."

The driver's door was locked, as well as the back hatch.

Leon made a tunnel of his hands and peered through the glass. "Have you got a jimmy or a window punch?"

Alain shook his head. "I've got a tire iron."

"Get it and call for CPS." The deputy pulled out his jackknife and opened it. He got on his knees to probe at the rusted area along the edge of the van's slider near the lock. Years of winter road salt had eaten away the metal. It crumbled and flaked off as he dug and twisted the blade.

"I think—" Leon began. He stuck two fingers into the hole he'd made and caught his tongue between his teeth as he strained to reach something. The lock popped. "Gotcha."

Alain went for the radio inside his truck. He watched through the windshield as Leon opened the side door, reached in and came back out slowly holding a baby carrier. The tenderness with which he held it, firmly by the handle and steadying the bottom so that it didn't tip, seemed strangely natural for him. Alain knew that he had at least ten nieces and nephews. Maybe it was catching.

The baby's dirty face, smeared with snot, grime and what looked like ketchup, stared up at them as Alain joined Leon.

"It's too cold for him to be out here without a hat." The sharp voice made both of them jump. A woman with gray hair and a wicker basket of clothes stood ten feet behind them watching the scene. "Mr. Gilhall, I would expect you to know better."

Leon looked like a ten year-old boy caught stealing a comic book. "Yes, Mrs. Piche."

"And a t-shirt," she continued. "My word, whose child is this?"

The baby's filthy shirt read: *Got Milk?* It barely covered a leaking diaper. Alain knew nothing about babies, but those little legs looked swollen and red with cold or a rash.

"Becky Lemieux," Leon said. "Back in school her name was Devord. Graduated right after me."

"I taught her," Mrs. Piche said, as if it had been last week that she'd had the girl in her high school math class instead of a dozen years ago. "She did not seem the type, but that is no matter now." She set her basket on the ground, marched forward and took the baby carrier from the deputy. He let go and took one involuntary step backward.

"Find a diaper bag. I am taking the child inside and out of this chilly air." It was not a request.

It took less than a minute to get the retired teacher installed in the laundromat with the baby to wait for Child Protective Services. Trash filled the van almost to the level of the windows, but they managed to find some baby wipes in the debris. She was in the process of fashioning a diaper from one of her husband's chamois shirts when Alain and Leon went back outside.

A bone-thin figure leaned into the van's open side door, digging through the junk. It wore filthy overalls. Ragged, hacked-off short hair and the shapeless garment made it difficult to tell the gender.

Leon picked up his pace.

Alain reached for the deputy's elbow and missed. "Easy there, cowboy."

"We're good," Leon said with fake joviality, "all good. Becky!"

Becky froze. After a moment her hands twitched. She slowly reached into the van to touch a broken TV antenna, then a stuffed animal.

Leon took hold of one overall strap and spun her around. "You aren't going to say hello to an old friend?"

Small moist sores pocked the pale skin of her face and neck. Alain could see the same on her scalp through the thinning hair. Her eyes were sunken, and her jaw seemed to protrude as she ground her teeth together. Her eyes lingered on Leon's face, flickered to Alain and back.

"Hey." Non-committal. "Hey, you—" Recognition came in slow waves. "I know you."

"What's my name?" Leon asked.

"You tried to date me." Her face carried a shadow of the girl she'd been, until the exposed, rotting stumps of teeth ruined the image. "Sucked at basketball."

"What's going on out here today, Beck?" Leon asked.

"Collecting my stuff. It's mine." She looked back at the piled junk in the van. Her fingers curled.

"Do you have it all?" Leon asked. "You haven't lost anything important, have you?"

That seemed to wake her up. Becky's brow creased, and she began to touch her treasures one by one.

"Ms. Lemieux, are you missing any items?" Alain asked.

33

The woman shook her head. Her fingers came up to pick at one of the sores on her face.

"You're sure?"

"Get off my ass." Spittle flew from her mouth when she spun toward him.

"Whoa, easy," Leon said. He reached out as if to steady her and snapped a cuff onto her wrist.

Alain grabbed the other arm. He applied pressure to the elbow to make her twist away, allowing Leon to affix the other cuff with her hands behind her back. Alain expected her to fight but she seemed to switch off as soon as she realized what had happened. With the meth-heads it was always impossible to tell which way they would jump. They patted her down and then seated her on the running board like a poseable doll.

"I assume we don't need to search the car?" Alain asked.

Leon shook his head. "Let impound find the pipe."

They both knew that if she had any drugs she'd have been smoking it when they drove up.

"You went to high school together, I gather?" Alain asked as they waited for a patrol car to transport her to the hospital for a drug test, then to the drunk tank.

Leon watched Becky rock from side to side on the running board. He chewed his lip before answering.

"You wouldn't even have recognized her," Leon said. "Cute as a bug . . . too smart for me although it didn't stop me from trying. Married some dipshit from our class, lasted maybe ten years, then she hitched up again with a salvage diver working the harbor. He ran off before the baby was born, and she probably started using right about then."

Leon's knowledge of the local population ran in deep, tangled skeins. Alain didn't have high school memories of his own. The forests and swamps, the lakes and streams had been his institutions, his uncles allowing him to run free as their own version of homeschooling with a GED test as his ticket to college, but he remembered the girls he had grown up around and assumed he might marry. Crushes die hard. This was the reason that State Police were never posted in the county where they'd grown up: too many ties, grudges, debts. Alain had never been immersed in any community the way Leon and most of the deputies were. He couldn't convince himself whether it was good or bad to have so many people knowing your secrets, your flaws, as well as you knew theirs.

The quiet stretched out between them until the patrol car arrived for Becky. The social worker had shown up in less than five minutes. Alain let the silence go on until they'd seen her Miranda-ized and loaded up. He and Leon climbed into the cab of the truck.

"It's a good thing you recognized her car," Alain said.

Leon flipped the heater vent up and down, then looked out at the shitbox van.

"I gave her a warning not two weeks ago," Leon said. "She'd left him outside the grocery store to go dumpster diving. Fifty degrees out. I believe my mistake was in thinking that there was some good part of Becky left in there to listen to the warning. There isn't. Not when she's doing meth. It's someone else. Something else."

He cleared his throat.

"You know how they get the sores?" Leon asked. "Bugs. The meth makes them think there are bugs under their skin, and they try to dig them out."

We hear of a strong young man from Black River made idiotic by the use of tobacco. At last notice he had made the firm acquaintance of a fine oak tree in all facets of the term, and endeavored to spend a great deal of time in its presence.
2 August, 1898. The Palladium Superior.

Chapter Seven

Trooper Brett Vullonen waited on the front steps of the single-story square house where Aimee Henderson had lived. The white siding appeared to be crooked. Willow Lane bounded one edge of the area known as the student ghetto, a cynical title for a place where the worst crimes were littering, noise complaints and the occasional streaker. Alain parked over an empty beer can floating in a puddle on the dirt driveway.

Brett had the white milk complexion of his Dutch ancestors, and he never spoke a single word more than necessary. Shyness seemed like it would be a hindrance to a cop, but Brett learned more through simply listening to witnesses and allowing them to talk themselves out than three chattier officers could glean from the same folks.

"Pro?" Alain asked. One thing the U.P. did not have was a lot of well-paying jobs so several groups, extended families mostly, spent their time industriously relieving students, tourists and vacation homeowners of excess belongings. Everyone knew who they were, but as long as they didn't steal from locals it was unlikely anyone would drop a dime and turn them in.

Brett turned and headed for the back of the house by way of answer. It meant "see-for-yourself." The back of the house overlooked a muddy scrap of yard. Alain ran the beam of his flashlight around the edges of the space. Rusted chain-link had provided a backstop for the usual rubbish that floated on the wind in the student ghetto, mostly plastic cups from keggers. A rusted grill and two trash cans roughly cordoned off a tiny wood deck. Alain glanced at Brett. They'd gotten a budget memo from the idiot governor to conserve everywhere, which included the use of crime scene tape.

The back door hung loose and crooked on one hinge.

Alain inspected the boards. A welter of footprints outlined in mud covered the surface. They'd get some photos, but picking out an individual track would be hell. He stepped up onto the wood, keeping close to the wall and off the tracks. The door handle had scratches around it, as did the deadbolt, which looked new. Aimee had taken her security seriously, but it hadn't done any good.

36

"Looks like someone tried to pick it, then got pissed and ripped it open," he said.

Brett nodded, hands in pockets.

Alain pulled on latex gloves and eased the door open. The remaining hinge gave way, and it crashed to the deck.

"Hi Mom, I'm home," Leon whispered.

Same old Leon. He seemed to have shaken off the encounter with the meth-head. The darker things got, the bleaker Leon's humor. Laughing at the devil.

Alain entered the house, stepping near the edge of the doorsill. He figured Brett would have checked the house for occupants, then withdrawn to wait for him, standard procedure. Leon followed him in, trying to walk in his footsteps. He gave a low whistle.

Not a stick of furniture stood upright. Posters had been torn from the wall, cupboards and drawers emptied onto the floor. Shredded clothing lay strewn across every surface; thick textbooks had been ripped to pieces and hurled about the rooms. A tiny kitchen, living room, bedroom and bath made up the entire place along with an enclosed front porch.

"Usual stuff is still here," Brett noted, pointing to the smashed TV/DVD combo and portable stereo.

"Computer?" Alain asked. All three of them scanned the house. They found a power cord for a laptop but no computer. A stack of cardboard file boxes lay tipped over next to the desk. Leon knelt and began to sift through the folders splayed across the floor.

"These are organized by date, but nothing more recent than last semester," he said.

"Maybe she keeps them at school," Alain said. None of them believed that. In fifteen minutes they were done. A fold of cash and a credit card in Aimee's name were still tucked into a broken jewelry box with some decent pieces that a burglar would have snapped up.

Alain stood in the center of the living room and closed his eyes. What would a folklore student have that someone would want so badly? Sex and drugs were the usual culprits in human excesses. The house smelled like baking and flowery air freshener, without even a whiff of pot. No paraphernalia, either. He opened his eyes to find Brett and Leon watching him.

"Let's check with Marvin at the university, see if she was dealing," Alain said.

Leon snorted. "Marvin wouldn't know if *he* was dealing."

"We have to ask. He's surprised me before," Alain said. "Can you follow up on that tomorrow, Brett? I'll pump her prof for some more info, see if she had any clue to what the girl was up to."

Leon knelt to pick up a torn-off textbook cover. He handed it to Alain.

"You might need this," he said.

Alain glanced at the title. "Female Sexual Roles in Folklore of the Middle Ages?" he asked.

"Got to speak their language," Leon replied. "Besides, you are officially middle-aged now."

A gabble of voices bled through the thin wall on the street side of the house.

"Jeez, can you imagine trying to sleep here?" Leon asked.

Brett parted the blinds on the front window. "Something's happening out there," he said.

Alain leaned to see through the gap. Dusk had given way to night. A small knot of people clustered under the lone streetlight on the block. All had cell phones to their ears and were talking. Two lanky boys ran past the house and up to the group. Someone let out a short, sharp scream.

Brett's radio flared with static, then the sound of the dispatcher's voice calling available units to the intersection they were looking at. General disturbance, which could mean anything.

"Call us in, on scene," Alain said.

Leon already had the front door open.

"Should I stay?" Brett asked. He held the mike for his radio.

"Come out front," Alain threw back over his shoulder. "There's nothing here. Let's see what's going on."

Kids made up the crowd, all college-aged students in hoodies and flip-flops despite the chill.

"It was a bear," one of them said.

"A guy in a costume," a tall white kid said. His mangy dreadlocks bobbed in agreement. "I saw it on cable. They remade the Zapruder film or something. It moved weird, though."

"The Bigfoot footage, moron."

Alain held up his badge.

"What did you see?" he asked.

That was a mistake. They shouted over one another: more bears, sasquatch, a guy in a suit . . . mothman, whatever the hell that was. They weren't all stoned. He heard one "Saint Bernard," which was the most reasonable thing he'd heard since dawn. Here was his big dog.

Alain held up his arms to quell the noise.

"Fine," he said, "good. Which way did it go?"

Every arm pointed north. Leon was halfway to Alain's truck. Alain whipped the keys to him, and after unlocking the doors Leon tossed back Alain's handheld radio.

"One block west," Alain told Leon. "Roll slow, check the alleys. Brett, one block east. Everybody else go home and lock your doors."

He asked dispatch for more cars to block from the north and south. It would take a few minutes to get them in place.

A kid took Alain's picture with a cell phone.

"Go!"

Half went. Alain put them out of his mind and started trotting up the middle of the street. He hung his badge on the front of his jacket and pulled his flashlight. He scanned the side yards, between cars, even flicking the beam into the trees occasionally. More kids milled in loose bunches, sensing that something had happened. Alain wondered how long he had before the news vermin showed up.

Clouds lined the sky from horizon to horizon, choking off any moonlight.

One block, then another passed. At each corner he waited for the bracketing vehicles to catch up: Leon on one side in the truck, Brett's cruiser on the other.

The kids he encountered initially pointed in the same direction, but now those on the street began to ask him what was going on.

"It's out of sight," Alain said into the radio. "Between me and one of you two. It has to be. Slow up. Maybe it went to ground in one of these backyards. It could be our dog, which means it's killed once already. Brett, get the DNR out here with their bear trap, just in case."

"We hit campus in another block." Over the radio Brett's voice sounded canned. "The cemetery's across Wright Street, then nothing but the river. If it gets that far—"

This scream hurt Alain's ears. It sounded like blood in the air. He broke into a sprint. The unearthly noise came from a heavy woman standing in the front yard across the street. She wore only a baggy shapeless dress but did not seem to feel the cold night. Another shriek tore out of her, this one with words he couldn't make out, something foreign.

As he reached the yard, her eyes fell on his badge and she clutched at it, yanking it off, clip and all. With that in hand she clung to his arms, patting him, talking rapidly in Spanish. Gray hairs had pulled loose from a heavy braid to cast a corona of street light around her head.

"Uh. Shit," Alain said. "*No se . . . no, no hablo.*"

He tried to get free of the woman to point, to try and get an idea from her of where the animal had gone. She latched on again and towed Alain to the side of the house. A screen door was ripped open crossways, the frame bent from the force, the thin wooden inner door splintered. Inside, toys and dolls, a tricycle on its side, a tiny red nylon jacket, a cot with blankets thrown aside. No dog had done this.

"*Nieta*," the woman said. "*Mi nieta.*" She wrung her hands over his badge. It sounded like a prayer. Alain felt sick.

The "a" ending meant female. Alain remembered that much from a single semester of college Spanish. Everything else he'd learned seemed to be gone.

"A little girl. Ah . . . *a niña? Uno?*" he asked. "One little girl?"

The woman nodded. He couldn't look at her face, the hope painted there. Now she pointed, northwest in a line cutting across the yards.

Alain hurdled the first fence, staggering on the other side. He fed a running stream into the radio.

"Leon, pick it up, it's between you and me, cutting toward campus. Brett, get up to Wright and swing west hard. Cut it off. Lights and sirens. The animal took a little girl. Dispatch, send me everyone: fire, rescue, the dogcatchers, I don't care. Everyone."

Sirens tore open the night on both sides.

He took another fence at a leap and almost crashed into an above-ground pool, skidding on a slick layer of downed leaves. He could still see Aimee's ripped face. Not another little girl in the same day. His truck roared by to his left, Leon hunched over the wheel. Across the edge of campus now, threading between benches and trees, rounding a utility building.

His side locked into a cramp. He hammered it with his fist as he hit Wright Street and kept going toward the cemetery. The animal was headed somewhere. If it wasn't a dog or a wolf, it had to be a bear although he'd never heard of one picking up a child.

Leon wheeled up to the gate in Alain's truck.

"Get around the back," Alain yelled. "Do whatever it takes. If it gets to the river, it's over."

Beyond the Dead River lay a million acres of forest. They couldn't search it with all the help in the world. Leon put the truck into four-wheel drive and plowed along the outside of the cemetery's perimeter fence. Alain rattled the gate once to be certain it was locked, then began to climb. For an instant he teetered at the top over the iron spikes, legs shaking, his balance rolling back and forth as the gate moved. With a final lunge he half-fell inside the walls of the Holy Cross.

The strobing lights from the police cars licked the top of headstones, painting monuments in blue and red. Alain turned his radio volume down and tucked the unit into a jacket pocket. Trees blotted out the trickle of sounds from the city. He drew his pistol, tried to listen, to sort out breathing and footsteps in here with him. Nothing. He moved in short rushes, flashing the light for an instant then running to a new spot while the afterimage still burned in his eyes. A pink tube of fabric lay in the middle of a cemetery lane, a sock perfect for a little girl. Alain tucked it into a pocket. Sweat slicked his torso under his jacket. She was here. If it hadn't eaten her yet.

An opening creased the trees to his left. Beyond a ring of statues he could see the dim truck lights in the distance as Leon powered across the rough ground to circle behind the property.

Alain gulped a breath and pushed on. Even if he couldn't stop the animal he had to get the girl. *Nieta.* Granddaughter, that's what it meant. It wasn't a name. Idiot. He gave up on the cover and ran down the center of the lane, slashing the beam of his flashlight from side to side.

"Hey asshole, I'm coming to kill you," he said. "Here boy. Good dog."

Alain halted and switched off his light, listening and watching for a reaction.

There. Shadows shifted a hundred feet ahead. He hit it with the light. Waving branches but no wind, which meant something had pushed through.

"Drop her," he yelled. Running again. Why was he yelling at an animal? It came out like a chant. "Drop her! Drop her! Hey bear, drop her."

This part of the cemetery was older, the headstones simple granite plaques only few feet high. He clipped one with a boot, pinwheeled his arms and managed to stay up and hang onto his gun. Through the branches, the pines whipping at his face. Alain slid to a stop. Mausoleums arrayed side by side. Even in death the rich had their own neighborhood. He could see the back wall of the burial ground, with nothing but wilderness beyond. Leon had to be close.

Alain filled his lungs and bayed like a bear hound. They still hunted with packs of dogs in the U.P., and nothing made bears flee like that belling bark. He pounded through the streets of the dead city, barking, baying, aiming light and gun into each shadow as he ran. A pink granite crypt had a small statue in front of the double doors. It turned its head. The gun in his hand came halfway around before his brain lit up with what he was seeing. He let the muzzle drop, turned the flashlight on her.

41

She wore a sweatshirt with a duck on it. Her pajama bottoms were filthy; the mate to the pink sock in his pocket hung off one foot. He scanned the area with his light, holstered his weapon and knelt by the little girl. She watched him without making a sound.

"*No miedo*," he said. No fear. He couldn't remember the damned word for police so he said it in English. Her grandmother still had his badge.

She might be three. He didn't know much about kids. He used his free hand to pat her down, checking for blood. Head, chest, limbs, all clear, not a tooth mark on her. On her back he found thick slime, drool. It must have carried her all this way by the back of the shirt. He'd need a sample of that for DNA. Alain scooped her up. She weighed nothing.

Her eyes were huge and wet, brown, her mouth tight and pinched. She looked as though she was trying not to cry.

"*No miedo*." Alain felt like a fool. He needed to get her out of here. He struggled to pull out his radio. When he shifted the little girl's weight she locked her arms around his neck.

"The girl's with me. Leon, what have you got?" he asked.

"I got nothing," came the reply from the handset. "Lots of dark nothing."

Alain scanned the inside of the cemetery. No mud on the inner wall where anything had climbed out, but it was gone. He could feel it. The animal had escaped.

"Damn it," he said quietly.

The girl hiccupped.

He had no proof that he'd been chasing his killer, but it was crazy to think that a wild animal would come straight into town and grab a child. And what about the thumbprint on the camera? But the coincidence, this thing showing up while they were at Aimee's house, as if someone was following the investigation . . . He hated coincidences.

"Shit," he said.

She had silently withstood being stolen from her bed and carried through the dark, but the little girl had apparently had enough. At the sound of the second bad word sobs shook her birdlike body, tears spilled down her cheeks, she opened her mouth and began to howl.

Residents report viewing bright and active lights high in the sky over the town waterworks for a good length of time yesterday evening. Has an excursion balloon company come to town early for the Independence festivities? The sheriff and other authorities have suggested that what was seen was merely a miasma of swamp gas rising into the air. This editor will not grace that reasoning with a reply.

5 May, 1898. The Palladium Superior.

Chapter Eight

Alain's house sat in the gloom under the oak trees, gables casting deep shadows across its face. The clock on the truck's dash showed one a.m. He left each day not knowing when he would return so leaving a light on seemed like a waste. Alain used his flashlight to locate the proper key and get the front door open, then navigated to the kitchen in the dark. If felt good to know his way around.

Until he nailed the desk.

He swore as he dug out his flashlight and illuminated the piece of furniture. It stood squarely in the middle of what had been a formal dining room. Since Alain didn't do anything formal, he used the room as an office. The desk—a simple slab of mahogany on thick legs, scratched and worn but still grand—he'd found shoved under the eaves in the attic soon after he bought the house. When he'd left that morning, it had stood firmly up against the wall twelve feet away. The flashlight also revealed his ladder-back chair set squarely on top of it.

Alain backed to the wall and drew his pistol. He listened. The house creaked in the wind as it always did. Light in his left hand, pistol in his right, he gave each room a momentary bright flash using the push-switch on the butt of his flashlight. Kitchen: clear, the back door locked, no sign of entry. The old doors and windows in the house were a joke for security, so he left a few small items— a birch leaf, an owl feather—in places where they would be moved if anyone had been there uninvited. Everything was where it was supposed to be.

He took the back stairs slowly, his flashlight beam twisting long shadows down from the upstairs hall. The first room on the right was the library, complete with worn Oriental rug, fireplace and huge built-in shelves. He felt for the catch that released the hidden door. A section of shelves swung out silently, and he shone his light into the narrow passageway behind the walls of the second floor. Nothing. He'd bought the house without seeing the inside, and it had taken him three months to find this space. Old Horace Ganderson had had his secrets.

He holstered his pistol and flashlight and lifted his Mossberg twelve-gauge shotgun from its pegs behind the library shelves. Pistols were great for concealability, but he'd rather have a long arm in a gunfight. Someone had been in his house. His house, damn it. He racked it quietly then removed an extra shell from the ammo carrier and slid it into the magazine. The shotgun had a tactical light built into the fore-end, and he used the same flash-and-clear method to move back out into the hallway.

He quickly scanned the rest of the place.

Alain stood at the top of the main stairs and slipped the shotgun's safety on. Why would someone break in to move two pieces of furniture? It could have been Leon playing a joke on him. As far as he could tell, no one else knew about the spare key he kept tucked in the crotch of a tree in the yard. He'd changed the locks after moving in. Had they touched his food? He wondered about his toothbrush, the half-carton of milk in the refrigerator.

Glass shattered on the steps below him. Alain snapped the shotgun to his shoulder and triggered the light. He swept the stairs and saw nothing, played the powerful beam over the entry hall and found nobody.

The light caught something glittering halfway down the stairs. He started down, keeping the light on it. A picture had fallen from the wall and broken. The face of Horace Ganderson looked up at him from the steps, surrounded by shards of glass. Alain lowered the gun and kept the light on.

"I'm getting jumpy, old man," he told Horace.

He knelt and picked up the picture, sliding the bits of glass off into a neat pile on the step. Horace had been up in the attic with the desk, and Alain had decided to hang him in a place of honor over the steps. He'd built the house, after all. He was a handsome devil, with a twinkle in his eye that Alain couldn't remember ever seeing before in such an old photo. The man had character to spare, it seemed. Alain had done some research on the house after he bought it, and once he found the right town folks to ask he had gotten a load of stories about the old man. He'd been quite the rake, always hiring attractive young women to work in the house at generous wages. Perhaps that explained the secret passageway connecting the library to the servants' quarters. Horace had left a mark on the city of Marquette, the kind that DNA tests might still be able to find in local families.

Alain swept up the glass and tried to put the picture back in place. He found the hole where the nail had been, but no nail. He left the Horace propped up on the hall table, determined to fix it in the morning. The desk . . . the desk was whatever, something odd but he could find a reason if he looked for it.

He woke at six, unable to sleep any longer. The case tumbled in his head: Aimee's body, the animal track, the cemetery—assuming that was part of it. A thread had to tie some of it together, and at the moment all he had was the missing laptop. What could a graduate student be working on that was so important? He made a mental note to ask Dr. Bourbonnais . . . Stephanie. If it didn't have to do with school or money then all he had was sex or drugs, or nothing but random violence.

Alain stooped to pull on a pair of sweatpants but halted still half-bent. His palms were covered in dirt. The cemetery, maybe, but, no, he remembered washing them when he'd gotten home. He stood in the center of the room, pants forgotten, staring at his hands. If he brought them closer to his face, he knew what he would smell . . . wet fur, an undercurrent of blood. He crashed open the door to the bathroom with his shoulder and scrubbed them until they were pink and tender and had stopped shaking. The roil in his guts gave him a spare second to crash down in front of the toilet before everything came up.

Coughing and panting he curled down to the floor. The chill of tile felt good against his skin. Feverish? Maybe. Alain never got sick. He hadn't felt like this since the State Police academy. After his failure to stay in the Lower Peninsula for college, he'd feared the need to live in Lansing for weeks on end. The regimen had helped at first—the blitz of physical training, classes and practice filling the gaps he felt when he left home—but the sense of wrongness had accreted in his body. It was stronger than when he'd gone to college a few years before. By the end of the first month he would get dizzy easily, had headaches that he struggled to hide from the instructors and other students. On his first weekend pass he'd driven north in a fever dream until he reached the Upper Peninsula. Crossing the Straits on the Mackinac Bridge his heart had soared above the water. He took the first exit in St. Ignace, swerved to a stop along the shore and collapsed to the welcoming ground for what felt like an eternity.

Now moving as if in a trance he got himself up off the floor, dressed, still feeling loose and hollow, laced up his running shoes and headed out the front door. Time to run, just chase out whatever was in his system. Horace's picture still stood propped on the table.

Even after daylight savings time kicked in six a.m. meant darkness this far north. His jacket had brilliant reflector tape on it that caught headlights and glowed in silver streaks. It did make people slow down, although likely they thought him a deer rather than a runner. He could feel last night's chase in his tight hamstrings, the ghost of a stitch in his side. One beer too many at the Walleye. If he was in better shape he might have caught the thing last night and ended this. If he quit drinking altogether maybe whatever was happening to him would stop.

Alain slipped on a patch of ice, caught himself and ran on. The case. Forget the dreams and focus on the case. His stride settled into an easier rhythm, the lope that had carried him down hundreds of miles of logging roads and forest trails in Chippewa County as a boy. The children of the tiny Bay Mills community knew he wasn't truly Ojibwa and had offered stones and fists as often as friendship, but no one, not even the older boys who ran track at the big high school in Sault Ste. Marie, could keep up with Alain for long. He'd spent days running in the woods, not going anywhere in particular, simply finding what was beyond the next sandy curve of two-track or over the farthest hill.

Waagosh, the old man who'd originally found him and raised him as a nephew, didn't ask any questions when the boy returned from his personal marathons. He spoke more often to the flock of crows who gathered in the pines at the edge of the bare dirt yard. Alain never heard him say anything special to the birds, at least not in English. Waagosh would ask the birds about the weather in English, then slip into Ojibwa after the largest crow answered him.

Alain's route took him back to the base of the hill upon which his house stood. He watched his footing as he started the climb, sweating freely. A thin line of snow leftover from an early October storm ran in the gutter, crested now with dirt and pocked with the occasional dog turd. Dog tracks, too, lots of them.

He stretched his stride, reaching for an extra bit of ground with each one. The air cut his lungs like glass and stung his heart. His gait felt long and lean, flying as if the slope was down rather than up, streaking through the trees lining the road. He staggered to a sudden stop as he realized what he'd seen. Tracks. Dozens of them, clear and sharp and patterning over one another into a mix of pad and claw.

Alain was not half the tracker Bob was, but he could follow sign like this. The snow captured full imprints, then he could trace their route as they wove across the sidewalk to impressions melted into the frosted grass of his neighbor's yard. The tracks must have been made last night. Many animals, and all of them heading for his house. A pack of dogs, it had to be. A loose conglomeration of mutts that slipped out at night . . .

He followed them through the trees until he reached his truck. He unlocked it with the keypad, felt behind the seat and slid his hand into the hidden sleeve that ran along the back. His groping fingers encountered the cold wooden stock of a rifle and he drew it out. His M14 might be considered old school by the new troopers, all of whom carried the state-issued AR-15s, but Alain liked older, reliable weapons. He'd carry a lever-action like the one he'd learned to hunt with if regulations allowed it. As it stood, the fifty year-old battle rifle served him just fine.

He pulled a magazine from its pocket on the rifle sleeve, loaded it into the weapon, chambered a round and released the safety.

Fifteen minutes later he stood in the front hall again feeling stupid. He'd stalked all around his own house following the tracks to each door, every ground floor window, even finding some muddy prints several feet above the ground on the stone walls where they must have stood on their hind legs. No animals, just tracks.

47

Alain clicked the safety on and removed the magazine from his rifle. The round he'd chambered spun through the air as he pulled the bolt back to clear it. It landed and skipped across the carpet into the shadows of the front hall.

The phone shrilled. Alain jumped.

He passed through the office, eyeing the chair still stacked atop the desk in the middle of the room, and answered the phone in the kitchen.

"Logan here," he said, laying the M14 across the kitchen table.

"It's Stephanie Bourbonnais. Is this too early?"

"Not at all," Alain straightened his posture. He heard his own voice drop a little lower in register. She was lovely. She was also the only suspect he knew by name. "What can I do for you?"

"I've been thinking about Aimee's . . . well, her death, and I have some questions for you. Can we talk?" she asked.

"Of course." No need to let her know he expected information from her in return. "How about the Trackside?" he asked.

They agreed to rendezvous at the diner in twenty minutes. He hung up the phone and headed for the stairs, planning to catch a quick shower, but something in his peripheral vision made him turn. The desk stood neatly against the wall with the chair tucked under it. Standing on end in the center of the desktop, like a good little soldier, a rifle cartridge glimmered in the half-light.

Stephanie had pulled her dark hair into a ponytail. Her face was striking behind her glasses, with high, fine cheekbones. Her hairdo exposed a very soft-looking neck. He'd always liked necks.

"Detective Logan."

"It's Alain, Professor."

"Assistant Professor, but if you're Alain, I'm Stephanie." She cocked her head. "What's the matter? Another death?"

Alain sat, unfolded his napkin and placed it on his lap as he thought about his answer. She could read him like a movie poster. "Nothing like that. It's been a rough morning." He scrubbed his hands against the napkin.

"Hmm." Her lips were full when she pursed them.

The waitress rescued them from the awkward pause and they ordered coffee and various combinations of egg, potato and pork.

"You wanted to talk about Aimee?" he asked.

"It's more about her work. I was half joking when I said she studied monsters in the woods, but last night I looked over her proposed dissertation topic. She left it with me before going on her trip." Stephanie toyed with her spoon, stirring her coffee even though she took it black.

"You have her files for this semester?" he asked, pulling out his notebook.

"Files? No. I mean, I have her notes on the topic with some supporting materials, and a paper she did earlier, but I wouldn't call them files," she said. "Why?"

"No matter, please go on," he said. "What made you call me?"

She twisted in her seat, and tucked a loose strand of hair behind one ear. "See, this is the hard part. You're going to think I'm loony. The lonely scholar has too much time on her hands. She loses a student, a friend, and comes up with a conspiracy theory."

"The easiest way is to say it straight out," Alain said.

She bit her lip. When the words came, they poured out as if she wanted to get it over quickly. "Do you know what a loup garou is?" She gave it the hard Quebecois pronunciation of "loo ga-roo."

He thought of the tales Waagosh had told during the long winters of Alain's youth. "Some kind of French werewolf?" His uncles had scorned the superstitions carried down by the white men from Canada, but their own tales of witches and shapeshifters were held as dangerous truths. To be honest Alain had thought they all sounded ridiculous.

"Exactly. Every culture has them, but the French tale has particularly deep roots in the trials and persecutions that took place after the Reformation. At least ten thousand people were burned at the stake in France, many accused of being werewolves as well as witches. It didn't stop until the middle of the seventeenth century, less than twenty years before the French settled Sault Ste. Marie."

She continued. "Settlers carried it with them from Europe, and while it eventually died out back home, in the north woods it gained in strength and popularity. It hit a peak in this area with the height of the logging camps, but is still told today using some of the same language."

"Aimee studied werewolf legends?" Alain asked.

"Not legends, folklore. Legends are old and dead, and they usually have some moral lesson. Folklore is what people tell each other about what happened, what is taking place now and will happen in the future. If legends are a history text, then folklore is a newspaper."

"But there are no such things as werewolves," Alain said.

Stephanie shook her head. More of her hair escaped the ponytail holder to lie in a fine dark net against the skin of her neck. The boys in her classes must have a hard time concentrating.

"The fact that men don't turn into animals is immaterial," she said. "It's the belief that matters. Let me put it to you this way: Do vampires exist?"

"Never seen one," Alain replied. He found himself fidgeting with the rifle cartridge that had appeared on the desk. When he'd first picked it up it had been warm to the touch. He'd dropped it into his pocket without thinking when he left the house immediately after hanging up the phone. The desk had been in the center of the room, and then it wasn't. He'd seen it. So, he was crazy or it had moved. Anything else was impossible. Alain didn't feel crazy. He touched his fork, which felt solid as a utensil should.

"I would say no," she continued. "However, there are groups of people who like to act like vampires, and some of them may actually believe they're vampires. The fact they are not undead doesn't make those people in black mascara who drink blood disappear."

"I've heard about those," he said, "and there have been a few murders connected to those groups when their rituals got out of hand. What does this have to do with Aimee Henderson?"

"Her dissertation topic is about groups whose members believe themselves to be werewolves. Real loup garou. Here in the U.P." She chased a lone hash brown around the plate with her fork.

"Here?" Alain's skepticism must have been plain.

"I'd never heard of them either, but in her notes she mentions hearing rumors beginning a few months ago. She thought she was getting close to some of the members, and she wanted to interview these crazy people."

"And you think they killed her?" he asked.

"I don't know." She pressed her paper napkin flat, then began to shred it. "I want to help, and I thought this might be important."

"Are there any names in her research?" he asked.

"Of course not," she snapped. "That would be too easy." She dropped the napkin and pulled another one, tissue thin, out of the dispenser on the table. "Shit. Ah, pardon my French. I feel stretched out. You know, worn." She sighed. "I can give you the names of the people she collected stories from here in town, one good lead over in Grand Marais. Maybe you can track the loups garou down. You are a detective, right?" She managed a smile, oblivious to the fact that egg yolk from her napkin dotted one of her cheeks.

He pointed to his own cheek until she figured out to put the napkin to its intended use.

"Christ, I'm a mess. I have to get to class," she said. "I'm free this afternoon to try and set up some appointments with Aimee's subjects. I'd also like to do some research into this on my own. I'll be at the library on campus after four, if you'd like to meet me."

"That sounds good," he said. He followed her to the front where they paid separately, then walked her out to her car. When he held the door she pursed her lips again.

"How long does the gentleman act last?" she asked.

"As long as it needs to," Alain replied. "Exactly as long as it needs to."

He watched her drive off. He'd go along on her wild goose chase, for the time alone with her if nothing else. Stephanie Bourbonnais's connection to this case was very interesting.

"Don't you have something more important to be doing, Alain?"

He turned to find Dr. Philemon, the retired sawbones from the bar the night before, standing a pace behind him and also watching the departure of the other doctor.

"Mel," Alain said by way of greeting.

"I've heard about what happened," Mel said. He tilted his head back toward the diner. "The current coroner gossips like a harpy. Fishes like one, too." The county didn't have enough deaths for a full-time coroner, so the duty rotated among the physicians for a year at a time.

Although retired, Mel Philemon kept his nose deep into the town's business. He had been a part of the welcoming committee when Alain had moved to Marquette and had passed along more information about Alain's new town than anyone else he'd met since, all in a manner that seemed casual but could have been a smooth line of bullshit. He knew everyone and had likely seen them naked and heard their secrets.

"We're working on it, Mel," Alain said. He hesitated for a moment. The man was a doctor. "What do you know about sleepwalking?"

"You think a sleepwalker did this? Not from what I heard, unless bears sleepwalk."

"No, no." Alain regretted saying anything, but he was into it already. "Me. I woke up at the head of the stairs yesterday. Didn't tie one on the night before, either."

Mel cupped his chin in his palm. His gray whiskers made a rasping noise against the calluses of his casting hand. "First time?"

"Yes."

"You remember anything?"

"A strange dream."

Mel waved that away like a mosquito. "Can't fix dreams. Could be stress . . . this case. Your first homicide in our fair county, eh? I wouldn't worry about it. Lots of weird things happen up here, dreams, everything."

"What do you mean?" Alain asked.

Mel gave him a measured look and scanned the parking lot for listeners before leaning in. "You haven't noticed it yet? You struck me right off as a young man with his nose to the ground. Someone who notices."

"Notices what?"

Mel pushed his toque up and rubbed at his forehead. "Ah, maybe it's the job. I thought being a cop was the same. Look, I moved up here right after interning in Detroit, right? 1960s: a war zone down there. I get here, and it's so quiet, so . . . different, that I wrote off the things that happened for a long while."

Alain wanted to ask a question, but Mel went on.

"The random crazies, sure, the ones who think the blizzard is talking to them through the walls or the ELF signal is killing their sperm. It's a long winter and people get shack-wacky."

"ELF?" Alain asked. He felt a little lost in the face of this outpouring.

"Not fairies," Mel said. "Extreme Low Frequency radio waves. Over in Republic there's a 32-mile long antenna the Navy built into the ground that is pumping out an ELF signal. They use it to talk to submarines underwater, all over the world. Who's really crazy?" He took out a pipe and began to pack it with Captain Black tobacco. Alain recognized the smell. Waagosh had smoked the same brand.

"Some years it seemed all I was delivering was girl babies. Then a long run of boys. Not every year, but, I don't know, cycles. I wasn't the only doctor in town at that point, but close enough. I check the records, and sure enough: in 1971 not a single female child was born in Marquette County. The teachers down at the school will back me up. The thing that really got me, though, was the diseases," Mel said. "They would only happen here. I'd check the papers and there was nothing in Schoolcraft County, not a damn thing going on in Wisconsin, but right here in this little pocket of the world old diseases would occasionally show up, things that had been knocked out for half a century—yellow fever, cholera, even tuberculosis—like time was looping back on itself. I figured out what was happening, even if I didn't know why, so I hit all the old medical books and learned what to look for. I didn't lose a single person past the first victim." The doctor popped a match against his yellowed thumbnail and held it to the bowl, puffing until he had a brazier glow. He took a long draw then pointed the stem at Alain. As he talked smoke leaked out the corners of his mouth and wreathed his head. "This is a special place. Special good, and special bad. Things can happen here that don't happen anywhere else, and it might be good if you kept that in mind, Detective."

Mel pulled his coat close and turned to go. Almost too low for Alain to hear he repeated, "Never lost a second victim."

The butcher died of a nine-day nosebleed. He had become a great eater of meat.
7 September, 1898. The Palladium Superior.

Chapter Nine

Alain reached the post by eight a.m. Janet's small SUV already sat in the parking lot in her accustomed spot closest to the door. A sheriff's cruiser pulled in behind him and honked. The window slid down to reveal a grinning Leon.

"I've found your dog," he announced. White clouds billowed from the car's tailpipe in the chill morning air.

"You've been detecting in your spare time," Alain said. "How do you know it's our beast?"

"It huge, enormous from what I've heard. Which reminds me of something my wife used to say—" Leon continued.

"Where?" Alain asked.

"Well, usually right there in the bed she'd say it, but one time in the church parking lot after the Shrine circus. She has a thing for clowns."

"Obviously," Alain said. "It's cold out here. How about if I shoot you? Will you tell me then?"

"It's at Hope Pines Farm, you impatient twit. No one appreciates a good story."

"Let me check in. You can spin your yarn on the way." Alain sprinted up the steps and through the front door.

Janet stood at the copier wearing her dispatch headset. She handed him the top sheet off the stack of copies, a summary of everything new in the case. It comprised a scant half-page.

"I'm going—" he began.

"Hope Pines Farm, I know," Janet said. "You don't think Leon could keep his mouth shut on the radio, do you? Go on, I'll log the trip."

"Thank you, ma'am," Alain said. "I don't know what we'd do without you."

"And what exactly do you think you'd do with me?" she asked, "or will you not have any time left over from your private lessons with the professor?"

Alain was speechless. He'd forgotten how small of a town Marquette could be. Janet's laughter accompanied him out.

Leon handed Alain a paper cup of coffee when he climbed into the patrol car, then spun the tires in the gravel as he pulled out.

"So where and what is Hope Pines Farm?" Alain asked, sipping at the powerful gas station brew as soon as the danger of wearing it had subsided.

"It's on Thoney Point, not too far from Buckroe, and it's a canine sanctuary," Leon answered. "It's like a rest home for dogs too old or sick to be adopted."

"Sounds fancy," Alain said.

"It's a couple of dykes with a house trailer and a barn on some logged-over acreage. Good folks, especially if you're a mutt."

"Leon, I don't think you're supposed to call them that."

"Mutts?"

"Dykes."

"Ah yes," Leon said, nodding. "The hick is being insensitive again. How about: vagina-oriented?" He swung onto the highway heading north and ran the cruiser up to eighty.

"I think lesbian is acceptable."

"My wife says Rhonda and Rhee call themselves dykes. They're . . . uh . . . reacclimatizing the term, or something."

"Reclaiming?"

"Yep. That."

Hope Pines Farm had a cheerful hand-painted sign portraying a pile of snoozing mutts. The neat gravel drive changed after a quarter-mile to a dirt road newly carved out of the jack pine forest. It twisted back into the woods, rutted and muddy.

"Apparently," Leon said, "it's all about appearances. If they make the place sound prosperous and idyllic, they get donations online. If they flat out tell the truth, that they're barely scraping by, they get squat. So, they have a lovely website and a nice sign by the road for photos."

"What about this big dog?" Alain asked, crumpling his coffee cup and tucking it away. His stomach still felt weak from the retching this morning. He studied his palms. He didn't dream the dirt, so he must have been outside at some point. Alain hated this feeling, not knowing.

"It's a long-shot, but it's all we've got," Leon said. "When I asked around at a backyard breeder's place, he talked about this monster that the girls have taken in. Apparently it hurt some troll down in the 'burbs, and it's been exiled up here to the frozen north." Trolls were denizens of the Lower Peninsula, so-called because they lived "below" the Mackinac Bridge that connected the two peninsulas.

The road got worse; the cruiser fishtailed as Leon gunned it through the muck. At the end of a sharp curve a steel gate blocked the road, with "DRIVE SLOW OR GET SHOT" stenciled across the top bar. Alain jumped out to open it, and took the opportunity to check his Sig in its holster. Leon pulled through. Alain closed the gate behind the cruiser and got back in.

"Friendly," he said, jerking his head at the gate and its message.

"I believe these two may like dogs quite a bit more than people, and I can't say that I blame them." Leon pulled up to a sagging single-wide trailer and honked. "I've never heard a dog complain."

A cacophony of barking erupted from the barn fifty yards behind the trailer, and in seconds a swarming wave of dogs in every shape and size surrounded the car. The taller ones put their front paws against the doors and peered in. The small-to-mediums hiked legs against the tires and added their scent to the new arrival. They all barked and wagged: big tails, little stumps and everything in-between. Alain had never seen so many happy dogs in one spot. He cracked his door, and four noses intruded into the car at various heights. He plowed in and headed for the trailer. If anything, the barking and howling increased in pitch and intensity.

These dogs had a strange response to him. Some sat and watched from a cautious distance or went down on their bellies, while others curled and wound around Alain like he wore a suit of bacon. His jeans were covered in hair and nose juice inside of five seconds.

His foray into the pack gave Leon time to get his door open and escape the car. No answer at the trailer, but he heard a voice call from the direction of the barn. As one, the dogs turned and hurtled back toward the sound.

The new center of the pack rounded the corner of the trailer, set down a shovel and nodded by way of greeting.

"You must be the state trooper," she said to Alain. She was a solid, square woman in a tattered barn coat.

"Yes, ma'am," he answered, which earned a snort.

"Ma'am, eh? Call me Rhonda." Her speech was pure U.P., which meant it borrowed heavily from Ontario.

"Rhonda, I'm Alain, and this is Leon." He had a sense that using their titles would push this conversation in the wrong direction.

Leon tipped his hat and eased away a greyhound whose inquisitive nose hovered at an uncomfortable height.

"You come to see Daisy." Her tone made the question into a statement.

"Daisy?" Leon asked. "The dog I heard about is a male."

"Daisy is a boy. What's in a name, eh? He come with that one, and he don't answer to nothing else. C'mon . . . in the barn." She turned without looking to see if they followed. At first glance Alain had thought her to be in her fifties, but upon closer examination she couldn't be older than thirty-five. Life had taken a toll. Her face showed the telltale lines of skin grafts, along with the lack of expression common among burn victims. Her chopped, dirty-blonde hair held heavy laces of gray. She favored her right leg, and grunted with the effort of walking.

He got a closer look at some of the individual dogs as they loped alongside. Some were missing a leg or an ear. A brindle pit bull had only one eye, and a mass of scar tissue on its neck. Rhonda followed his gaze.

"Fighting dog," she said by way of explanation. "State gonna put him down. Ain't that right Maxie? Too vicious for polite society, he is." She hugged the ugly head, and Maxie whined in delight. Rhonda scratched the stumps of his ruined ears. "Should've gassed the bastards on the outside of the ring."

The sliding door on the barn rolled back to allow a tall redhead to step into the morning light.

"These cops are here to see Daisy." Rhonda jerked a thumb at the two of them.

"Rhee Taylor." The redhead extended her hand to Alain, then Leon. "Why do you wish to meet a specific member of our little resort?" Her accent was pure Bryn Mawr. The cultured tones were pleasant to the ear, but Alain heard iron beneath the velvet.

Rhonda reached into a pocket, and the dogs went wild. They quieted when she pulled out a glove rather than a treat, although one or two had to sniff to be certain it wasn't edible.

"That Christian Laine, he complained, didn't he?" she asked.

Leon put on his cop face, which meant she'd probably scored a hit.

"Trouble with one of your neighbors?" Alain asked. He took a step closer, making the circle more intimate.

"He's got those poor Labrador bitches churning out litters like machines," Rhonda said. "Five million gets put down every year in the U.S., and he's making more to sell to the suburbs."

Rhee rested a hand on her arm. At the touch, Rhonda turned away from the men.

"We don't see eye-to-eye," Rhee said, "and there are rumors about what we do out here, who we are. Remember: a small town is where people go to church on Sunday to see who didn't."

Alain waited. He always gave people a chance to talk themselves out.

Rhee gave him back a bright, shallow smile.

57

"You may as well see Daisy," she said, "since you've come all the way out here. There truly can't be any harm in it."

She led the way into the barn, towing Rhonda by the hand like a willful child. Together the two of them ushered out the pack except for one lap dog, old and waddling, who looked as if he had some Corgi in him. The inside of the barn held pens and cages ingeniously connected by ramps and ladders to use every possible inch. A woodstove provided heat, insulation lined the walls, the construction a combination of new wood and scavenged old lumber held together with scrap metal and wire.

Something rustled in a box stall built for a long-gone plow horse. One by one, starting at the ground and moving up toward the ceiling, a shadow rising within the pen blotted out the light from the cracks in turn. Waist-height, head-height—the thing had to be seven feet tall. Panting like bellows came from behind the stall door, nails scratched the weathered boards. Rhee turned to look back at the policemen.

"You ready to meet Daisy?" she asked.

Both men took a half-step backwards. Getting a better shooting lane, Alain told himself. The women were perfectly at ease. Maybe Daisy only ate men.

She looked through a gap at face height. "Get off the door, you monster. I can't open it when you're leaning on it."

The shadow dropped. They could feel the impact through the raised wooden floor.

Rhee swung the door open.

"How's my baby boy?" she asked.

The panting grew louder but the dog remained out of sight in the stall.

"Sorry," Rhee said over her shoulder as she stepped into the stall. "He's shy."

Coaxing noises came from the stall. Rhonda stepped forward to help.

A nose appeared at the edge of the door, four feet off the ground—a nose bigger than a salad bowl, followed by the rest of the dog's face. Massive brown eyes settled on Alain. The head disappeared again as Daisy retreated.

"Come on, you big baby," one of the women said. "Moe! Come get Daisy."

The chunky Corgi waddled to the door of the stall, tail wagging. The head re-emerged and leaned down to touch noses with Moe, who stood about ten inches high. Rhee stood in the doorway, leaning against Daisy's shoulder because she could not fit past.

"Moe is the only dog he's made friends with so far," she said.

"What kind of dog is that?" Leon asked.

"Daisy is an English Mastiff. Seven and a half feet long, nose to tail, and he weighs two hundred sixty pounds. We had to use the cattle scale at the vet."

Moe barked and crouched, begging the big dog to play. He retreated as Daisy came out of the stall. The huge dog's tail wagged, but he seemed wary of the men.

"Stand still and let him get used to you. He'll come around." Rhonda had emerged from the stall as well, and she stood with her arm around Rhee's waist as they watched the dogs play. Daisy held still and tried to follow Moe's movement. Moe ducked and wove through his friend's enormous paws, barking up at him. Daisy drooled.

"Whoa," Leon said, amazed at the volume.

"Mastiffs do that. It's part of their charm," Rhonda said.

Charm, thought Alain, as the thick slime hit the floor. Moe got involved with a stuffed squeaky toy he found in Daisy's cell, and the big dog turned his attention to Alain. He stood still as the mastiff approached and lowered his head to sniff Alain's hand.

"Relax, officer," Rhee said. "Dogs can smell fear."

"He doesn't want to scare the dog," Rhonda said.

"I'm sure that's it," Leon chimed in.

Alain ignored them, and held his other hand out in front of Daisy's big snout. He turned it over, and Daisy nosed his palm gently, looking for a treat. Moving slowly, Alain reached up and began to scratch the dog's ears. Daisy sidled closer.

"Look out!" Rhee and Rhonda called in unison.

Too late. Daisy dropped his hind end to the floor and flopped against Alain with all of his weight, ramming his head into the kneading of Alain's hands. The shift in weight overbalanced him, and Alain crashed to the barn floor with the dog on top of him, both thrashing and kicking. A thick rope of slime slapped him across the face. One paw the size of a quart jar clipped him in the groin.

Leon bent double, holding his sides, giggling like a little girl. Rhee gathered herself to offer assistance but Alain had already extracted himself from underneath Daisy's crushing weight and made it to his hands and knees. The dog rolled over onto his back and presented his belly for rubbing, four feet sticking up in the air. Alain obliged. Leon wiped away tears.

"That's why he's here," Rhonda said. "His last owner got a little old and fragile. One time he knocked her right down and broke her hip."

"You want me to get your . . ." Leon gasped for air, "your walker out of the car, Alain?"

Rhonda ignored him. "She called us. She'd been a donor, and couldn't stand the thought of him in a shelter."

Daisy panted, drooled, stretched and passed a cloud of truly toxic gas. Alain gagged.

"More mastiff charm?" he asked.

Daisy chose to stay in the barn and play with Moe as they ventured back out into the silver autumn morning.

"Satisfied?" Rhee asked.

"Daisy's colon may be an environmental hazard, but I don't think he's dangerous," Alain said.

"You tell that Mr. Laine he can stick his complaint right up his bung, eh?" Rhonda chimed in. "And tell him to have a litter or two of pups himself, see how he likes it."

"Now that I would pay to see," Leon said.

"Detective, you still haven't told us why you're out here. It seems like a lot of attention for a dog complaint," Rhee said.

"We're investigating a murder, and very large dog tracks were found. You seem to have the largest dog in the area . . ." Alain said.

"How big?" Rhonda asked, interested.

"Bigger than Daisy's," he replied. He'd checked when the two of them had finished wrestling.

She scoffed. "Impossible. Mastiff's the largest breed in the world. There ain't nothing bigger. You're looking for a wolf."

"Our state biologists thought it more likely that a dog--" Leon began.

"Bull shit," Rhonda said, making it two distinct words. "Wolf. I heard it."

"When? Where?" Alain pulled his notebook from his jacket pocket, discovered his pen had bent in two when Daisy had flopped on him.

"Up there." Rhonda pointed away from the lake and into the Huron Mountains. "Last night. Big one running solo."

"It couldn't possibly have been a coyote?" Leon asked.

Rhonda turned her you're-an-idiot glare on him. "Coyote don't sound nothing like a wolf. Dogs know the difference. Coyote calls, the boy dogs want to go out and fight it, and the girls they want to go love it. When the wolf howls, you can't pry them dogs outside with a crowbar. They get so close to the stove some of them singe their tails, but they ain't going outside for nothing. The wolf call, that's the old wild talking—the part dogs don't got no more. Look almost the same, but totally different. Like people facing off a gorilla. Scare the shit right out of them."

The old wild . . . Alain scanned the pine-dark slopes of the ancient mountains to the south and west, lying like recumbent beasts, and he wondered what might be looking back down at him.

Chapter Ten

Both men were quiet as Leon bumped and skidded the cruiser back out the lane. Alain had left his contact information with the women and thanked them for their time. He also surreptitiously dropped a folded twenty into the donation box on the porch of the house-trailer. He caught Leon doing the same before they left. They didn't say a word about it.

"Ten o'clock already," said Leon, "and what have we got?" He concentrated on biting at a hangnail, and nearly slid the car off the narrow lane into a stump.

"We've got a big goofy dog that is definitely not our killer. We've got a dog lover that says it's a wolf and a wildlife expert that says it's a dog." Alain ticked the items off on his fingers. "The whole dog angle feels like a dead end to me now. The victim was hung up on werewolves—"

"Hang on a minute," Leon stopped him. "Back up. Werewolves?"

"She planned to do her dissertation on the loup garou. Modern ones, not old stories. Her professor thinks a cult of people who believe they're werewolves got her."

Leon toyed with the front of his shirt, and Alain figured he touched the small crucifix that hung over his sternum. The chain was the right length to keep it hanging over the round scar that marked the spot where Leon had been shot by a bank robber. "I guess we really are chasing monsters, then, eh? I always wanted to be one of the good guys. We need to stock up on torches and pitchforks."

"Wrong monster. For these we need silver bullets," Alain said.

"My grandma told me the loup garou ate up boys who didn't bring home deer meat. That toothless old woman scared the hell out of me up until my first hunt, all because she had a taste for venison." Leon shook his head and returned to the present as they left the woods and reached the solid paved road. "It still doesn't explain last night, does it? Some crazy in a suit running through the student neighborhood, then snatching a kid . . . What are you going to tell the fellas?"

"Let's get them together after lunch and see if anyone else has anything," Alain said. "Last night could be unrelated. I still think it could have been a bear."

"Bears don't do things like last night," Leon said.

Alain knew that, and it irked him.

"There are sick and crazy animals just like there are sick and crazy people," he said. "You never know what they're going to do. If we've got someone in a suit . . . that's . . ."

He let it trail off. Speaking of crazy. Alain didn't even know where to start with that one. It had to be an animal. The girl's sweatshirt had been covered in saliva. Was Daisy capable of wandering through town with a little girl in his huge mouth? He might not be a killer, but he was certainly a serial drooler. The women had sworn he'd been in the barn all night so they'd have to be lying or dim. He hadn't gotten the feeling either was likely.

"We'll go over the break-in and the cult idea, and split them up," Alain said. "If there are people around pretending to be werewolves someone has to have heard something. We'll get the greenies working on actual wolf sightings, see if there's anything to what Rhonda told us. And bears, I guess, so we can rule it out."

"Sounds good," said Leon. "I can call my wife, see what she knows about the cult thing. If there's a rumor she hasn't unearthed in this half of the state it's not for lack of trying."

"Fine," Alain said, "but don't tell anyone else how you handle your detective work if you want a raise, though. The higher-ups will start calling her first and cut out the middle-man."

Leon held up his hands defensively. "It's not my fault that I'm married to the best source in town. Ah, shit. I've got to meet with Captain Campus Cop after lunch to talk about drug dealers . . . his favorite topic."

"I think it might be his second favorite, behind parking infractions," Alain said. Leon considered that.

"If we could a get a drug dealer enrolled at the college who liked to double-park, Marvin would walk around with a stiffy twenty-four seven," Leon said.

Alain snagged the radio from the dash mount and called into the post. Janet seemed surprised to hear from him.

"I've been trying to raise you on your cell phone and the radio for the last thirty," she said over the air. "Are you a mind reader, Detective?"

"The dog farm must be in a dead spot," he said. "We're back out on 28 and heading into town."

"Trooper Beatty is looking for you," she said, "as is the professor from the university." Beatty was the trooper from L'Anse, the young lady who had taken over interviewing the witnesses last night. Janet spoke formally over the open radio channel, but her tone added volumes of meaning. "Both are eager to see you as soon as possible."

Alain filled her in about the meeting he wanted and asked her to put out the call to gather the officers at the post at one p.m. He got the specifics about Beatty, who wanted to see him at the victim's residence, and asked Janet to pass along the word to Stephanie that he would catch her at the university library at four.

Leon concentrated on his driving with a bit too much precision as Alain replaced the radio mike.

"Yes?" Alain asked.

"Nothing. Nothing at all," Leon replied in a saintly manner. "I heard you broke bread with the young doctor—what is the name, again?"

"Bourbonnais," Alain said.

"Ah yes, Bourbonnais, a lovely name. I heard you were seen having breakfast," Leon lingered over the word, "this very morning. It seems remarkable that you would need to interview a witness twice in one day. That's all. I'm only mentioning it. Polite conversation." Leon could be a study in innocence.

"Why is everyone so interested in my dealings with women?" Alain asked.

"Well, you're the second-most handsome man in town, and I'm taken. It's a small town, there is nothing else to do and we all have a lot of money riding on the outcome."

The car banged through a pothole.

"You're betting on my love life?" Alain asked.

"Sex, marital status, divorce, second wife: the whole shebang. There's an outside leaner bet on sexual orientation, but personally I think those are mean-spirited shots from a few girls and maybe a boy or two you've rejected." Leon polished an imaginary speck on the inside of the windshield.

"You are kidding about this, right?"

"Does eighteen hundred sound like we're kidding?" Leon asked. "Not many have lasted single in this town as long as you, and we're very concerned, both about your well-being and our possible winnings. Long winters, my friend. Personally, I'm going to buy a snowblower and a hot tub when you fall desperately in love with a certain hefty but sexy farm girl this winter and are settled down and making little detectives by the spring thaw."

Alain leaned his head into his hands and turned to watch as the car lots of beautiful Marquette unrolled past the window.

Leon swerved to the curb across from the Willow Lane house. Beatty stepped from her state police Chevy Blazer on the other side of the road and waved them over.

"You're going to want to see this," she said perfunctorily. She led the way between the houses. She didn't turn into the yard behind the house Aimee Henderson had rented. It gave off the violent emptiness of a crime scene. Beatty reached the edge of the woods, dug the toes of her boots into the sandy bank and began to climb. The hillside rose steeply here and soon they were breathing heavily and looking down on the roofs of the student ghetto.

"I haven't visited the murder scene, but I've seen the pictures," Beatty said, stopping at a spot where a natural depression in the hillside formed a shallow bowl. "Does this look similar to you?" She stepped aside as Alain and Leon gained the edge.

Claw marks had raked the earth, torn and thrown about great clots of dirt and rock. Half-buried in the lowest part of the small bowl he saw the remains of a medium-sized dog. Alain realized that his eyes deceived him. Not half-buried. It looked like half a dog.

"Do we know whose? How long it's been gone?" he asked Beatty.

She checked her notebook.

"Meatwad," she said.

"Excuse me?" Leon asked.

"The dog's name is Meatwad," Beatty said, "or was Meatwad, I suppose. Two roommates I talked to last night said he'd been missing for a day or two."

She swung her notes closed with a snap.

"They were a little . . . unclear," she said. "The kind of unclear that leads to the munchies."

"Where's the rest of him?" Leon asked, sounding as if bile rose in his throat. Dead people didn't bother him.

Beatty shook her head. "I took a quick look, but I thought you might want to check for tracks. No sign of the, uh, the remainder."

"Good work, Beatty," Alain said. "Let's get Bob or one of the other rangers out here, see what he can find," he went on. "You want to tell the kids?"

"I'll do it," she said.

"Here." Leon held out a business card he must have swiped from the porch at Hope Pines. "These ladies can help if they're looking to take in another one, and they'll make sure the kids are fit to be owners first."

Beatty stepped away to call dispatch and get more people on the way.

Leon shook his head slowly at the scene in front of them. "Alain, my friend," he asked, "how does a weirdo who only thinks he's a werewolf tear a seventy-pound dog in half?"

Alain had no answer for that one.

In his cubicle at the post Alain swore at the paperwork in his inbox, then began to swiftly initial and sign everything Janet had marked for him. The phone messages from the press were tossed aside. He'd have to deal with them soon and release a statement. A heavy envelope in the middle of the stack caught his attention: thick cream-colored stock with his name in cursive, the wax seal imprinted with a signet of stylized curves. It could be a river. Or hills. Who the hell still used wax seals? Alain dug out his pocketknife and slit under the glob to preserve the imprint. He was thoughtfully turning the single page the envelope contained over in his hands, feet up on the desk, when Leon arrived a few minutes early for the briefing.

"How long does the full moon last?" the lanky deputy asked by way of greeting.

"One night?" Alain guessed. He didn't glance up from the note.

An expedient resolution to this matter would be appreciated. —HMC

Nothing more. The paper smelled like money.

"Exactly. And do you know which night that might be?"

Alain set the note on his desk. "I get the idea you're going to tell me."

"It's tonight." The deputy had his hat in his hands, and he tugged at the brim with both hands as though trying to reshape it. "Full October moon: the hunter's moon."

Alain cleared a stack of training forms off his guest chair and gestured for Leon to sit. "It wasn't full last night? Sure looked like it."

"Last phase before the full moon, called the gibbous moon. It's so close that it's hard to tell the difference," Leon said. "I looked it up in the Farmer's Almanac. The wife buys them. Boils."

"Your wife boils the Farmer's Almanac?"

"She gets boils. Makes her mean. Meaner. The Almanac tells you if it's going to be a bad month for boils, and it's got folk remedies and shit."

Alain let that drop. "Giblet moon last night, full moon tonight. Got it."

"Then another *gibbous* moon as it starts to wane," Leon continued, "and the whole thing starts over again. Twenty-eight days until the next one." The deputy's big hands clenched into fists.

Alain saw where Leon was headed. "So you think if it's a lunatic with a werewolf fetish, he started up when the moon got full. It's important to him . . . her . . . it. So we have until tomorrow night to catch this critter, or we lose him for a month and he could end up who knows where."

They both understood the consequences of the killer going to ground for four weeks. Other cases would demand attention, clues degrade. The culprit might disappear for good, move to another area and get away with murder.

Janet stuck her head into the cubicle. "Hey Leon, how's tricks?"

"Gibbous," Leon answered. He slumped in the chair.

"Where are my autopsy results?" Alain asked. "And I need the warrant for the subject's financial reports."

"Tomorrow," Janet replied, in a tight voice.

Leon twisted his hat further out of shape and tried catch Alain's eye.

"Sorry," Alain said. "I'm—"

"An asshole under stress?" Janet asked. She smoothed his hair behind his ear then pinched the lobe painfully between two perfect nails. "Forgiven. This time. Right now you've got a meeting to run."

Chapter Eleven

Leon slouched into a desk at one side of the room while Alain took the podium. He noticed Harold missing—Hell, now, with Leon spreading the nickname the poor kid didn't stand a chance—but everyone else present. At his request Beatty recapped her report on the new site where the dog carcass had been found. The similarity of the torn-up ground seemed interesting, but no new evidence had been found on the hillside yet. Copies of last night's report made their way from hand to hand around room, then were dutifully clipped into binders. The door-to-door work progressed, slow and fruitless so far. All the big dogs they could locate had paws too small to leave the track found in the woods. Rhonda had been right. It didn't seem to be a dog.

Janet stopped in to report on the phone calls they'd taken about the crime. "More crazies than usual," she said.

"Crazy how?" Leon asked.

"Along with the usual old ladies afraid that bikers are coming to gang-rape them, we've got missing chickens, scary dreams and a bearwalker," she continued.

Leon sat up at the last word, as did a few other men and women among the officers. Alain knew Janet came from Indiana, meaning she hadn't grown up with Ojibwa.

"Leon will take the, uh, the last one." Alain didn't want to say it aloud. A bearwalker: a powerful magician who could float through the woods as a ball of light or assume any animal shape. They breathed fire and could curse anyone with Ojibwa blood to a slow, wasting death. He didn't believe in them, but his uncles had urged him never to say the word. The fear they'd instilled in a ten year-old kept the word lodged like a bone in his throat. "Beatty, you've got the chicken thief. Look for similarities to the dog site. We don't have to worry about dreams or biker gangs. Yet."

The calls were a longer shot than the door-to-door work, but if he couldn't find his dog he'd need a new theory. Alain sketched out the duty roster for the evening patrols. He wanted twice as many cars as normal on the roads after dark, circling wider than usual into the woods surrounding town. If any giant squirrels, bearwalkers or even Homo sapiens showed, they'd be on top of them in a hurry. His overtime budget for the extra manpower only lasted another twenty-four hours. Any longer than that, and he'd need to start sending team members back to regular assignments. Something had to break.

Alain cut the meeting short. He caught Janet on the way back to her desk.

"Harold Burke call in?" he asked.

"You mean Hell?" she asked.

"Whatever he's going by these days. Did he call in sick?"

"As a matter of fact he did. He wants to help if he can. Asked where you were, then gave me the story about his wounded wing. Poor Hell," she said. "I told him about the dog farm. Maybe you could find him something on a desk until he heals?"

"Yeah, sure," Alain said. His stomach growled. Checking out the site of the Meatwad's death had made him miss lunch. "Figure out what he can do. Maybe call the surrounding counties, check for animal complaints. We need everybody on this one."

The short meeting meant Alain had a few hours to kill before he'd planned to meet Stephanie at the university. He stopped at a drive-thru for a sandwich and coffee and then began to wander. When he couldn't hike or run an aimless cruise seemed to help his subconscious percolate and sift through the layers of information he'd taken in. The troubling note on the fancy paper rode shotgun. He had no clue what it meant or who *HMC* might be. Alain had gotten hate mail before, but never such nice hate mail. He wove in and out of the town limits, following pavement to gravel forest service roads before looping back through the small grid of downtown. The long slope of Front Street reminded him of the sepia photos he'd found in the attic of his house showing the same buildings a hundred years in the past: the clock tower on the bank building that cast its shadow across the street today, the public library like a crouching limestone lion. Old scenes superimposed themselves over the present in Alain's eye, making him feel as though time itself could be malleable, the horses and streetcars still a part of the traffic like layers in sediment.

He made stops at a few locations for conversations that specifically avoided the words "loup garou" or "werewolf." He sprinkled in terms likely to get the talk started: weirdos, freaks, tourists that appeared more strange than stupid.

Two liquor stores netted him nothing. At the tiny grocery that processed most of the poached deer in the county the owner, who resembled Santa to a disturbing extent, shook his head and lamented the general existence of them damned people. It seemed that he meant everyone.

Alain drove the county line road all the way to the washed-out bridge. It had been gone for over three years now. The county planned to fix it in a good tax year, which might fall in the next decade or the one after. On the way he passed a small, run-down resort that had closed the first summer after the washout had suddenly located it on a ten-mile dead end. The cabins seemed to hunch in against themselves like a drunk trying to act sober. He noticed the chain that used to block the drive lying loose in the dirt.

Alain pulled into the parking lot for the propane filling station—the very last building at the end of the road—and got out to survey the damage. He'd seen it several times already, but the raw destructive power of nature always gave him a sense of awe, a good idea of his insignificant place in the natural world. The twisted metal wreckage of the bridge had been removed, but he could still see chunks of concrete and snakes' nests of rebar scattered through the brush along the high banks for fifty yards downstream. The water flowed in a deceptive rippling calm. Footsteps approached behind him.

"Ice dam," the owner, proprietor and delivery driver of the station said, before leaning over to spit into the stream. "Morning it went, I thought I was back in the war. Must have been twenty ton of ice broke up all at once and come through here like the devil on a freight train." He'd been starting conversations the same way since the accident. Alain nodded.

"You still on that city electric for heat?" the man asked.

"Haven't froze yet," Alain said.

"They're stealing from you. Big drafty house like that. There's the crime you ought to be looking into." Sales pitch delivered, the owner turned away from Alain and trod into the oversized garage past the flat snout of his propane truck.

Alain followed. He'd come, as all the locals did, for the smoked whitefish the owner's wife sold on the side.

The garage connected straight into the house through a screen door. As Alain paid for his bag of double-wrapped fish, the gas dealer came up with a new topic.

"Got neighbors," the man said.

"On this side?" Alain asked. What a stupid question, he thought immediately.

The wife wiped down the counter, making slow circles with her sponge.

"Bought the Shore-Breeze Resort." The owner slid by his wife, nudging her rear with his hip in the process, to reach the refrigerator and take out a pop. He waved one at Alain.

Alain shook his head. "Do you know where they're from?"

The man took a long pull before answering. "Chicago. They're FISH." Fucking Illinois Shit-Heads. "Say they're going to put in solar, for chrissake."

"So you've talked to them? What are they like? How many?" Alain tried to calm down. Probably just a couple of yuppies who planned to open another antique store or a gift shop.

"I've seen three," the owner said, "and believe me you cannot tell who's doing what with who."

"With whom. And it's four," the wife said. "The one guy is nice. Ryan something. The women and the other guy are freaks."

69

The screen door to the garage banged shut behind Alain.

Alain climbed into the truck. He dropped his fish on the floor and grabbed the radio to get back-up rolling in his direction. It couldn't be this easy. "Freaks" might cover a wide array of behaviors not normally seen in the U.P. Still, he had a feeling in his gut that this could be real. Luck, in his opinion, was nothing more than probability taken personally. If he flipped a coin ninety-nine times and got heads each time, the chance of it being heads the hundredth time was still fifty-fifty. He'd had cases break in odder ways.

He started the truck, then shut it off again. He couldn't drive in without back-up. Nothing, however, prevented him from taking a look around.

The cluster of cabins that made up the resort sat scattered throughout a clutch of tall pines. As Alain approached through the woods he could see places where the cheap log facade on the walls had rotted away or come loose to expose the plywood beneath. One of the trees had fallen recently to smash a cabin to kindling. It still lay there: trunk bisecting the roof, branches shattered like shrapnel, the base uprooted, roots clotted with the gray sand that covered this part of the U.P. He could smell the sap in the jagged, broken wood. At the center of the loose assembly of buildings stood what must have passed for a lodge, larger than the others, with a screened porch attached the front of the building and an empty concrete pool along the side. The mud-streaked silver SUV parked out front had Illinois plates, but Alain couldn't make them out at this distance. He watched from behind a tree.

After a few minutes the side door of the lodge banged open and a bearded young man shambled out, yanked down his sweats and began to urinate into the pool. He stood with his back to Alain, all of his attention on weaving his stream through patterns in the air.

Alain moved one tree closer, then to another within ten yards of the porch. The Mercedes SUV shielded him from the boy's view, but several windows on this side of the lodge made it impossible to move any closer without being exposed. He stood motionless, memorizing the license plate and considering his next move. Back-up had to be close. He needed to get inside before the cruisers arrived. Even innocent people acted differently with police present, and Alain wanted to see these transplants in their natural habitat. Alain heard the side door open and close. A quick lean and peek around the truck told Alain that the boy had gone back inside.

He took a deep breath, let it out, scrubbed a hand through his hair to muss it and then stepped into the open with purpose, heading for the porch. The screen door rasped as it dragged across the boards. He knocked on the inner door. It had a crude symbol painted on the surface of the wood at eye-level, a Greek delta superimposed over a theta. Alain glanced back to the Mercedes. Sorority girls? Four litter boxes lined one end of the porch.

Footsteps vibrated through the floorboards. The door swung open to reveal the urinator. His sweats bore the name of an expensive store silk-screened down the leg in looping swirls.

"Yeah?" the boy asked. If surprised to have someone appear on his doorstep out of thin air he covered it well. His face remained open, his tone mild.

"Hi." Alain had allowed his shoulders to slump forward. He dry-washed his hands together in front of his stomach, and let his voice creep into a higher register. "Have you seen—this may sound weird—but have you seen a Labrador? My dog ran off." He waved one hand in the general direction of the forest beyond the lodge property.

A girl joined him in the doorway. No, not a girl. She dressed like the boy but had to be at least ten years older. Maybe more.

"A pet?" she asked. The corners of her mouth twitched into a hint of a sneer.

"His name is Meatwad," Alain said. He shrugged and grinned and leaned forward.

The couple took an involuntary step back, and Alain moved closer. One more time and he'd be inside.

"I didn't hear anyone calling a dog," the woman said.

Shit.

"He's kind of shy," Alain said. "If I can get close enough to see him he'll come because I have treats, but if I call he keeps running."

"Your pet runs when you call him?" She wore a cashmere sweater, her face carefully made up. A silver pendant on her necklace had a nicer version of the symbol that appeared on the door. The word "pet" sounded dirty in her mouth.

A tiger cat stalked past the open door. Alain could see a drift of what had to be cat hair in the corner of the room. Stacks of paper covered a sagging ping-pong table in the middle of the floor.

"It's kind of a game." Alain leaned in again, pointed at the cat and asked, "This your little guy?"

The boy stiffened as if expecting to be hit.

"He lives with us," the woman said. "We do not own animals. Cats make their own decisions."

"You folks just moved here, huh? It's nice," Alain said.

She sniffed. The boy made a see-saw motion with his hand.

71

"I thought four people lived here," Alain said. "What's all this?"

He took a small step forward into the room and gestured at the table. The woman frowned but she made room.

"My work," she said in a clipped cadence.

"Luke and Summer decided to go back down to the city," the boy said. "They left after two weeks. Summer saw a snake."

She shot the boy a nasty look.

"They weren't dedicated enough," the woman said. "We'll build the retreat without her. Without them."

"So the two of you are going to re-open the resort?" Alain asked. He scanned the room. Decades of cigarette smoke had yellowed the walls. Twin doors in the back wall led deeper into the building. He could smell marijuana and the ammoniac underlayer of cat piss.

"Retreat," she corrected him coldly. "A spiritual retreat: a place for a few chosen people. We've had a lot of interest already. Now if we can only find a contractor willing to actually work in this flyspeck place, we can still open in time for next summer."

The boy handed Alain a pamphlet from the table. It read "Superior Glade" across the top and featured high-quality shots of the Pictured Rocks, carved sandstone cliffs along Lake Superior that appeared in every scenic Michigan calendar ever published. He flipped it over. The back had contact info but no prices or any mention that the area pictured on the front was sixty miles away.

"Ryan—" she shook her head. "I'm sure he wants to be on his way to find his pet."

"Oh, Meatwad's fine," Alain said. "He does this every other week or so."

Her lips came together into a tight pucker.

"Have you considered the fact that maybe he doesn't want to be a servant?" she asked. "That he has a soul? Animals are superior to humans in many ways."

"Well, he's a good boy but he does like to roll in dead things and eat his own poop from time to time," Alain said. "What kind of special people?"

"It might be difficult for you to understand," she said.

"Sylvia," the boy—Ryan—said.

Alain could hear gravel crunching under tires in the driveway. He had only a few more seconds as the guy with the lost dog.

"Try me," he said.

Sylvia's eyes glittered.

"People who are human only in appearance."

"Oh really?" Alain asked. "That's neat."

Ryan stooped to look out one of the low front windows. He turned back into the room to speak, but stopped short at Sylvia's expression.

"We keep a low profile, out of necessity. Humans don't understand us, and vice versa." Sylvia said.

"So, um, what are they if they aren't human?" Alain asked.

Heavy knocking sounded on the door.

"Syl, there are cops outside," Ryan said. He said the same way a kid might announce the arrival of an ice cream truck. Alain adjusted his estimate of the kid's age downward, at least his mental age.

"Shit, what now?" she asked. "This godforsaken place."

Neither one of them seemed nervous. Curious, yes, but there were no shared looks or any increase in tension. Alain felt his own excitement ebb. His lucky hit was dead in the water. Whatever these two whackjobs were up to, they hadn't killed anyone. He needed to get back on the road.

Ryan shrugged and opened the door. The trooper on the porch stepped inside as soon as he saw Alain.

"What the fuck do you want?" Sylvia asked.

The trooper stopped short. He looked at Alain, who shook his head minutely.

"We, uh," the trooper said, "Well, we're conducting an investigation in this area, and—"

He looked for help again. Alain studied the ping-pong table. Sylvia saw something she didn't seem to like. She whirled on Alain.

"You didn't lose any dog, did you? You were spying on us!"

Alain held his hands up between them. Her shift from sarcastic to aggressive had happened in an instant.

"Whoa, easy, it's a routine investigation, ma'am," he said.

"Oh shit," Ryan said under his breath.

"Don't you ma'am me, you cocksucker!" Sylvia shrieked. She snatched a handful of brochures from the table and flung them at Alain. They scattered into a glossy airburst as soon as they left her hand. He flinched anyhow.

The trooper keyed the radio mike on his shoulder and said "Contact." A splintering crash at the back of the lodge meant at least one more officer had entered the building.

"She's off her meds," Ryan yelled. "Don't hurt her!"

The trooper got the woman in a bearhug from behind as a local officer came through one of the twin doors with his pistol drawn. She went berserk: kicking, flailing, screaming and crying.

Alain spun to face Ryan. "Let me see your hands!"

Brochures spiraled down to settle across the wooden floor.

Ryan had never moved from his spot by the front door. He raised his hands obediently over his head. He watched the struggle as the two officers tried to get Sylvia under control. She knocked one leg out from under the table while thrashing. It collapsed.

"Syl, stop," Ryan said. "Don't spit."

"All you fuckers are against me," she yelled, "all of you. Fuckers!"

Her mascara ran down her face in a jagged mask. They'd gotten cuffs on her and rolled her onto her stomach. The trooper had gone to his patrol for leg shackles and a spit mask while the local officer held her pinned. He still wheezed from the fight.

"You want to tell me what's going on here?" Alain asked Ryan.

"Don't!" Sylvia yelled.

Alain stepped in front of the boy to block his view of the woman being trussed for transport.

Ryan shuffled his feet.

"Has a young lady visited here recently? A student?" Alain asked.

"Amy, something?" Ryan asked. "Sure."

"You wanted to fuck her," Sylvia muttered. "I knew it. Put your penis in her."

Ryan blushed.

"No, Sylvia, I told you. Not then, and not now," he said. He lowered his voice. "Please don't listen to anything she says. Sylvia got back from a, a rest, at the hospital this morning," he said. "She hasn't taken anything since then, though, not like she's supposed to."

"How long was she there?" Alain asked. He pulled his notebook out and jotted a reminder to check intake and release records at the hospital.

"Three days," Ryan said. "This time."

"And where were you during those three days?"

Ryan glanced around him at the woman on the floor. They hoisted her to her knees. She'd gone limp and seemed unconscious. The two men had to support her weight between them.

"Here," he said a little louder, with emphasis. "I stayed here."

He looked at Alain and shook his head in a tiny waggle. After the officers had staggered out the door with their burden, Ryan let out a deep breath he'd been holding.

"Jesus," he said.

"So?" Alain asked.

"I went down to Traverse City to meet my dad's lawyer. He's on a golf trip, but he agreed to help me out of this mess. I've got to get clear of this craziness. My dad's already pissed that I co-signed the note on this shithole."

"When did you leave and return?"

"As soon as I checked her in I took off, and I barely got back in time to retrieve her this morning. That is a long-ass drive. There's a lot of nothing up here," Ryan said.

74

Alain let it slide. FISH. He took down the lawyer's name, the hotel the boy had used in Traverse City and wrote another note to have the traffic cameras checked on the Mackinac Bridge for the Mercedes. If the story held up and he'd been gone for the last three days while she'd been locked up, this truly had proven to be a dead end.

"Aimee came out here—" Alain said. He paused to let the boy fill in the rest.

"Oh yeah," Ryan said, "last week. I guess she'd heard about the therian stuff."

"Excuse me?" Alain asked.

"This stuff." Ryan waved his hands at the brochures covering the floor. "Therianthropy. Sylvia got all excited to talk to her, at least until she decided that the girl made eyes at me. Syl's real persuasive when she's not, you know, screaming batshit crazy. I used to think there might be something to it. Anyway, I saw Aimee turn off her recorder after about an hour, subtle-like. She seemed nice, but not really interested."

"Have you seen her since that day?"

The boy shook his head.

"Therianthropy," Alain repeated it as he wrote it down.

"People who believe they're panthers or bears or animals on the inside."

"Wolves?"

"Sure, why not? You wouldn't believe what people will buy. Sylvia planned to charge people five grand a week to stay here and discover their animal under her guidance. Summer—the other girl—left when Syl told her she was a boanth."

Alain paused, pen held over the paper.

"A cow," Ryan said. "She tried to tell Summer her inner animal was a bovine. It didn't go over very well."

"These believers think they can actually turn into these animals?" Alain asked.

Ryan shrugged. "Not really. Spiritually, maybe, but even Sylvia didn't think she could turn into a cat. She believed she was a cat on the inside."

Alain closed his notebook. "Why?" he asked.

He gestured around to take in the whole run-down place, the collapsed table, the drool on the floor, all of it.

Ryan cocked his head like a dog and thought for a moment before answering.

"I don't know. Crazy sex is the best sex, I guess. Freaky. You ever been with a cat?" The boy gave a laugh.

"I'm going to need a customer list, people who got in touch with you. Stay put," Alain said. "I'm going to take a look around with one of these officers."

"Should I get my lawyer on the phone?"

"You're not under arrest." Alain said. "As long as there's nothing big here, I don't think so, but you're welcome to make the call."

"I'm cool," Ryan said.

He took a seat on the floor and surveyed the ruins of his first business venture.

It took Alain less than an hour to determine that this place had no clear connection to the girl's death. The boy didn't seem to even know about it, and he did not come across as smart enough to lie well. Alain tossed a pipe in the trash before the other officer found it and had to make the decision. Nothing else on the property seemed suspicious. He left the local cop to do a thorough search as a precaution.

Alain walked back down to the propane station and headed out on the long drive back to the highway with only a bag of smoked fish to show for his efforts.

This case was grinding on him. It didn't have a shape, no edges or cracks where he could get a grip, apply pressure, tear it open. The animal aspect skewed his process. If a wolf had killed the girl, who had left the thumbprint and erased the pictures? It certainly wasn't these ineffectual new-age freaks. Maybe someone had contacted them, someone who thought he or she was an animal on the inside, but they'd still need an actual beast to do the killing. He couldn't find the line that led from one step to the next. Of course, it didn't help that he was losing his own grip, sleepwalking and who knew what else. It felt as if he'd been on the case for longer than two days. While he screwed around and hit dead ends, the pile of meat and marrow that used to be a girl named Aimee lay on a metal tray in a lab somewhere to the south. His stricken dreams, the tracks, the cast of her cold eyes when he'd lifted the sleeping bag. It all made Alain want to hurt someone.

The North Country lost a champion this season. Trefflé Largnesse would walk another man's trapline in winter to feed that man's children. He would dog-sled fifty miles for the mail and sleep in a snowbank with his team, more comfortable than a Chicago banker with an iron stove and a hotel featherbed. Uncounted are the lost wayfarers whose first introduction was an uncomfortable hug from a hirsute man springing from the shadow of the trees. Half-bear, half-Québécois, dirt-angel, half-witted when it came to the fairer sex. Treff ran these woods like he'd been born to it, and we are all the poorer for his passing.
31 October, 1898. The Palladium Superior.

Chapter Twelve

Identical rows of hunched students filled the library computer stations, earbuds plugged into phones, but the stacks were empty. Occasionally Alain used his state ID to check books out here. He seemed to be one of the few. Stephanie waited in a carrel by the aging elevator, looking more alert than she had at breakfast— snappier. A stack of books and Xeroxed articles teetered on the desktop.

"I called Mama Bouche, Aimee's main interviewee. She can squeeze us in before she closes at five. I thought we'd pick up some reading material for the trip," she said. "I've got Aimee's notes, and a lot of her source material. The printed parts, at least. She hadn't turned in her tapes yet."

"Tapes?" he asked.

"Audio recordings of the stories she collected. She had to record each legend and tale from the original source. They're required for the folklore archives before she can get credit."

He helped her gather the books and papers, and tucked the few that did not fit in her bag under his arm. He could stand to do some research on wolves himself. During his years spent growing up in the woods he hadn't seen so much as a track. Then again, an hour tracking wolves with Bob might teach him more a week in the library.

Stephanie said, "If I wore your letter jacket, people would talk." She led the way into the stacks rather than toward the front door. "I have one more book to pull."

He didn't reply to that. "Ordinary cassette tapes? Is that what you use?"

Stephanie scanned the signs on the ends of the bookshelves and chose a row. She talked over her shoulder. "Some people use a digital recorder, but cassettes are still common. It seems to put older story-tellers at ease to see technology they understand. Students bring the tapes in and convert them to digital files after collection. I think Aimee has used both methods in the past. Why?" Stopping in front of one shelf, she ran a finger along the spines until she reached a gap. "Damn. The catalogue showed this one as available. Who steals folklore?" She turned on the heel of her boot and stalked out of the aisle, leaving him to follow.

Alain remained silent until they'd crossed the parking lot.

"We didn't find tapes at Aimee's apartment," he said slowly, thinking out loud. "Where else would she have kept them?" Aside from her laptop, they seemed to be the only thing possibly missing.

"We can check her office in the English building, but I don't think she'd leave anything important there. She shares it with a dozen other grad students." Stephanie climbed up into the cab. As he shut his door he caught a faint breath of her scent. Not flowery or fake, but something nice. Vanilla?

The graduate student office turned out to be a dingy room with two desks and a window painted shut. A Chinese take-out menu tacked to the door had hand-written commentary and copious footnotes. According to the prevailing wisdom the moo-shoo must be avoided at all costs.

"Thirteen people share this?" he asked.

She shrugged. "The liberal arts are under-funded. If we could score hockey goals or pull in Department of Defense grants, we'd get more space. As it is, they leave us alone because we don't ask for much."

Alain rifled the drawers. No files of any kind. This was a place to grade papers if the walk to the library proved too far. He stared at a ceiling tile with a water stain the exact shape of Norway. Some wag had added a small Norwegian flag on a pushpin and a sign that read "Fjord parking only."

"Why would someone steal old stories on tape?" he asked the ceiling.

Stephanie had long legs. She wore a knee-length skirt and kept shifting position with a great deal of thigh and smooth calf adjustment. Mama Bouche, whoever she might be, lived an hour's drive southeast in Munising. Highway 28 followed the lakeshore for part of the trip. In spots where the dips and undulations and yearly migration of the sand dunes had gotten the better of the state engineers the route curved inland for long stretches.

Stephanie worked her way through the literature she'd brought. She occasionally referred to a three-ring binder containing Aimee's thesis notes.

"There's a flood myth tied to werewolves," she said at one point. "The human king Lycaon tricked Jupiter into eating human flesh. That made the king of the gods a little pissed off and he transformed Lycaon into a wolf as punishment. That's where the word lycanthropy comes from."

"So, Jupiter was a vegetarian?" he asked.

"He obviously wasn't a humanitarian. The whole mess made him decide to destroy humankind and start over," Stephanie replied.

"I've had days where that seems like a good idea," Alain said.

Aimee had tucked loose index cards into her thesis proposal. Stephanie caught one in mid-air as it fell out and drifted toward the floor. "Moonlight is the wolf's sunlight," she read, before flipping it over to show him that it only contained the one line.

"Solzhenitsyn," he replied. "A Day in the Life of Ivan what's-his-name, I think."

One of her auburn eyebrows went up, but she simply said, "Hmm," and tucked the paper gently back into the notebook.

He saw her fingers linger on the page, on her student's handwriting. He wanted to know what the girl had been to Stephanie. She seemed proud like a parent might be. There was something else there. Competition for a man, a woman, a grant . . . Why was she so interested? The simplest explanation would be that she missed her friend but his job had drummed that kind of naiveté out of him years ago.

She caught him looking. Her eyes were bright with suppressed tears.

"If you say anything," she said, "a single word that makes me cry right now, I will stab you with a pencil someplace uncomfortable."

"You mean like in a kayak?" he asked.

Stephanie almost laughed. Some of the tension seemed to go out of her. She returned to her reading, seemingly engrossed, and he caught another glimpse of her legs. He couldn't help it.

"Aimee's work focused primarily on sex," she said.

He swerved back into the proper lane.

"Right," he said, nodding.

"Werewolf tales are fraught with sexual tension," Stephanie said. "They're all about lusting after the flesh of tender young girls. Devouring them."

Alain could feel her watching him. She made no move to tug her hem back into place. He cleared his throat. "So this Mama Bouche, what does she do that requires an appointment?"

Stephanie said, "She sees the future. And she knows everything about everyone. I've collected tales from her in the past, and I suggested her to Aimee as a starting point."

She was taking him to see a psychic. Alain hoped Leon never got a hold of this story. He'd never hear the end of it.

Munising, a harbor town like Marquette and every other town of any size in the U.P., had been born even before the shipping trade took hold. Grand Island sheltered it from the worst of Superior's winter wrath, a fact recognized by everyone from the natives to the French voyageurs to modern tourists. Vestiges of the town's history remained, but only enough for a paragraph in the tour guides.

Stephanie directed him off the main drag into a residential area, to a brick ranch like any other if one ignored the lavender neon sign shaped like a hand in the front window.

They walked to the front door together. Alain had the feeling that he'd done this before, déjà vu that hovered at the edge of consciousness like a buzzing insect. It evaporated when the door swung open to reveal a solid but tiny woman in a shimmering purple warm-up suit. She sported short gray hair, sparkling earrings and new white tennis shoes, and she checked them both out from head to toe.

"You still single." A Quebec childhood still spiked her speech.

Stephanie stepped forward and kissed her cheek. Mama Bouche held her at arms' length for study.

"Good hips, nice high bazooms. What's wrong with those university fellas?" she asked Stephanie. "Shut their peters in a book and put it on the shelf, maybe?"

Stephanie didn't seem to have an answer for that.

"Who dat?" Mama Bouche reached out and tugged at Alain's jacket, pulling him down to her level. Her eyes were green, brighter than any he had ever seen. In an instant the twinkling grandmother look was replaced by a look that a twenty-year veteran of the police force would have envied. Mama Bouche looked at and through him, and not for a million bucks could he straighten up or take her hand from his lapel or do anything but return her gaze. Her brow creased. She didn't seem to like what she saw.

Mama Bouche muttered something that sounded like 'the blood.'

"I heard 'bout you," she said. "Wonder when you come see Mama. We got much to talk." At that she turned and waddled into her house, leaving them to follow.

A décor heavy in pastels included Kincaide paintings on the walls, idyllic country settings. Alain had never liked the painter's work—too warm, fuzzy, just plain too happy. He'd never found a scene in real life that came close. Mama Bouche took a seat in a blue leather recliner.

"You got twenty minute," she said. "Them Indians got the shrimp at the casino buffet tonight and I aim to get some before the old folks eat 'em up."

"This won't take long." Stephanie took a seat on a couch that matched the recliner. Alain sank in next to her, trying not to dwell on the image of the periwinkle cows that must have given their lives for this furniture.

"You ain't seen them old folks eat the shrimps," Mama Bouche said. "Like the bear in the honey tree."

"We came about the loup garou," Alain said.

The slope-shouldered clock on the mantelpiece ticked, dividing up the ensuing silence.

"Loup garou ain't nothin' for you," Mama Bouche finally said.

"You shared stories with a student of mine—" Stephanie began.

"Where that get her?" Mama asked, settling back in her chair. She seemed to know the answer already. "I warn that sweet little girl, leave the loup garou alone I tell her. Young people don't always listen to Mama. Think they know better. Mama sees." She leaned forward and looked to the carved wooden crucifix hung over the fireplace in stark contrast to the soft atmosphere of the room, a bloody, suffering Jesus with ribs protruding like a ladder to heaven. Mama Bouche turned back to face them, her eyes hooded. "I told that girl, and now I tell you. Them old loup garou was gone like the real lumberjack. That's the old days. Now they back. You the one, boy, should know maybe some thing about the loup garou. Found in the woods, little baby all alone in a cabin."

Alain felt as if his bladder had filled suddenly at her words. He wanted to rock forward to ease the pain and pressure but couldn't move. How did she know?

"No mama, no papa, *que le bébé* on a table with the door wide open. Nobody knew that cabin even out there. Old man lost while hunting find you. Stupid old man, Waagosh, and he don't wonder why they ain't no bear, no coyote come looking for a tender baby. He take you in like it happen every day, take you out that forest to raise you up." Her voice expanded to fill the room with more than sound.

Stephanie had not moved an inch since Mama Bouche had mentioned his origin.

"The forest give you up, boy. Waagosh take you home, yes, but he only a part of it. You not what I 'spect but maybe you not what I fear neither." She shook her head as if to clear it of whatever she'd seen when she looked through Alain.

"Loup garou stay in the forest, in that dark. Make a deal with Lucifer, does the loup garou." She crossed herself in a slow and stately way before continuing. "That one way to do it, man trade the soul for power, do evil for him so he give you something."

Alain struggled to breathe in the close, over-decorated room. This was not what he wanted. The details of a three hundred year old legend did him no good in a murder investigation. Her casual revelation of his orphaned beginnings had struck him like a punch, though. The words wouldn't come out.

"How?" Stephanie asked.

Mama Bouche turned her emerald gaze to the professor.

"Spell. Piece of the Word."

"Scripture?" Stephanie pressed.

Mama Bouche nodded. "Like a bloodstopper, one of them folks can say a verse and stop up any cut, even a gunshot. I seen it. Got to be a special verse for the bargain with Lucifer, though, and a way to say it perfect. Might be a piece of the Word backwards or in Greek or Latin, maybe. No telling. I don't mess with no loup garou. I had me a dream after that girl come."

Alain had taken his notebook from his pocket, but returned it after catching a glimpse of the look on Mama's face. He tried to get a grip. His head felt like it was caught in a propeller.

She continued. "Wolves in the churchyard, they was. Circling. Put they paws up on the door, then come down and go round again. Then they yell, but it ain't like the wolf. It's a woman screaming every time they try to howl. Circling and screaming. I woke me up and knew the loup garou come back."

Mama Bouche sank back into the recliner, a tired old woman in her own living room. The clock ticked again, or maybe Alain could hear it clearly now.

"Time," she said, looking directly at Alain, "old man Time, he don't walk in a straight line. Like any fool man lost in the woods he circle back on his own tracks, touch the same tree a dozen times. Old things, them things you think is gone, they come round again, too, more than one sometimes." She seemed to blame him for whatever had confused her.

"How," he began. "How do I—"

"Kill him?" she asked.

No. That had not been his question, not at all. What the hell had he been about to ask?

"Don't need no silver. I seen that boojum nonsense on the TV. Someone make a deal with the devil they tough but they ain't no immor-tal. The Dark One, he fix them up some when they do the change back and forth, but not everything. Old man here by Munising, one time thirty year ago he shoot a big black dog standing in his pasture, blew the leg clean off and the next morning his neighbor had a little limp. Old Lucifer, he don't want no weaklings. You get you a good gun and do that wolf right. Blast him in the ass and keep shootin'."

Mama Bouche stood up. "Now you got to go, and I get me some shrimps. Them Indians won't save me none. They still pissed off about something, like I the one take they land." The old woman's laugh had no joy in it.

She seemed anxious to get them out the door, but as she herded them she pulled Stephanie back to whisper something. Alain stopped, still numb, facing one of the Kincaide prints in the foyer while the women conferred, and for the first time he studied one up close. Annoying saccharine light still flooded the scene but the thatch-roofed cottage seemed to hide something—a secret or shadow—living in plain sight in the middle of a perfect village.

Stephanie gathered him by the arm as Mama Bouche hustled them out the door. They thanked her for her time. She simply waved a be-ringed hand in dismissal as she turned away. As the two of them climbed into the truck Alain saw the living room curtains twitch.

"What did she say to you?" he asked.

"Two things. She said the name of a priest—Father Avius—and that he's currently posted in Marquette. She gave me the name, but not why he's important."

"And?" he prodded.

"And what? We go see him. I thought you were the detective," Stephanie answered.

"Not that. What was the other thing she told you? You said she told you two things. The priest is one, and the other is . . ."

"Girl talk," she said. "No boys allowed." She crossed her legs and settled deeper into her seat.

Leaves tumbled across the pavement as he threaded through the quiet streets back to the state highway and aimed northwest. A beer sign flickered to life in the parking lot of a roadside tavern, the last outpost at the edge of Munising. This trip seemed like a bust. The old woman had stories and superstition, nothing more, even if she did know too much about Alain.

"You want to grab dinner here before we drive back?" he asked.

She studied him from beneath dark lashes.

"As a matter of fact," she said, "I do."

The barkeep, a balding man in a Packers jersey, waved a free hand toward a cluster of empty tables when they walked in. His other hand stayed steady on the tap, filling a mug for one of the mill workers at the bar. Alain scanned the beer pulls, and pointed and held up one finger when he spotted the Leinenkugel logo on the tap in use. Stephanie gave him a not-too-gentle elbow in the ribs. He changed it to two fingers. The barkeep nodded.

Stephanie led the way to a booth. Outside the window the dense pine forest began only a few feet away. Fading daylight gradually choked off into an early night among the thick trunks. Shadows reached out toward the warm light of the bar.

The proprietor set two schooners rimed with frost on the table and dropped menus in front of them.

"What's good?" Alain asked.

"All of it," came the answer. To complement his football jersey, the proprietor wore a spotless apron over chinos.

"You're the chef?" Stephanie asked.

He nodded. "I used to make awful food. Real slop. No one bought it so I decided to try something new, eh?"

Alain expected the usual burger and fried fish menu. The long list of Italian dishes in tiny print came as a pleasant shock. Stephanie made a throaty little sound as she discovered the same. They settled on calamari and a shared dish of chicken and sausage in white wine and garlic. The barkeep dropped off salads and crusty bread before leaving them alone. Stephanie held out the rim of her beer glass to touch his.

"To the loup garou," she said.

He sipped. Telling her this had been a waste of time would ruin the rest of the evening. Maybe the priest would have an answer that didn't involve magic.

She placed her glass on the table and traced sigils into the frost on the side.

"All we're doing is talking to people," she said. "When does the excitement start?"

"Most of this job is talking. You push and you push, and hopefully something breaks loose, one tiny thing you can put together with another piece," Alain said. "Excitement is overrated. This part is good, too, like hunting. The shot at the end is a small part of the whole, almost insignificant. Stalking is the thing."

"Is that why you do it? Because you like to hunt?" she asked.

"I'm good at it. I think this is what I'm supposed to do."

The calamari arrived. Alain watched her eat and wondered when she would ask. She must be dying to find out.

"Mama Bouche said something about a cabin," Stephanie said.

Bingo.

"I'm an orphan, and I got lucky," Alain said. "That's all I know. Some babies get left on church steps, I was dumped in a cabin. Everything else is only a story that people have told me. Waagosh found me, he and his brothers raised me. Where he found me is not important."

He left out a lot. There hadn't been any formal adoption until Waagosh passed away in his nineties, when Alain was fifteen. Then the state got involved and discovered that the boy seemed to have appeared out of thin air. They started making noises about foster care, and one of Waagosh's cousins, also elderly, adopted the boy. The cousin thought it a great joke, and introduced his "white son" to all his girlfriends.

"Well, it is in the sense that it's entered the canon," Stephanie said, "the consciousness. Mama Bouche knew who you were right away."

"She probably knows some local Ojibwa," Alain said. "There's a lot of intermarrying with the people who raised me, visiting back and forth."

"Story-telling," Stephanie said.

"What people say doesn't change the truth. I'm not a story."

"Of course not," she allowed, "but the circumstances are remarkable enough that a tale has begun to form around them. It's not complete yet, because you're still alive and known to too many of the tellers, but eventually it will slip those bonds and have less to do with you. Let me put it another way. Do you think George Washington actually chopped down a cherry tree?"

Alain used his fork's tines to drag streaks of marinara across his plate. He stopped when he realized he was making claw marks.

"I don't know," he said.

"Neither do I," Stephanie said, "but we've both heard it. Something happened that set that story off. You'll likely be a part of the local folklore in some way, no matter what you do."

"Wonderful. Me and the loup garou."

Stephanie slid her spotless salad plate aside as the proprietor approached with a platter. The entrée touched down in the center of the table. The aroma of garlic curled around the two of them.

"Look at it this way. You get to be the hero with the mysterious past," Stephanie said. "You do catch bad guys."

"There's more folklore about monsters than heroes, isn't there?" Alain asked.

"Well, yes," she said.

A sense of Mama Bouche's stultifying living room still seemed to be with them. Alain remembered the calm certainty on her face as she'd told them about the old ways coming back. He'd be willing to bet that Stephanie was thinking the same.

85

"No one ever believes that they're the monster, though," Stephanie said. "I had a professor who told me that everyone is the hero of their own story. People are capable of terrible things in the name of love, religion, and whoever did this thinks they were justified."

That troubled Alain. Who could justify what had happened to that girl? Why had Stephanie said that?

Outside the window the temperature dropped while the forest waved dark branches that went ignored.

Alain unlocked Stephanie's door and held it open while she climbed in. He circled around the front to slide behind the wheel. When she pulled her coat tighter he flipped on the heater.

Highway 28 cut a smooth line through the woods almost empty of traffic. He set the cruise at sixty and kept a sharp watch for deer. The wind swirled, pushing the truck from side-to side, causing the pines to bow and twist.

"So we go see this priest tonight," Stephanie said. She seemed to relax in her seat as the warmth from the vents trickled through the cab.

"We can try," Alain answered. "I'll call ahead." He scooped his radio from the dash mount and raised it to speak. He caught a flash of green reflected in the weeds at the side of the road. Eyes.

He dropped the mike and hit the brakes, flinging a protective arm in front of Stephanie. A canine shape slunk out of the undergrowth and flowed across the pavement, keeping head and tail low, turning to glance at them without any apparent concern. Its eyes seemed to meet Alain's, and for one snapshot instant it blocked the center of the highway. The anti-lock brakes kicked back against the pedal, juddering as the truck slowed to a crawl.

The animal disappeared as fast as it had come. The entire encounter lasted only two or three seconds.

Stephanie released her grip on the armrest. "Holy shit. Was that—?"

"Coyote," Alain said. "Wolves are twice that size. Run with their tail out straight, not hanging down like they're embarrassed. That's the best way to tell them from wolves. Coyotes always look guilty."

Headlights appeared far back in the rearview mirror. Alain brought the truck back up to highway speed.

"I've never seen one before," Stephanie said.

"They're everywhere," he said.

"Out here, right? Not in town?" she asked.

"Everywhere," he emphasized. "If people leave their pets out at night, coyotes will snatch cats and little yappy dogs out of the neighborhoods right in Marquette like it's a Chinese buffet. Usually they stay out of sight, though. They're smart. It's odd for one to mosey across the road like that right in front of us."

Alain replayed the image burned in his memory, the animal turning to look at the approaching truck as though it had nothing to fear. They were becoming more aggressive, Bob had said. Or perhaps something in the woods made traffic seem negligible by comparison.

The lights of Marquette appeared in the distance along the shore, hovering at the bottom of the windshield and growing larger by degrees as if they chased a slow-moving UFO through the night. He felt as though he should try to get more out of Stephanie, but the warmth in the truck, the meal, something about her made him want to sit in companionable silence for a few more minutes. He wasn't doing his job.

He cut inland at the first cross street, automatically plotting the shortest route to the rectory. Gravel ground under the tires as he swerved into the parking lot and brought the truck to a halt. He killed the ignition. They sat listening to the wind.

"Feels like Halloween already," Stephanie said, her first words since the coyote's sudden appearance.

"Four days," he said. "My favorite holiday."

"Really?" she asked. "Why?"

"It's old and primal. You can feel Halloween in the air," he said.

He wished the moon would roll out from behind the clouds. At this phase it would be bright enough to cast shadows of the truck and the stacked stone wall surrounding the churchyard. The second night of his investigation. At some point he'd have to go to sleep and face his dreams.

Alain asked, "Do you know what the moon is called right after it's full?"

"Gibbous."

"Am I the only one who didn't know that?"

She slid out her side and waited for him at the tailgate.

"I looked it up," she said. "Knowledge is power."

He led the way through a gate in the wall and up a neat, cobbled walkway to the door of the rectory. He stopped, turned to face her under the weak bulb of the entryway light.

"You did a lot of good at Mama Bouche's place. I think it helped the investigation," he said. He hated lying to her.

She took a step back and looked him in the eye. "Why do I feel like I am getting the brush-off?"

"You're not," he continued quickly, "definitely not. But I need you to let me do the talking and don't touch anything. There's a chain of evidence to think about now. You wouldn't want to help catch Aimee's killer only to have him or her go free on a technicality, would you?"

She shook her head.

"And there's your safety to think about," he said. "If we're following the right chain of clues, it will lead to someone who has already killed at least once. The second time is easier for most of them."

"Are you trying to scare me?" she asked.

"Scared and alive isn't bad. I don't want to put you in any danger."

Stephanie cocked her head at that, just a hair. He could smell that scent again, the vanilla.

"I need you for this, though," he went on. "The folklore angle is the only place where anything is moving. I need you." He felt like he was lying to her. He did need her, for the folklore, and because he couldn't scratch her off as a suspect.

"I want to help," she said after a moment.

"Good."

Alain turned to the door, but she stopped him with a hand on his arm.

"Thank you," she said.

He lifted the wrought-iron knocker and let if fall onto the heavy door. Once, twice, three times. He couldn't hear footsteps, but after a few seconds a fumbling at the latch led to the portal slowly swinging inward. It revealed a portly woman in a faded dress, a shapeless cardigan sweater.

"Father's out," she said by way of introduction.

"That would be Father Avius?" Alain asked.

"Well Father Bennett is visiting his sick mother, isn't he?" the woman replied, "So of course it's Father Avius."

A moth head-butted the outside light fixture repeatedly.

"He's out," she repeated.

"Do you know when he might return?" he asked.

"Late," she said. "It's always late. Since he got here, out every night. It's not the drink, though, not this one. You're that cop." Her stream of consciousness seemed to run shallow and straight.

"Detective Logan," he said. "And you are?"

"Broomsell. Edna Broomsell. You been after my boy. Got it in for him."

Alain ran the name through his memory, masking his reaction when recognition hit. Ivan Broomsell aspired to someday be a small-time hood. So far his greatest caper was burglarizing a pawn shop and then trying to sell the goods back to them. It hadn't taken much detective work.

Edna's mouth drew into a tight angry line as she blocked the door to the rectory, her doughy arms folded across a forbidding bosom. Enough nice cop. Alain needed a new lead in this case. It was making him angry. He took a step forward, crowding her against the door jamb. Up close she smelled like a damp dish sponge.

"When did Avius get to town?" He tried to make his voice as cold as the iron door handle.

Edna opened her mouth, changed her mind and closed it again.

"Tell me," Alain snapped. Edna jumped. Seemingly of their own volition her fingers plucked at the sleeves of her ratty sweater. Stephanie stood still.

"Week. Maybe ten days—," Edna said.

"Where does he go when he's out?" he asked, cutting her off to push the pace.

"I don't know," she said. She looked down.

He let anger creep under the surface his voice. "Edna. Where?"

"I said I don't know," she met his gaze this time, and he thought she told the truth. "Driving, he says one time when I ask him. Driving around. He says he wants to know everything about this area. He's got old books and maps of the U.P. and he goes out to see places where old things happened. Gets all excited about the history." Her lip curled as she said the last word, as though it rhymed with something dirty.

"May we see these books?" Stephanie asked.

Alain's hold on Edna broke at her polite tone.

"You got to have a warrant. I know that for sure. You ain't got a warrant, you can't come in." She directed the last straight to Alain, bolstered by her hard-earned television legal knowledge.

"Wait," Alain said. He strode to the truck and retrieved his binder for the case. An eight by ten of Aimee's school picture took up the first page. He returned to the door and held the picture under the light.

"Was this girl here? Did she visit Avius?"

Edna reached out with one hand to touch the picture.

"Yes, she come here. The only night he stayed in, she come. They talked and talked. I didn't pay no mind."

"They talked about history? About Father Avius's books?" Stephanie asked.

Edna said, "It's too cold to be standing out here." She stepped back into the doorway and began to swing the door shut.

"Edna we're not done," Alain said.

She watched him with a cunning piggy smile as the door closed. A heavy bolt rattled home.

Alain headed for the truck.

"Why didn't you stop her? Arrest her or something." Stephanie dogged his footsteps.

"Chain of evidence," he said.

Stephanie stopped on the path. He rounded on her.

"If I arrest her she'll clam up. If we barge in there and he turns out to be our guy, nothing we find is admissible in court. I don't like it any better than you, but there are other ways."

"I want to find Aimee's killer," she said in a low voice.

The moon shone through filtering thin clouds now, and he addressed it rather than her.

"Finding him is only a part of it," he said.

She touched his arm, and the hot and tight sensation in his chest eased.

"Would you like me to take you home?" he asked.

"Are we done?"

The blue light of the moon shone curved on bits of broken glass beneath a dark streetlight.

"For tonight," Alain said. He shouldn't even have her here.

"Okay, Alain," she said after a hesitation, "tomorrow then. Would you drop me at my car?"

He held the door of the truck for her. The drive to the university parking lot took only a few minutes. He waited as she unlocked her Mazda and got it started. She pulled up next to his truck and put her window down.

"Thank you for a pleasant evening," she said. "Given the circumstances."

"Call me if you think of anything else I need to know," Alain replied.

The light of the sodium arc lamps in the parking lot illuminated only the bottom half of her face, so he could see her perfect teeth as the window slid up.

After she rolled out of the lot, Alain called in and asked dispatch to send patrols past the rectory every half hour and note the time that Avius got home. He'd talk to the man tomorrow, but wanted to know how long he stayed out. If his story didn't match, Alain might have something. He held the mike to his forehead, thinking, before adding a request for the patrols to look up Stephanie's address and do the same for her. That made his stomach feel loose. It was the right thing to do.

He needed a shower, a beer and a bed in that order, although he would entertain the idea of drinking in the shower to save time. The winding drive leading up to the front of his house uncoiled pure black under the trees. The moon lost at peek-a-boo with the clouds again. The trees roiled in the grip of the breeze, and white pine he parked under seemed to reach down and pat him on the head with a branch as he got out.

Alain paused after unlocking the door to listen—an old house talking in the wind, nothing out of the ordinary. He threw his jacket at a coat hook on the tallboy, then eased his holstered gun out of the back of his belt and tucked it into the hidden compartment in the grandfather clock that stood in the entryway. Like the passageway upstairs, this secret had taken him months to discover. It had slid smoothly open one day as he moved the clock from the dining room to its present position. He didn't know what Ganderson had kept there but it proved handy for a pistol. Given the old boy's free hand with the ladies, he may have kept a six-shooter there himself for parlaying in the parlor with the occasional irate husband or outraged father.

He retrieved a bottle of Leinie's from the refrigerator and took a swig before sitting to remove his boots and socks. His office was undisturbed. If the desk and chair had been wandering during the day, they'd made it back to their respective spots before he got home. He really was losing his mind. He sat with his head between his knees for a minute, unwilling to climb the stairs. It wasn't exactly that he was afraid to go to sleep. Not that.

A knock at the door made him sit up straight. The likely candidate list for a late-night visit had few options: Leon or a stranger. Alain padded to the office window on bare feet and moved the curtain aside an inch. One of the porch supports blocked the view of the door. Damn Ganderson and his huge pillar. Alain let the curtain fall and entered the foyer. He flipped on the porch light and saw Stephanie framed in the front-door glass. Elaborate scrollwork in the pane outlined her face. Eyes wide and hair blowing loose in the wind, she stepped forward as he opened the door and spoke before he had a chance.

"I've thought of something else you need to know."

She kissed him. Hard. Her arms slid around his neck, and her body folded into his. The cold air wrapped them but neither felt it. The door banged open against the wall, and they broke apart long enough for her to close and lock it. Her eyes sparkled.

"I parked right out front," she said.

"What will the neighbors think?" he asked.

"Screw the neighbors," she answered, dropping her coat. Stephanie pushed him back to the base of the stairs. She climbed up on the first step, matching his height, and kissed him again fiercely. Her hands roamed—unbuttoning and tugging at his clothes. He ran his hands down the curve of her back, then up under her sweater. She shivered and broke off the kiss.

"What is it I need to know?" he asked. Her skin was smooth heat under his hands.

"First," she said. "I don't do things like this. This is totally inappropriate. I barely know you. What have you done to the wall?"

His home improvement project—currently a three foot hole in the plaster—gaped alongside.

She stripped off her sweater and brought his hands between the cups of her red lace bra. A fine gold chain held a small cross at her throat.

"Second, you need to know that this opens in the front," she said. "I wore my good lingerie tonight. Don't wreck it. God, you must think I'm a slut."

She slapped at the ornate wall switch at the base of the stairs. The hall light went out and only shafts of moonlight through the tall windows remained.

Slap. Lights.

She took hold of his chin and looked him in the eyes.

"This is crazy," she said.

Lights off.

They fumbled their way up, dropping clothes along the way. Stephanie lost patience and pulled him down to the deep risers.

"There are beds upstairs—" he began.

"Shut up, Detective," Stephanie said. She knelt before him in the dark and ripped open his fly and there were no more words out of him, only a long intake of breath. He laid his head back on the step and looked at the shadow-swept ceiling as the blood pounded. She seemed to enjoy the control she had. He took her head in his hands, ran his fingers through her heavy hair.

Stephanie released him. Alain sat up and started to rise, but she pushed him back with one hand on his chest and straddled his thighs. She reached down to take a firm grasp and guide him into her, settling with a series of short thrusts. Then she kissed him again, eyes open, setting a rough and insistent pace with her hands on his shoulders to hold him down. Her hips rolled and she arched her spine. He cupped her breasts, gently at first until she covered his hands with hers and squeezed to let him know what she wanted.

Stephanie's breath came short and sharp, rising until she threw her head back and dug her nails into his chest as she ground against his body.

"Damn, Detective," she panted, "I needed that."

He raised up on his elbows and kissed her.

"We're not done yet," he said. He cupped his hands beneath her bottom.

"You can't—" she started.

He looked past her bare shoulder down the long fall of stairs to the door. His jeans were still a tangled knot around his ankles.

"Live to fight again another day," Stephanie said as she slid off him and stood.

He kicked the jeans free and took her hand to lead the way upstairs.

"Hmm," she said, "holding hands on the first date?"

"Never let it be said that I'm not a romantic."

Lumberjacks in the employ of the Mackenzie camp learned a thing or two about spirits when they attempted to sleep off a drunk in the haunted and abandoned way station on Yellow Dog Trail. Not a one of those strapping boys will say what happened for certain, but witnesses report that they returned to cutting Monday morning in their union suits rather than go back inside for their clothes.

7 January, 1899. The Palladium Superior.

Chapter Thirteen

Stephanie lay curled on her side, head tucked into Alain's shoulder. She kicked the rumpled ball of sheets onto the floor.

"That was informative," he said. He felt lucky and stupid at the same time. She was a part of the case, the only name he could attach to Aimee at all, and he still hadn't established whether or not she had an alibi.

She bit him on the shoulder.

"Is there going to be a test?" he asked.

She nodded, and draped an arm across his chest.

"Ow," he said when she hit the scratches her nails had left.

"Did I do that to you?" she asked, tracing the marks then continuing to outline his pec and bicep.

"It wasn't a werewolf," he answered.

She bit him again, harder, then growled and sniffed at him.

"Whoa," she said, sniffing again.

"We reek of love," Alain said in his best Barry White voice. It made both of them laugh.

"You smell manly. I, on the other hand, smell like a herd animal after a wildlife special. A true lady might glow after intercourse, but I seem to work up a hell of a sweat when I fuck. I'm going to use your shower."

She hopped off the bed and strolled out. He admired the limited view available in the semi-darkness. He could hear her opening doors as she progressed down the hallway.

"Third left," he called out.

"I didn't hear that." she answered. "This is a perfect excuse for being nosy."

Lights flipped on and off, and her footsteps grew fainter. He heard the water begin to run before he dozed off, then something like singing, although that may have been part of a dream. Stephanie came back into the bedroom wearing a towel after what felt like only a minute.

"Very funny," she said, leaning over and kissing him. "What did you do, run back here and jump in bed?"

"Hrmm?" Alain said wisely.

"Fine. You can pretend if you want to," she said. "Considering the circumstances, I don't mind if you want to see me naked with the lights on. You could have at least handed me my towel, though."

Alain didn't have all his numbers adding up yet, but something about what she'd said didn't make sense.

"What? Towel?" he said.

"When I got out of the shower and stood there starkers? I had water in my eyes, but I saw you in the hallway. You gave me a nice wolf whistle and headed back here," she said.

Alain snapped awake. He rolled across the bed and groped on the floor for the heavy aluminum flashlight he kept there. He held a finger to his lips and crept toward the door. Stephanie's eyes went wide as she realized that it hadn't been him. She recovered quickly and followed along behind him on tiptoe, fists clenched, angry rather than scared.

He flashed the light toward the stairs. Nothing. The same in the other direction. No footsteps. No creaking floorboards. He felt a flare of rage at this second intrusion. This was his house. He handed the light to Stephanie and pushed her back into the room. She knelt behind the bed. He covered her with a blanket, gave her the handset of the cordless phone from the dresser and put his mouth close to her ear.

"911," he whispered. "Say: 10-70, one undercover on scene, code 2." He pulled back to look at her face. "Stay down on the floor until I come to get you. Flat as a pancake. No peeking."

Alain slipped into the hallway on bare feet, bare everything, setting his toes down first before shifting his weight each time. He stuck his head into the library and waited until he felt the vibe of an empty room before stepping in. Alain retraced his steps to the swinging bookshelf and retrieved his shotgun again. This story kept repeating itself. He racked the slide slowly to move a shell into the chamber, letting the sound stretch out over a few seconds to make it harder for an intruder to identify in the quiet house. The wind thrashed a tree branch against the window and moaned at the frame. Alain stepped back to the doorway and flashed the shotgun's tactical light quickly each direction before exposing himself. When the wind died he could hear Stephanie murmuring into the phone. Cavalry on the way: code 2 meant no lights or sirens. Hopefully they could trap this bastard.

A splinter of light at the top of the stairs caught his eye. He raised the Mossberg and crept toward it. Then a ball of light the size of a walnut drifted out of the first-floor arch leading to the kitchen and hovered three feet off the ground. Alain blinked, trying to clear his vision. He swung the barrel back and forth as he scanned for a source. He didn't want to trigger the flash and give away his position.

The ball was difficult to see if he looked at it directly, appearing and disappearing every few seconds. He found he could track it better with his peripheral vision. Not a laser dot or lightning bug. It bobbed and wove, seeming to dance around the foyer before stabilizing and rising up the stairs toward him. Alain aimed at the little glowing light automatically, although he wasn't about to blast Tinkerbell or whatever the hell. He tried to control his breathing. The wisp advanced halfway up, hovered for a moment then blinked out. Gone.

So he stood naked at the top of the stairs pointing a shotgun down at nothing when the front door exploded.

Splinters of hundred year-old glass, Brazilian mahogany and antique hardware flew in all directions. Time slowed for Alain and he saw the portal bulge and expand like a huge blister before it burst. A dark shape filled the frame moving fast *holy shit so fast* and someone must have driven a truck into his house but the truck ran at him and he put the sights on it and squeezed the trigger. The twelve-gauge bucked against his shoulder and he racked the slide and rode the recoil down and re-acquired the target ten feet inside the house already *so fast* fired again and it changed direction and disappeared through the arch into the dining room. Light, damn it, use the light. He squeezed the fore grip of the shotgun and lit up the entryway. Clouds of dust and a jagged hole open to the porch, but no . . . battering ram thing.

The house shook with thunderous footsteps. He started down, racking the slide. The crashing at the back of the house sounded like glassware. He flashed the light again to see the kitchen door closed but hanging from one hinge before his light flickered and died. Damn. Where the hell was his back-up? A piece of the front door frame clattered to the porch. Alain moved toward the silent kitchen.

More massive stomping rocked the house but not heading toward him. The thing pounded up the servants' stairs. Stephanie. Alain took the front steps two at a time with the shotgun at port arms feeling old and slow. He came up the last three in one jump and aimed the barrel down the central hallway, locked the stock into his shoulder and saw the eyes. They shone orange in the moonlight, flaming eyes on a fluid black form tearing down the hallway straight at him. Boom. The Mossberg kicked almost of its own accord and he racked and fired and racked again as the eyes suddenly dropped three feet lower. He thought he'd knocked it down but the eyes kept coming. The thing ran on all fours.

Alain felt rather than saw it gather itself for a leap. He felt strangely calm . . . relieved. It wasn't him. There really was an animal. And he fired and *two rounds left only two more.* Eight pellets of .33 caliber buckshot traveling at over a thousand feet per second turned it aside. The thing slid, scrabbling at the wooden floor in the hallway, into the library followed by a crash of glass. Alain hit the doorway right on its tail but saw only a broken window and trees thrashing outside. A shadow streaked across the rear driveway but he had no clear shot.

He pounded into the hallway and down the back stairs, yelling at Stephanie to stay put, stuffing spare shells from the shotgun's sidesaddle ammo carrier into the magazine. Alain ran down past the ancient carriage house, across the alley and his neighbor's yard and into the next street. He looked north and south, scanned the quiet houses, and saw his neighbor's wife walking their yappy dog. At least she had been walking, until he burst out of the bushes, naked with a gun.

He lowered the Mossberg and thumbed the safety on.

"Maria," he said, angling the shotgun stock to provide what little coverage it could. "Did you see a big, um, dog or animal run through here?"

Maria Setzler, a seventh-grade math teacher, was difficult to render speechless. She slowly shook her head while trying to keep her gaze safely above his neck. Even the yappy dog stood silent and watched him.

"Have you seen anything unusual this evening?" he asked.

The grin started at one corner of her mouth and spread. Again, the headshake.

"Thank you," he said with as much dignity as possible. "Have a pleasant evening." Alain began the walk back to his house, painfully picking his way across the gravel in the alley that hadn't even slowed him down before. Alain looked back to see Maria still standing frozen under the streetlight. Her grin had grown into a full-blown smile. He approached his house from the rear hoping to slip in unnoticed, but now it had police cruisers front and back and lights spilling from every level like a birthday cake. The cavalry had arrived.

His house looked as if it had lost a fight with a bigger, meaner house. The library window from which the intruder had leapt gaped like an empty eye socket. Alain walked through the cops at the back door without a word, ending their conversation in mid-syllable. The wooden treads of the back staircase held deeply gouged evidence, so he tiptoed through the broken glass on the kitchen floor before cutting through the office to use the main stairs. Brett Vullonen examined the hole where Alain used to have a front door. He stopped when Alain appeared, his demeanor the same as if they'd bumped into each other at the coffee shop, which meant a curt nod. Alain handed him the shotgun and turned to climb the stairs without a word. Clothes still lay strewn across the risers and he gathered them up as he climbed. The justice system didn't need every single detail of the evening. He couldn't stop the gossip, but it would be better for his case and his career if this part didn't make it into the official report.

An earnest young sheriff's deputy with an AR-15 rifle guarded the door of the bedroom.

"I got a look at her quick, and she's not bleeding but won't come out," he said. His Adam's apple traveled up and down his scrawny throat as he swallowed. "I don't think the lady had any clothes on."

"Stephanie," Alain said through the door, "it's okay."

The door swung wide, revealing the professor dressed in a pair of Alain's jeans and an old button-down shirt he wore while mowing the lawn. Wide eyes, her face pale and streaked as though she had been crying. Her hair was loose, disheveled and he wanted to sink his hands into it again. He made himself step past her into the room, handing her the bundle of clothes from the stairs, and began to dig in the dresser for something clean to wear. She sat on the end of the bed holding the clothes as he tugged on a pair of briefs, then black cargo pants and t-shirt while the deputy stayed at his post outside the open door and pretended to be invisible and deaf.

"You did everything right," Alain said. "You stayed out of the way so I could do my job without having to worry."

"It's not dead." She said it as a statement rather than a question.

He stuck a pair of clean hiking socks in a pocket. His boots might still be downstairs in the entry hall, the last place they'd been before the door exploded. He went to the closet and took down from the back of the door a wide nylon belt that held his speed holster, sheath knife and spare magazine holders and buckled it around his waist. At the dresser he filled one cargo pocket with a half dozen spare batteries for his flashlight.

"Not yet," he said. Alain left the room and headed downstairs to get some firepower.

Brett had taken charge of the scene at the bottom of the stairs. He looked politely away as Alain retrieved his Sig 229 pistol from behind the hidden panel in the clock. Alain removed it from the concealment rig he carried on duty and slid it into the Galco Combat Master quick-draw holster on his right hip, drawing a few times to be sure the tension felt correct and the gun wouldn't stick if he needed it. His single spare magazine went into the holder on his left side. He'd pick up more from his locker at the station or from the stash in his truck.

"Where's your perimeter?" he asked Brett as he began to hunt for his boots, stepping lightly through the debris in bare feet.

Brett shrugged. "Well, it's hard to say at the moment."

"What do you mean? You don't have the town blocked off?" Alain struggled to keep his voice even, the one boot he'd found dangling forgotten in his hand. Standard operating procedure included setting up a perimeter for a call like this. With the extra cars on patrol tonight it should have been child's play.

"The situation's a bit confused," Brett said, "what with everyone answering the first call at St. Peter's."

"What?" Stephanie had come halfway down the stairs trailed by the deputy. She'd changed into her own clothes.

"Dispatch planned to call you, Alain," Brett continued, "but your 911 call came in before they had a chance. It took a minute to sort it out, and even then you took a backseat." He cast a glance at Stephanie. "A double Henry," Brett used the old code for a homicide, "at the rectory. By the time we got cars to both, dispatch had no one left for a perimeter. I sent two cars back out to run some fast loops. Haven't heard a thing yet." He cast a look around the ruins of the entry hall. "This is quite a trespassing case, I'll admit. Moose, maybe?"

Alain redoubled his efforts to find his other boot. When it turned up under the remains of an umbrella stand twenty feet from where he'd left it, he sat on the steps to yank on his socks and then the wayward pair. His jacket hung in the same spot he'd left it, ripped almost in two. He fished his flashlight and notebook out of the ruined coat and added them to the pockets on his cargo pants.

"We've got a scene here, Alain. They've got it under control over there."

"And you've got this one. I'll give you a statement later at the station." Alain found his car keys and cell phone still in the bowl on the antique tallboy, the only piece of furniture upright at the front of the house.

"Let's go," he said to Stephanie. "You're staying close until we get this sorted out."

Her nostrils flared at the command. She seemed to have regained a bit of her color and composure after the initial shock.

"Please," he said. "I may need your help. We have to look at the good Father's desk and bookshelf. These legends are the only thing holding this together. If our guy wants them, so do I."

She held his gaze before nodding, and was able to walk side-by-side with Alain through the hole into the night.

Alain hit the flashers and sped through the city toward the rectory. He drummed his fingers on the steering wheel, lost in thought, driving too fast on reflex and memory.

"Mama Bouche," he said suddenly.

"What?" Stephanie asked.

"She gave up the priest to us," he said.

"To me, you mean."

"Right, right, to you. She could be in danger. You have a cell number for her?" he asked. Stephanie shook her head.

Alain pulled his cell phone out and dialed the direct number to dispatch. He didn't want anything important on the radio tonight.

"Detective Logan," said the night dispatcher, a talkative retired auto worker named Ernie, "did you get your prowler?"

"No time, Ern, I need you to raise the Munising city patrol and have them pick up a Mama Bouche." He read off the street address from memory. "She might be at the casino."

"Sure thing, Alain," Ernie said. "You got an arrest warrant?"

"Protective custody. She can go home, but she needs someone with her at all times. It'd be better if they could stash her someplace until tomorrow morning, or, no, bring her here. I want you to call on the phone, not the radio, okay? No names on the radio. You got it?" They came up on the rectory. City, county and state cruisers parked at all angles in the small parking lot and across the lawn, and an ambulance idled, lights dark, in front of the door. "I also want to know if anyone on the street sees anything. Dog, deer, elephant, asshole, you call me at this number about it."

"Consider it done, Detective," Ernie was gone.

"You think someone's listening? Using a scanner?" Stephanie asked.

Alain nodded as he slotted his truck between the ambulance and the coroner's car and killed the flashers.

"I need you to stay in the truck," he said.

"What?" she looked around the parking lot, as if the thing that had attacked the house lurked in the shadows. "Why?"

"Evidence," he said, "I can't have you stepping in something that might get a killer off the hook. Look, you're surrounded by cops. I'll send someone out here to sit with you. My friend Leon will be here any second. You'll like him. He's a mess. If I find something we need you to identify, I'll come for you."

After a moment she nodded. Her calm after the attack had slipped for a moment, but she had it back. Impressive.

"I'll be right back," he said as he climbed out and made a show of engaging the locks before closing the door. A gray-haired Marquette city cop bundled in an oversized patrol coat guarded the door, thumbs tucked into a straining gun belt. At a word from Alain he sauntered over in front of the truck and gave Stephanie a cheerful salute through the glass.

Using the term "door" to describe the entrance to the rectory might be optimistic. The old ironwood had resisted better than Alain's decorative portal, but it still ended up as a pile of splinters and shards no bigger than a TV tray. He ducked under the crime scene tape. The blood started six feet inside the door.

"Booties," he heard from behind the door. His reflexes must be shot from the hangover of his massive adrenaline rush. He didn't even flinch, just felt drained and slow. If that person had wanted Alain dead he'd be toast.

Alain did turn in time to catch a plastic bag with a pair of paper shoe covers in it. The trooper who had stopped him turned back to tagging and sampling smears of blood on the wall behind where the door had been. The area of the spray looked enormous. He looked up and saw dark streaks of it on the ceiling, at least nine feet off the ground. Carotid artery severed, maybe; those could really gush.

He stopped to pull the flimsy covers over his boots to minimize tracks and contamination of the scene before continuing into the house. Beyond the entryway, a dining room full of warm bodies and one cold one. Camera flashes, quiet conversation, one braying laugh as someone probably made a sick joke—a murder scene like a hundred others, except for the shattered door and the blood on the ceiling. The first victim: the housekeeper, the same Ms. Broomsell who had been so forthcoming and helpful a few hours before. He recognized the sweater covering the largest intact part of her. She sprawled face down, the table shoved against the window and chairs smashed or strewn about the room. Alain looked back down the hallway, tracing her path. A bloody handprint hung on the wall where she had held herself up to stagger forward a few more steps.

"Running from it," he said half to himself.

"That's what we think," the trooper next to him said, pausing in his camera work. "She didn't quite make it." Alain could never remember the guy's name, and tonight he didn't even try.

"Where's the other one?" Alain asked.

"Study." A thrust of the jaw indicated the direction through another arch, deeper into the house. Alain stopped to examine deep gouges in the plaster on each side, cut in far enough to expose the lath underneath, huge claw marks like the ones on the back staircase at Alain's house. He stretched out his arms and tried to touch both sides at once but came up short by a foot either way.

In the study the heavy oak desk lay flipped on its side. He couldn't see a body behind it, but the stances of the men and women standing in a circle told him it had to be there. A fire burned on the hearth, sweltering in the crowded room. The air stank of a hot perforated bowel. Alain took his time crossing the room, trying to find the path the killer had taken. A couch overturned, an end table legs up in the corner, kicked, perhaps. An Oriental rug covered the center of the tile floor. It had been a good one thirty years ago. The shredded fabric told Alain what he needed to know about the claws on the killer's feet . . . or paws. In the darkness of his house he'd really only seen a huge form with had orange eyes. It ran on four legs. Useful stuff, that. Too bad a trained observer hadn't been on the scene, such as a detective. He could feel the shotgun buck against his shoulder again. Be sure of your target—that's the first rule—but he'd opened up without knowing what he was shooting at. Even with the micro-second glimpse he had, though, the thing felt wrong, not human or bear or anything he had faced on the streets or in the woods. It had seemed twisted somehow, and his reptile brain took control of the trigger finger long enough to burn off five shells in self-defense or fear or both.

While skirting the hearth he noticed bits of paper at the front edge of the fire. They looked like corners, singed but not wholly burnt, thick and uneven paper which made it old or modern hand-crafted stuff. He picked the scraps up by the edges and brought it with him.

The crowd made room for him in the circle, a few nodding in greeting while the others gauged his reaction to the body.

The priest—Father Avius, Mama Bouche had called him—had seen death coming. He'd died face up. Well, at least up. His face hung by the side of his skull, torn almost completely off except for shreds of muscle along the jaw. It looked as though he'd gone down swinging. A poker folded in two lay under the body, handle clutched in his hand. It would have been an impossible angle except for the extra joint his forearm now sprouted halfway between elbow and wrist. His crucifix lay close to the other hand, the chain broken and smeared with blood. He had tried the word and the sword and neither had saved him from being disemboweled. Below the sternum his abdomen gaped open and mostly empty. The gut pile across his legs didn't seem big enough to contain everything that had been inside the good father. Whoever had done this had spent a little more time with Avius, and might have taken souvenirs. Or snacks.

The youngest-looking EMT popped her gum, seeming determined to appear jaded. "I think I know the cause of death." Pop. "Liver on floor."

Eyes flicked to her and back to the body. No one spoke.

Alain borrowed an evidence bag from a deputy and sealed up the bits of paper he'd found. He turned away from the dead man and looked over his books. Avius was filling in for the regular priest, so Alain left the shelves alone and concentrated on the disheveled stacks littering every horizontal surface.

"Bloodstoppers and Bearwalkers," he read quietly aloud off one cover. He'd heard Mama Bouche mention bloodstoppers, the folks who could stop a wound from bleeding by speaking a Bible verse. Not any verse but a special one that had power for the right person. He picked up the book and scanned it. Folklore, and he had a specialist right outside. This case circled around and around this shit. He still didn't have a motive or a suspect, only stacks of old stories and two dead scholars: Aimee, now the priest. Edna was collateral damage. The answer was in here or it was related. He felt it. Most of the titles were similar, tales and local histories of the U.P., some so old they looked hand-bound. He couldn't bring Stephanie in, though, not and have her see what might have happened at Alain's house. If he hadn't been chasing lights and shadows when the attack came, she and Alain would be lying at the cold centers of their own circles of uniformed authorities. Some odd timing, that. Hell of a coincidence. He hated coincidence.

Alain gathered up as many of the oldest books he could carry, especially those with notecards tucked into them by, he assumed, Avius. He added two notebooks scattered in front of the overturned desk, then collared a city cop standing around with nothing to do.

"I'll log these as evidence. I want the rest of the books in this room that are not currently on shelves boxed and taken to the post."

The cop looked like he was about to argue that it wasn't his job. He swallowed it after catching the detective's expression.

"Where the hell is Leon Gilhall?" Alain asked the room at large. No answer other than a few shrugs. "Nobody's heard from him?" He got blank looks in return. Leon should have been all over these calls. The hair on the back of his neck bristled. Alain headed for his truck with the books and evidence bag forgotten in his hands.

"That was a quick stop," Stephanie said when he jerked open the door of the truck. Alain didn't answer. He cranked the ignition and threw the shifter into reverse. The books were discarded on the seat. He popped the shifter into drive while still rolling backwards, spraying gravel on a few patrol cars as he slewed the truck out of the parking lot and onto the road.

"Where the hell are we going now?" Stephanie asked. She clutched at the oh-shit handle over the passenger window.

"You're getting dropped off," he said, taking a hard corner and letting go of the wheel long enough to slap the switches for lights and siren. He speed-dialed dispatch again and got Ernie on the first ring.

"Detective!" Ernie sounded delighted. "I've got your Mama in custody. Munising P.D. is driving her up here."

The man actually chortled. Alain had thought that a made-up word until he heard Ernie do it. He hit another corner, tires shrieking, working the brakes into the curve and then the gas until the truck straightened out.

"Ernie, I'm dropping some important things off for you. Then I need you to raise Deputy Gilhall."

"On the phone, still?" Ernie asked.

"Phone, radio, foghorn, whatever you've got. Roll a car to the Walleye tavern, and I'll check his house. Unlock your front door." He tried to fight down the rising tide of cold in his gut.

The trooper post approached fast. Alain slid into the lot in a controlled skid, aiming the passenger door at the steps. The truck fetched up short and rocked on its suspension. Alain shoved the untidy stack of books at her.

"Take these in. Read them. Find me something to go on. I don't have time to explain," he said. "Please trust me and wait here until I get back."

She took a look at the expression on his face, and, amazingly, didn't argue. She hopped out the door loaded down with the evidence and he rolled out again, careful not to spray her down with gravel. He probably had enough to atone for without that.

In the rearview mirror he watched as Ernie let her in and locked the door behind the two of them. He killed the siren and flashers, boosted the headlights to high and put the gas pedal on the floor.

Leon lived four miles outside the city limits toward Negaunee and south of the Dead River. The V8 howled as he pushed it through the night on the two-lane highway. The 4x4 suspension, too high and soft for a hundred miles an hour on the curving road, felt like driving a mattress. Alain let off the gas and allowed the speedometer to drop to ninety. He tried to relax and scan the ditches for movement. The swaying branches played tricks on his eyes, and his heart leapt into his throat a handful of times when he saw a deer about to bound out in front of him that turned into a branch or reflector post. Leon would have called it a sphincter-pucker drive if he'd been along.

He heard Ernie try to raise Leon on the busy radio a half dozen times. A check with the other officers on the air verified that no one had seen him. He didn't have duty tonight, but like most deputies he took his cruiser home and had been known to stick his nose in if anything interesting happened. He should have shown up at the murder scene, or definitely at Alain's house. His fingers drummed a rapid tattoo on the wheel and shifter. His cell phone rang. In trying to answer it he almost threw it across the cab.

"Alain."

"Nothing, Detective," Ernie said, "not a peep. You want me to roll another unit to you?"

"Have you got anyone heading to the Walleye yet?" Alain asked.

"In a few minutes. The party's breaking up at the rectory," Ernie replied. "By the way, nice package you sent me. Perfect dimensions."

"She's not sitting there, is she, Ern?" Alain asked.

"Ladies room."

"Try saying that to her straight," Alain said. "She might tie your business in a knot." It felt forced and hollow in his ears.

"Good to know," Ernie said, "really useful information."

Alain dropped the phone. The turn-off for the dirt road Leon lived on came up faster than he recalled. He stood on the brakes, the back end breaking loose when he swung into the curve. He rode it out on the throttle again. The washboards rattled his fillings and vibrated the truck, but around sixty miles an hour the tires began to float over them, spending as much time in the air between bumps as actually touching dirt. Alain dropped the headlamps to normal, then cut them down to his parking lights and slowed considerably. The road curved through a draw between short, steep hills. Thick tree cover made it pitch black. He nosed into a pullout along the road used by anglers on the Dead and killed the engine.

Leon's driveway lay a hundred yards ahead, the cabin itself set back from the road about the same distance. Alain had no intention of rolling up and making a target of himself. He climbed out of the truck and popped the rear half-door. He slid his M-14 rifle out of its sleeve, grabbed the magazine and groped for the thick plastic ammo box. He found it slid partway under the front seat and popped the latches. An extra magazine for his Sig rode on top. One full mag in the pistol and two spares gave him thirty-seven rounds of hollow-point .40 caliber. The box also held an ammo pouch which he clipped to his belt in the small of his back. It contained two spare twenty-round box magazines for the M-14. He loaded the rifle, drew back the bolt and let it ease forward slowly, chambering a round, then slipped the safety off.

Unlike his shotgun the M-14 didn't have a light attached to it, so he would be going into the woods blind unless he wanted to juggle flashlight and rifle at the same time. That triggered a thought, and Alain snagged his shooting glasses from the truck visor before quietly easing the doors shut. The glasses went on to protect his eyes from tree branches. Alain melted into the woods.

Slow going, testing each step for fallen leaves and branches that might snap. Once under the cover of the trees, Alain stopped to listen. The shouldering hills blocked the wind here but it still drowned out the background noise of the woods. Likely no one would hear his footsteps, but the flip side of that meant Alain wouldn't hear anyone hunting him. The wild movement of the air would also confuse an animal hunting by smell, like a dog, bear, wolf.

"I'm blind, he can't smell, and we're both deaf," he murmured. "Good odds."

He took a deep breath and exhaled, seeking the calm required for hunting. It eluded him, flickering at the edge of his grasp. His mind raced: the thing in his hallway, Avius attacked as well as Alain. Or could it be Stephanie the thing was after? Both? It nagged him like a splinter under his fingernail. People committed murder for power, sex and money, and occasionally the truly mad did it for fun. Animals killed when they got hungry. No one killed for old stories.

Trees thickened into black forms in the previously shapeless night as his eyes adjusted, the spaces between brighter. He looked not at any particular spot but past them, and his feet found a path. The breeze against his skin felt like the warmth of a fire. No noise. Alain hunted the night.

A pinhole of light, perhaps a gap between curtains at a window, revealed the cabin when he crested a rise. He began to angle a few degrees to the left, aiming to halve the distance before circling the structure. The direction took him into a kettle, one of the deep depressions gouged out of the ground by glaciers and left for early settlers to puzzle over. These pits had rounded sides and varied from a few feet to a quarter-mile across. The immigrants had attached names like "devil's soupbowl" to the largest, positive that anything so odd must be the work of dark supernatural powers.

The high sides of the kettle blocked the wind, dead calm at the bottom. The sky opened over the bowl, and Alain saw the moon for the first time since turning onto Leon's road. He stopped for a moment to allow his breathing and pulse to slow, maintaining the state of awareness he had gained in the woods by studying the silver orb. It had risen completely and now fell toward the horizon, growing larger as if reeling the earth in on a string. October: the hunter's moon, so called because the cold white light of the full moon made blood shine in the dark, allowing a primitive hunter to follow the trail of a wounded animal through the night.

The air at the bottom of the bowl thickened. Alain did not move. The hair on the back of his neck rose again, his ancient defense meant to make him appear larger in the eyes of a predator. He wasn't alone.

The search for Anissa Rodhette has ended. For the third time in as many months, a lass has failed to return to her home from a forest excursion. Armed parties have combed the dark woods and swamps of the county from height to end without finding so much as a lock of hair. What new thing must we fear?
3 March, 1899. The Palladium Superior.

Chapter Fourteen

The growl—thick, deep and edged with madness—unrolled from one of the shadowy scrubby growths scattered across the floor of the kettle. Alain remained still, looking over and past each dark area. There: eyes. Twin globes of green fire burned in the dark as branches stirred and allowed the moonlight to penetrate for a moment. Gone as quickly as they had come, but Alain had the spot marked. Fifty feet away, too close. He began to turn, achingly slow, thinking of the movement required to get a shot off before it could reach him. Rotate and set the feet while raising the rifle, acquire the target over the sights, squeeze the trigger. Slow-motion if the animal didn't move. If it charged, well, he'd try.

As the rifle butt began to glide upward, seeking the iron weld to his shoulder, the reflex born of ten thousand repetitions, it stepped forward. The clouds had cleared, driven out over Lake Superior by the vicious wind. Alain saw it plainly. The head first, sleek and powerful, the long snout of a wolf, eyes hooded, lips curled to expose canines six inches long, ears back against the massive skull. Alain thought it must be standing on a rock because the head hung at least four feet off the ground, too high for a wolf. Then the beast took another step forward, curling its paw up and forward before setting it down like a cat. It stalked him. Shoulders and chest broad as a phone booth emerged, black with a silver streak disappearing between the two front legs. The growl rumbled louder. Another step, and still the back half of the animal stood in the shadows.

Alain faced a black wolf almost able to look him square in the eyes. It had to weigh three hundred pounds. His mind ran through comparisons and discarded them as quickly as they occurred. It was the size of a pony, a carnivorous pony.

For a naked second under the moon Alain stared down a cave painting out of prehistory, what his ancestors had battled and hunted for thousands of years between waves of ice advancing from the north. He understood now that the beasts of today were pale shadows of the nightmares that used to stalk these woods, hunting their soft two-legged prey in the winters of the past. He felt a fear shared by generations, and at the same time the spark of courage the hunters that had stood in this contest before him had felt. The smooth cool wood of the rifle stock touched his cheek as he caught the wolf in his sights and felt the curve of the trigger under his index finger.

Then it stood up.

The head rose into the air—seven, eight, nine feet as though it wasn't going to stop. Alain's mind took careful note even as some small part gibbered that what he saw was impossible. It held its head awkwardly, hunched forward over the powerful chest. The elbows tucked in close, huge paws dangling. The animal towered over the scrub that had hidden it.

Alain's finger froze on the trigger, the rifle forgotten, a useless cunning stick against a monster. The wolf's eyes flared green again as they caught the moonlight. It turned and strode toward the edge of the kettle still in shadow, away from Alain. It walked away.

Bears stand on their hind legs to gain a scent and coyotes will rear up to bluff an attacker, but neither of those can stay upright for long. The standing wolf bounded at an astounding pace on its hind legs. When it reached the edge it scrambled upward in an odd combination of movement, transitioning from two legs, clumsily attempting to grasp handholds with its paws, to four legs and then back.

Alain sprinted forward toward the edge of the depression. He could make out the creature already nearing the top and drew a bead on its broad back. He didn't want to shoot an animal running away. He had no proof this was the thing that had been in his house. It had stood up and looked him in the eye, but had not attacked.

The creature reached the top and stood framed against the stars in the sky. It looked back down at Alain. The image of the priest with his bowels strewn on the floor ran before his eyes. Aimee.

He squeezed the trigger.

The muzzle flash from the .308 seared his night vision. When the flaring spots cleared from Alain's eyes the lip was clear, no animal. It felt like a hit, as though he'd gotten it high in the chest. He turned to his right and began to climb at an angle. The loose earth at the side of the kettle made him scramble, crudely using one arm to pull himself up while clasping his gun. Alain felt vulnerable and exposed, the spot between his shoulder blades itching as though a rifle aimed at him as he climbed.

Alain gained the top and leveled the M-14 at the spot where he'd last seen the creature. He stopped again to listen. The wind had picked up and he couldn't pick out anything from the melee of flailing leaves. The moon was setting, the light failing by degrees. Alain clicked on the rifle's safety and put the sling over his shoulder, drawing his pistol in the same movement. He dug his flashlight out of his pocket, forming an X in front of his body with light and gun aimed in the same direction. He started through the woods toward the spot where the monster should be. Blood shone on the white bark of a birch tree. He'd hit it.

Alain swore. A quick scan of the area showed scrape marks at the edge of the kettle where it had clawed itself over the edge, but the hard ground beyond the lip hid any other tracks. He had to follow the blood trail. Leaving the light on made him a clear target, so Alain used it only in flashes, relying on the dying moon and intuition.

He stalked in a semi-circle around the first mark, and hit another within ten yards. This one lower, drops of blood on the ground as if it ran on all fours again. Again he made the circle, not trusting the direction from only two signs. There, another splash running straight as an arrow toward Leon's cabin. Alain began to sprint.

Why hadn't he killed it when he'd had a chance? He could have taken the head right off when it first stepped out. Then it stood up and walked like a man. Alain didn't know what to do but run faster, heedless of the crashing noise and branches lashing at his face. He took the end of one in the throat, swerving by reflex at the last second to avoid impaling himself. It cut along the side of his neck and broke off, warm blood welling from the gash left behind. The night air felt cold on his skin now, chilling him where sweat had soaked through his shirt.

The trees gave way to the clearing around the house and Alain thrashed into the open.

"Leon," he called.

He couldn't hear anything but wind.

"Get your panties on and grab a big gun," he yelled, "there's something out here."

He stood behind the house where only a few dark windows looked out onto the forest. When he flashed his light inside he saw no one. At the corner he put his back to the wall before popping his head around, light and pistol leading. Cleared the side yard. Same thing at the front corner, keeping an eye on the woods as he moved. The snapshot showed him a familiar sight, the wreckage of a door, pieces strewn across the porch and small lawn. Alain crossed in front of the windows moving fast.

An overhead light burned in the living room, perhaps the same one he had seen from outside before encountering the wolf. Heavy log furniture, much of it handmade by Leon, lay tumbled about, some smashed to kindling. Alain quickly passed through and cleared the rest of the small cabin. Only the front room showed damage. No sign of the occupants. Some of the tension trickled out of his quivering muscles.

He re-entered the front room. Clawing and raking gouges marked the walls in a manner he had seen far too many times in the past forty-eight hours. There was more here, though, a shape torn out of the wood next to the door, a symbol: overlapping triangles pointing down before curling back up at a final "v." It made him feel queasy to look at it. The strength, the madness required to rip out the seasoned chunks of wood . . . Alain traced the shape. The wood still felt warm to the touch, hotter than the air around it. He snapped a photo with his phone and tore his eyes away from the design.

He tried to use Leon's landline phone, but got no dial tone. His cell likewise had no service, and he'd left his radio in the truck because he knew the handheld unit wouldn't pick up anything in this dead spot.

Something caught his eye: fabric sticking out from under the ugly Realtree camouflage couch, the only piece of store-bought furniture in here. Alain kept a wary eye on the door as he moved it aside, but forgot about the danger and dropped to his knees when he uncovered Leon's uniform shredded and stained with what looked like blood, the leather belt snapped in two.

Alain's stomach twisted. He holstered his pistol and slid the rifle off his shoulder, knuckles white where they grasped the stock. The front door gaped. He took it.

Alain cleared the yard for the darkness of the trees before stopping. The wind smothered all other sounds. He had no way of locating the beast now. Alain burned to kill it, but he had no idea how to hunt a wolf. Trappers used bait. He didn't have any and the beast would be wary now that it had been shot. He could retrace his steps to the blood trail. Judging by the size of the drops it didn't have a mortal wound. It could be miles away by now.

He shook his head as if throwing off a dream and pulled in a deep breath. Alain allowed the scenes of blood and gore he'd seen in the last thirty-six hours to wash over him, that feeling of being the hunter borne on the night when he'd begun the stalk, the fear and challenge that had flooded through him when he'd faced down the monstrous wolf.

Alain threw back his head and howled.

Not the Hollywood howl that sounds more like a coyote, but a belling alpha male challenge full of pride and rage from deep in the chest. Possession of these hunting grounds, superiority, sex and food and power—he funneled them into sound, starting low but allowing it to grow and rise. Breathe. Again he hit it, pushing the note higher and farther and defeating the wind before letting it fade into the night.

He listened. The forest paused as the wind drew its own breath.

The answering call came from the south, carrying across the treetops. Anger and pain, it said. Fight. The wolf's call made his sound puny by comparison, a full-throated bellow that silenced everything and vibrated in Alain's chest and in his hunter's soul.

Distance was hard to judge. That sound had evolved to travel for miles, but he thought the animal still ran north of the hills on which Negaunee stood. Close enough, especially if he could draw it in for a fight. Alain shifted his weight and took one step toward the source of the challenge, all thoughts of back-up and procedures and evidence flown from his head and replaced with bloody revenge.

The second howl came from the north. Alain froze. Two of them . . . wolves hunt in packs.

The second wolf called from farther away. Suddenly the multiple attacks made sense—a timeline with two killers fit. He retraced his steps to the cabin at a trot. He wanted revenge for Leon's death, but it would have to be served cold. The driveway wound down through the trees to the gravel road, and he picked up his pace with the rifle held loose and low, running toward his truck, lights, radio, society, and reinforcements.

He crashed against the hood when he reached the truck, panting hard. The rifle went back into the sleeve behind the seat, unloaded with the ammo pouch tossed after it. As he swung onto the pavement he heard the calls for him over the radio. He snatched the handset.

"3-17," he said, "Returning to Base. Get the whole team together. Now."

Ernie knew when to talk back and when to shut up, and his calls for a rendezvous at the post took up the airwaves for the rest of Alain's drive. Ernie likely worked the phones at the same time since a meeting of the whole team would involve the Department of Natural Resources officers who weren't on call at night. So much for the overtime budget. Four murders already and two monsters on the loose meant he'd be hearing from the state if not the feds. Tomorrow was Sunday, and higher-ups still operated on a regular business schedule as if criminals punched a time clock. He might have one more day to clear this up locally. He damn well intended to do just that.

Alain squeezed the wheel, trying to force out of his memory the image of the wolf standing up. If he let down his guard for an instant he saw it again, rising up higher and higher. Beast, wolf-thing, standing wolf . . . he'd been skirting the issue since he saw it and now his brain wanted to make some sense of it. Mama Bouche had known what he would see if he kept chasing Aimee's killer. Loup garou, the werewolf.

Medieval legend carried to the New World, nurtured in the shadows of the north woods for three hundred years and now tearing people to pieces in his town. A human controlled the wolf, but Alain had failed to realize until now that he did it from the inside. His rational side had nothing better to offer. He shrugged it off. Serial killers were monsters, with or without claws. It had started as a man. His sworn duty was to stop it, arrest it or them as the case may be. Failing that, his job would be to hunt them down and destroy them. Alain knew which he'd prefer.

So why had the loup garou targeted Aimee Henderson? Could the girl have been simply in the wrong place at the wrong time? Alain doubted it. She researched the loup garou legend, and then one killed her. He didn't believe in neat and tidy answers. She'd found something, a secret or something of value and she'd paid for it with her life. Stephanie had said something that nagged at him, a hint about the research project Aimee had worked on. He couldn't remember what she'd said that had struck him as important. His brain felt mired in thick mud.

The lights of Marquette appeared out of the forest, and Alain slowed to a sane speed. Time to explain this to the troops, minus the part about the wolf standing up.

The post lot was filling rapidly with cruisers, Trooper Beatty's SUV and a scattering of private trucks and cars. Most of the members of the team were already on duty due to the expanded patrols. This case stretched them to the limit. The Marquette post had twenty active troopers responsible for patrolling an area of almost three thousand square miles—half the size of Connecticut—twenty-four hours a day. Even with borrowing troopers from other posts, like Beatty, and leaning heavily on the sheriff's deputies, Alain would rapidly run out of people able to stay awake.

The conference room smelled like scorched coffee. He saw no sign of Stephanie. Perhaps Ernie had unlocked an office with a couch so she could get some sleep. The officers present rubbed their eyes surreptitiously, thumbing through notebooks that hadn't helped a wink thus far. Bob and his replacement arrived, a kid straight out of the Marines in the Gulf. Ex-military always got preference for government jobs.

Alain leaned on the podium and launched into it without a preamble. "Leon Gilhall is missing."

Now he had their full attention.

"The door to his house has been smashed like the one at the rectory and at my place. If you haven't seen the pictures they'll be coming around," he said. "A crime scene team will need to visit that site immediately following this meeting."

Brett had burned the digital pictures from the scenes at Alain's house and the rectory to CD. He started a small battery-powered player around the room. Exclamations followed its path, marking those who had not been there to see the destruction and carnage first-hand.

"Actually, um." Something about Leon's door bothered him. He couldn't think. "Yeah. Leon is missing, and the whereabouts of his wife . . ."

A blockish deputy raised her hand.

"Yes?" Alain asked.

"I picked up Mrs. Gilhall at the Walleye Tavern an hour ago. She's in the lobby, and she said Deputy Gilhall should be at home," the deputy said.

"Good. Good," Alain said.

"She's angry."

"Glad to hear it," he said. That meant she probably was fine.

"We are looking," he continued, before anyone else could derail him, "for at least a pair of very large wolves, better than two hundred pounds apiece."

Bob snorted.

"Problem, Ranger Androtti?" Alain heard the tightness in his own voice.

"The biggest wolves max out around one-twenty. They might grow to six, seven feet long, but they're skinny. No such thing as a fat wolf. People always misjudge their weight," the DNR officer said.

"I suggest you take a look at the pictures of the crime scenes—" Alain began.

"Seen them. No wolf did that. They won't come into town like coyotes, and they sure as hell don't smash down doors," Bob said.

"I saw one of them," Alain said quietly. "It could almost look me in the eye. The thing was huge."

"Dammit, Alain, that's impossible," Bob said.

"I shot it. Twice, or two of them once each, actually. The one that broke into my house I finally hit with a load of double-aught buckshot. It didn't do a damn thing. The buckshot slowed it down, but it still ran off without missing a beat."

All heads turned to the door as it opened. Hell Burke came in late, his left arm in a simple cloth sling and his hair slicked back as though he'd just gotten out of the shower. He took an empty desk near the front. Good. Alain could use someone who wasn't about to fall asleep no matter how inexperienced he might be.

"The other one . . . at least, I think it was a different animal . . . I hit with a .308 high in the center body. That one ran off, and the blood trail didn't look strong," he said. "We need to bring these animals down. What you want is penetration. Ball ammunition out of a rifle, slugs from a shotgun maybe. Multiple shots. If your sidearm is loaded with hollowpoints you want to switch to something that will hit deeper," Alain said.

"Hang on a second." Bob's protégé stood up to speak. "You can't go around killing wolves if you feel like it. They're protected."

Bob rose and put a hand on the young man's shoulder.

"What Chris means is that wolves are federal jurisdiction," he said.

"Maybe if they're on national forest land," a trooper offered from the back.

"No, everywhere. State forest, national, private . . . doesn't matter. Gray wolves are on the endangered species list, and they're a purely federal matter. No one can shoot them without federal sanction, except in cases of grave personal danger. And that won't happen," he said, with a meaningful look at Alain, "because no one has ever documented a case of a wild wolf killing a human in North America."

"Bob, you need to stop by my place," Alain said, "take a good look at the front door, the back stairs and the hallway on the second floor. That thing came after me and I got lucky."

He felt bad about lying to Bob. Bob sensed something off, here, and if he did, likely some of the more experienced officers could pick up on it as well. The story wasn't simple enough to bear scrutiny.

Bob spoke from his seat this time. "I'm not saying you didn't see what you saw. I'm saying that anyone who shoots a wolf is going to be under the microscope. You'd better have your ducks in a row, career-wise."

The room got quiet in a hurry. The deputies wanted to be troopers, and the troopers wanted to keep their jobs. Aside from moving up in rank or jumping to the feds no higher plane of law enforcement existed.

"No one in here is going to shoot a wolf," Alain said, "aside from a case of, what, again?"

"Grave personal danger," Bob said, his face tight.

"That," Alain said. "But if we do pull a trigger we're going to do it with the right ammo."

He saw heads nod around the room. Wolves were a bit more endangered than usual in this corner of the north woods tonight. He'd gotten the message across. Alain glanced at his watch.

"Midnight. Night shift plus two. Can I get volunteers?"

Two deputies raised their hands to beef up the midnight to eight a.m. patrol. They both were kids with babies, eager for the overtime. Alain nodded.

"Keep your eyes peeled and call in every fifteen," he said. "I still need a crime scene team."

He culled four of the least bleary-eyed officers out of the pool that raised their hands, all of them anxious to put their name on the reports for a big case.

"And Hell," he finished, closing the meeting. Hell had not raised his hand, but he nodded at Alain.

"Bob, you have a minute?" Alain asked. The room filled with the scrape of chairs. Bob waited at the side of the podium with his young shadow—Chris, Bob had called him—until the rest of the team had filed out.

Alain let the time stretch out. Chris didn't seem inclined to leave. "There's something out there, Bob," Alain said quietly.

The wrinkles in the ranger's neck seemed deeper than the day before. The troopers complained about being spread thin, but Bob and the other Department of Natural Resources guys were usually one per county. Bob had been in charge of eighteen hundred square miles of forest, lakes and shoreline by himself for thirty-odd years, and only when his retirement became an inevitable reality did he get some help.

"I know," Bob said.

Chris shifted his feet, stuck his hands deeper into the pockets of his wool DNR jacket.

"You've seen it?" Alain asked.

"Not this time."

"Tracks?"

Bob nodded. "That, and a few other scenes. Deer . . . a porkypine. Cruelty, like an animal wouldn't do."

"You've got to be human to be truly evil, huh?"

"My gram used to say, when someone did us wrong, she'd say, 'Man is a wolf to man.' I never forgot that. I was 'bout as old as Mr. Angell here," he indicated Chris with a jerk of his head, "when I saw something I ain't never forgot either."

Cheap paneling and buzzing fluorescent lights made a surreal setting for this type of discussion. Bob's words thrust all three of them into some middle ground between normal and the twilight zone.

"I stayed out working one night, near dusk and way past quitting time. Mrs. Androtti missed me, for sure, in those days, but I was green and eager for the job almost more than what she had to offer."

Chris huffed and almost smiled before recovering his stoicism.

"It ran right across the road in front of me," Bob said, "on two legs. Covered in hair and tall as Goliath. Big sumbitch, whatever the hell it was. I found the deer it had been feeding on, roadkill likely, but I could barely make myself get out of the truck to look at it. That thing scared me more than anything I saw on Okinawa."

"It felt wrong," Alain said.

"That's it," Bob said. "Bad. Evil, like in a fairy tale or a kiddy book. I've felt the touch of that goddamn thing for almost forty years. Not always, but occasionally when I'm alone in the woods I get the feeling. Hair on the back of—"

"Your neck stands up," Alain said.

"Neck, hell, I think every hair on my body stood out. Damn it," Bob said. It came out as almost a sigh. "I'd hoped to make it to the end without seeing that thing again."

"You probably think we're both losing our minds," Alain said to Chris.

The hulking young man seemed to think over his reply carefully. "This is my land to take care of now. Why wouldn't I want to know what's really out there? I can't imagine it's worse than what I saw overseas."

Bob nodded his approval. He seemed proud of his replacement.

"It's out there. Two of them I think." Alain filled the rangers in on his attempts at howling.

"That was awful stupid, Alain," Bob said.

118

Alain shrugged. "It worked."

Bob shook his head, and nudged his newbie again. "Try not to be a hero like Mr. Detective, here. You'll live long enough to enjoy a really crappy pension if you don't take him as a role model."

Chris the Marine finally spoke. "So? What's next?"

Bob said, "We go after it, of course. If Alain tagged one or both of them, they might go back home to lick their wounds. We go to the last spot seen and track it, figure out where it's going. Damn. We're all a little bit dumb, aren't we?"

2:00 a.m.: The post still buzzed as Alain left the conference room with the state rangers in tow. He stopped by his desk, unlocked the bottom drawer and took out two small cardboard boxes.

"What have you got there?" Bob asked.

"Not a thing," Alain replied.

"Wouldn't be some of that hot ammo you're not supposed to use, is it?"

"Bob, I'm shocked, simply shocked you would think such a thing of me," Alain tucked the boxes of .40 ammo in a pocket, where they rattled against his leg during the walk to the parking lot. The state politicos frowned on Corbon DPX after a debacle in a wealthy suburb of Detroit. When the two officers on duty had faced a carload of armed robbery suspects firing shots in a crowded neighborhood, they'd used the hot-loaded penetrating round to ventilate the vehicle, unloading fifty-two shots into the car right through the doors. The Toyota looked like it had been in a war zone, and it got a lot of airtime as attorneys lined up to sue for excessive force. Apparently, if cops were going to shoot someone they should only do it a few times and use less effective ammunition. It kept things fair between the criminals and the police.

On their way out they passed the Lieutenant's office. He was still missing in action, which meant everything that happened on this case would be Alain's fault. He caught a glimpse of Stephanie with the volumes and notes from Father Avius's office spread out across the Lieutenant's desk. Mama Bouche was at her elbow. He almost stopped. Later. Not enough time.

Alain led the way in his F-150, followed by the rangers in Chris's Dodge 4x4, which the kid had tricked out with every gadget and bit of chrome possible. Alain felt around under the seat until he came up with a baseball cap, which he flipped upside down and placed in the passenger seat. While he drove with one hand, he tugged out his two spare pistol mags and emptied their hollow-point rounds into the hat, thumbing them out by feel. Briefly driving with his knees he unloaded the Sig, stripping the mag like the others before racking the slide to clear the round in the chamber.

He pulled into the turn-out where he'd stopped before, inching right up to the edge of the trees to allow Chris room to slide his shiny truck in behind him, then turned on the dome light and tugged the two boxes of ammo from his pocket. Bob popped the passenger door as he finished snugging the fat DPX rounds into the magazines.

"You got a license to be hunting this time of night, son?" Bob asked.

"What kind of paperwork do I need to hunt monster?"

"Statement of mental competence might be good," Bob said, "or possible lack thereof."

He seemed livelier than he'd been earlier that evening, certainly more talkative than usual. Bob could pass a day waiting for poachers on a half dozen words. The girl's death had been eating at him.

"You ready to go get these bastards before you ride off into the sunset?" Alain said.

"I believe I am."

"You have a gun?" Alain knew Bob hadn't carried a weapon on duty in years.

Bob pulled his jacket aside to show a Colt .45 automatic tucked into the back of his belt over his left kidney.

"That pistol a souvenir from Okinawa?" Alain asked. He finished reloading the Sig and holstered it

"Saved my bacon two, three times. I figure it might have one more in it."

Gravel crunched as Chris loomed out of the darkness. He'd been busy digging in his own truck, and it showed. The young ex-Marine sported a pistol in a holster strapped to one thigh, a knife bigger than Alain's on the other and a black nylon vest with what looked like fifty pockets bulging with gear. He carried an AR-15 rifle with a tactical light, red dot sight and a curved thirty-round magazine. Alain felt decidedly under-dressed.

The detective retrieved his own rifle from the back seat of his truck as well as the spare ammo pouch for it. He turned to face his little team.

"I'll show you where I lost the blood trail," he said.

Neither man questioned whether they ought to call their location in to dispatch. Bob knew this hunt didn't have any official sanction. It said a lot for Chris's level of trust that the kid stayed. Of course, how many times do you get a chance to slay monsters?

Alain pondered that as he entered the woods for the second time that night. This time he knew what his quarry looked like, and it scared the hell out of him.

The moon had set, and with it the wind had calmed as though it too had been driven by the white light. Now the breeze played in only the crowns of the trees rather than torturing them along their complete lengths.

Bob had a flashlight taped down to a pinhole, and by its faint light Alain led the three of them to the edge of the kettle. Leon's cabin shone brightly this time, illuminated by the crime scene team he'd hastily thrown together at the meeting. That was a problem he hadn't considered. If they encountered one or both of the loup garou close to the cabin and opened fire, the officers at the scene would hear them and investigate. All the more reason to finish this quickly.

Bob nodded to himself as if he knew the place. He'd spent over half a century walking these woods. If the old man's knowledge of this county could be distilled it would fill a shelf of books. His reaction to Alain's news about the loup garou had been a relief. Alain hadn't realized how heavy that secret had been until he'd told someone. If Bob had laughed or dismissed him, Alain didn't know what he would have done. Of course, he still didn't know about the dreams, what was happening to Alain.

The ranger passed by Alain, peering at the ground in the beam of his light, in his element, tracking a man who'd been hunting an animal. Bob followed Alain's footprints down to the bottom of the kettle, which had an easier slope on this side as opposed to the steep lip he and the beast had climbed to get out. Bob found the spot where Alain had stopped. He stood off to side for a moment, then began casting across the floor of the kettle in the general direction of bushes where Alain had first seen the wolf. In less than five minutes Bob found the spot where the animal had been.

"How did you know which direction to go?" Alain asked.

"You shuffled your feet, but the top prints were firm and aimed this way," Bob answered. "Had your gun on it, didn't you?"

"It stared me down over the sights," Alain said.

"Huh," Bob said from his hands and knees, examining the track. The question about why Alain hadn't shot hung in the air.

"It stood up," Alain said, "and I forgot to shoot. I froze until it turned and walked away."

121

Chris said nothing, continuing to scan the rim of the kettle through a small night vision monocular.

"That way," Bob said, indicating the direction with his head as he stood up and dusted off his jeans. He turned to Alain. "When I saw that thing run across the road in front of me all those years ago I pissed myself a little bit. I could have no more pulled the trigger on it right then than I could have flapped my arms and flown to the moon."

Bob easily followed the trail to the base of the steep side of the kettle. Alain slung his rifle and followed along, using his own flashlight now with a red filter clipped over the lens. The crimson glow preserved their night vision. Chris brought up the rear with rifle at the ready. Bob went down on his hands and knees again, head held low as he played his thin beam of light across the ground. He pounced on something and held it up: the brass from Alain's rifle. He held up one finger for Alain to see, asking silently: One shot?

Alain nodded.

Bob inspected the loose dirt of the slope before starting to climb, and stopped a few times to examine the marks left by the loup garou on the way up. Alain moved a few paces to the right and pulled for the top, moving fast to get up and provide cover for the other men. He hauled himself over the rim for the second time that evening and stood, unslinging his rifle before flashing his light over the edge twice, signaling Chris to come up. The taciturn Marine began his own climb making less noise than Bob. The kid seemed at home out here. If he had a head on his shoulders to match his woodcraft, the county might be in fine shape for Bob's retirement. As Chris's thick frame ghosted over the top of the kettle Alain almost felt sorry for the next generation of poachers who this young man would hunt. Almost.

A strange light washed over the trail, springing from yet another little device Chris had produced from his vest. It looked like an old crookneck army flashlight, but produced a brilliant purple-red colored light.

A hand-sized smear of blood glowed on the ground.

"Blood tracker. LEDs calibrated to the same color as blood to make it stand out," he said.

With a rattling of dirt Bob hoisted himself up to join them. Chris had his rifle tucked under one arm, barrel angled down but still ready to fire. He held the tracking light in his other hand. Bob followed and Alain took the rear, drifting back twenty feet and averting his eyes to avoid focusing only on the other two men.

The temperature had dropped. Alain wished he'd thought to bring a jacket. The cold washed over him, raising goose bumps. It might have been the cold. Separated from the others by the smallest of margins, he felt alone in the night again.

The forest had never been frightening before. It held dangers, of course: swift-running streams, treacherous cliffs and always the threat of insidious cold. Nature simply existed and did not care if humans lived or died. She would as gladly accept his body to feed and enrich the forest floor as she would see him survive. Alain became lost only once in his childhood wanderings. His uncles didn't come to look for him. When he returned home a day late, torn with briers, hungry and full of hot anger, two of them were working on an old car in the front yard. They'd nodded at him, as they did to other men, and returned to their attempt to remove a frozen water pump. If the forest had wanted him back, it would have taken him.

Now, though, the woods held a mystery, a shadow that seemed to watch from the darkness. There was the den he kept finding himself in his dreams, whatever he might be becoming. For the first time Alain understood the fear of people who had never spent a night camping farther than twenty feet from a car.

They passed the spot where Alain left the blood trail and crashed toward Leon's cabin. Bob pointed at him with one eyebrow inclined. It looked as though a wounded rhino had smashed through the brush.

"Trail's petering out," Bob said. "Had some pretty good smears at first, but now we're down to occasional drops. Where did you say you hit it?"

"High in the body, I think," Alain said. "It headed for the cabin."

"Nope," Bob replied, "it turns here and moves to the south." He indicated the trail with his hand and Chris illuminated it on the ground, but Alain couldn't see it. He knew he wasn't half as good a tracker as Bob. *Damn it.* The timing had been off from the start. The cabin had been torn up before he got there even though he'd been right behind the loup garou. That first howl had come from farther to the south. So, the thing must have killed Leon first and then hung around in the area until Alain arrived. That made no sense. The attack at the rectory had been a surgical strike with no witnesses. The animal at Alain's house had likewise disappeared immediately after it became clear that Alain was primed to fight. Why had this one stayed close?

"Can you follow it?" Alain asked.

"Maybe for a while. Be easier in daylight," Bob said.

"Let's go as far as you can," Alain said. "The clock is ticking."

Chris held up one hand, clenched into a fist: the sign for contact with the enemy, a demand for silence. He cocked his head, listening before slipping into the trees not making a sound. Alain followed, then Bob. The three of them moved through the woods in a sinuous line, the last two trusting the senses of the younger man to lead the way. Then Alain heard it, too. Groaning. In a small clearing in the woods where the ground was torn and clawed in a manner Alain had seen twice before, Leon Gilhall lay nude.

The deputy was caked in dirt. He groaned again, a low and guttural sound that grated on Alain's ears as he knelt beside him. His red beam bathed Leon in a hellish light as Chris gave him a quick check for wounds. He had no obvious broken bones or large wounds but they wouldn't know for sure until they rolled him.

"Leon," Alain asked, "can you hear me?"

Leon opened his eyes, his face streaked with tears, and began to sit up.

"Don't try to move," Alain said, putting his hands on Leon's shoulders. The deputy flinched away from his touch.

"Chris, Bob, take a look at this," Alain said.

A small puckered hole in Leon's left shoulder stood out against the pale surrounding skin.

"Bullet wound," Bob said. "Exit. Clean pass, straight through. You'll find the entry when you roll him, maybe a little lower but close by."

"Old," Chris agreed. "Five days, maybe a week. He'll be all right."

"What size does that look like to you?" Alain asked.

"Good-sized rifle. Not a .22, that's for sure," Bob said. "Deer rifle, I guess."

".308?" Alain asked. He felt a strange tightness in the center of his chest.

"Possible," Bob allowed. "You know who shot him?"

Alain nodded and got heavily to his feet.

"I think I did," he said.

Chris expertly rolled the deputy to check his back without disturbing the spine. As he slowly laid Leon down again, the deputy spoke.

"I'm sure it was a hell of a party, gentleman, but if you'll assist me with finding my boots I'll be on my way."

Leon's voice came out thin and weak. Chris took charge, asking Leon to wiggle his fingers and toes and follow a flashlight tracked in front of his eyes. After vociferous complaining and repeated assurances that everything hurt, but only a little, Leon was allowed to sit up. Bob donated his jacket and Chris produced a foil trauma blanket to cover Leon's lower half. Leon crinkled whenever he moved.

"What happened?" Alain asked.

"About to ask you the same thing," Leon said. "Did somebody knock me on the head? Last time I woke up like this I found myself married."

"Your head looks okay but I'd like to know how you got shot," Alain asked.

Leon craned his neck, trying to get a good look at his own shoulder.

"Is that what that is?" he said. "You would think I'd recall something like that, wouldn't you?"

"What do you remember?" Alain asked.

"The meeting. Getting in my car. Shit, when did it get dark?"

"This is no time for joking, you ass," Alain said.

Leon shook his head, wincing at the pain it caused in his shoulder. "I don't remember a damned thing since I last saw you."

He got creakily to his feet with a few helping hands, trying in vain to hold the space blanket around himself.

"Losing my dignity, already lost my mind," he said.

"How do you feel?" Alain asked.

"Like ten miles of bad road but I'm ready to get the hell out of here if I have to crawl."

Alain took one arm and they tried a few tentative steps. Bob led the way, choosing the easiest route over the shortest, and heading back toward the trucks rather than to Leon's cabin. Leon didn't question where they were going.

It took them nearly thirty minutes to cover ground that had taken ten on the way in. Leon moved like a newborn kitten. He stopped talking to save his breath. When they were still fifty yards from the road Chris handed his rifle to Alain and slung the lanky deputy over his shoulder in a fireman's carry. Leon didn't protest.

At the road they buckled him into the passenger seat of Chris's truck, tucked in the blanket around him and reclined the seat.

Bob pulled Chris aside.

"Take him to the hospital. You found him along the road on your way home, out by the east end of town. You recognize him from the team and can give them his name but other than that you don't know anything. Got it? Play dumb. We need time to figure this out."

Chris nodded and fired up his truck. Bob climbed into the passenger seat of Alain's Ford as the detective stowed his rifle yet again. Alain got them out of there before any of the crime scene team happened along to ask questions. He drove toward town at an easy pace.

Bob let the silence lay for a bit before clearing his throat.

"You got a theory?" he asked.

Alain nodded. His head felt far away, as if he was watching himself speak in a mirror.

"I do," he said.

The road unrolled in the headlights. Bob waited for Alain to figure it out. He seemed to grasp that a man can't be pushed to try to explain something he doesn't understand himself.

"I think Leon's one of them, the one I shot in the woods," Alain said.

"You didn't shoot him. That bullet hole's a week old, at least," Bob said. "If he took a .308 in the shoulder tonight he might be dead from blood loss."

"You know a Mama Bouche, down in Munising?" Alain asked.

Bob snorted.

"She told me the loup garou gets 'fixed up some' when it changes back and forth," Alain continued. "Maybe the switch healed the bullet wound, but not all the way. I'll tell you this: Leon didn't have a hole in his shoulder yesterday. He moved fine."

Bob dug in his shirt pocket, reaching for the cigarettes he gave up fifteen years ago. "That woman spends most of her time in the Indian casino, getting drunk and raising hell at bingo," he said.

"Doesn't mean she's wrong about this," Alain said. He didn't even feel ridiculous saying it now. In one night his world had changed, as though he'd walked out the door of his house and into a town with a different reality. What had the doctor told him? Things happen here good and bad. The only thing that hadn't changed was his job and he was going to do it until he couldn't any more.

Bob mumbled something unpleasant and turned his head toward the window. They came into the outskirts of Marquette as the green numbers on the dash clock reached four thirty.

Alain rubbed at his eyes. He'd been up for nearly twenty-four hours, during which he'd gone for a run, chased ghost lights through his house twice, met a psychic gambler who liked pastels, gone on sort of a date, gotten lucky, lost a front door, shot a werewolf in his upstairs hallway and another in the woods, investigated three murders (one fake), followed a blood trail and discovered that his best friend might be one of the werewolves he'd shot.

Filling out the daily report could take a while.

"I don't know Leon as well as you, I guess," Bob said.

Leon had to be one of the good guys. He fought crime, he didn't commit it. Certainly not murder. Alain racked his brains, trying to figure out where the deputy had been when Aimee died. He'd been unaccounted for after they'd hauled the poachers in. Alain had been, too, or at least busy sleepwalking. He wondered where Stephanie had been that night.

"The door at Leon's was smashed outward." Alain was spitballing now, thinking aloud. "It's been bugging me all night and now I can put it together. The fragments lay in the yard. He changed in his living room, tore it up himself and broke out of the house. Then he hung around until I got there and put a bullet into him, confused, not himself but not knowing what else to do. When the moon set he changed back." He could relate to not knowing what to do.

"You sure?" Bob asked.

Alain pulled into the post lot and shut off his truck. "No. We're talking about monsters, Bob. I'm not even sure the sun is going to come up in a few hours. I do know there's more than one of them. Two, at least," he said, "Leon's eyes reflected green, if that was him I shot and it seems like it was. The one at my house had orange eyes. Unless, you think they could change their eye-color?" He shook his head. "Hell, I don't even know how to think about this."

Alain wanted to tell Bob the rest of it . . . the dreams, the dirt on his hands.

"Rabies," Bob said. He stepped out of the truck and stretched, trying to work the kinks out of his back. "That's how I would frame it in my head. Your buddy is sick, and when he has a fit he's dangerous. The other one, I don't know."

"And what do you do with a rabid animal?" Alain asked. He traced the steering wheel with his fingertips.

"I didn't say it was a perfect analogy," Bob replied. "I'm sure glad I'm not the detective in charge of figuring this out."

The two trudged toward the front doors of the post. The lot had cleared as officers finished their reports and headed home to catch a few hours of sleep. It would be morning soon. They would all sit down in the daylight and make a plan to catch monsters, one of which might be a prime member of the investigative team. Alain wished he had an idea of what that plan might entail.

Olga Malthwait, 20, was taken with a fit of hiccups that has lasted for three full days and nights with no respite. Physicians fear that the condition may become fatal.
April 1, 1899. The Palladium Superior.

Chapter Fifteen

The bunkroom door had both tabs flipped up, which meant the two cots were occupied. Alain gave Ernie a half-hearted wave but avoided his attempt to snare Alain into conversation. He stood in front of the coffee machine for a full minute trying to decide if he should sleep or start hitting the chemicals to stay awake.

The Lieutenant's office door was closed. Stephanie probably was snoozing on the comfortable old couch. The supply closet that held sleeping bags was locked and Alain didn't feel like getting the key away from Ernie. His office chair held him in an upright position that would make it impossible to sleep.

He knocked. The Lieutenant's door opened slowly. Mama Bouche had changed clothes, either to visit the casino or she'd strong-armed some poor deputy into stopping by her house before bringing her into custody. The purple warm-up suit had been replaced by a simple black dress, a white shawl draped regally across her shoulders, silver crucifix and saints' medallions at her throat. He understood that it was her uniform, her battle gear.

"The blood, here" she said.

"Mrs.—um, Mama?" Alain said.

"I look at you, boy, I see the blood. Inside you, outside you . . . the blood. *Le Sang*. Nothing else. Is not right."

Alain couldn't grasp her words. They made no sense together. "I'm sorry?" he finally said.

Mama Bouche sighed as if he was stupid. "I look young man like you I should see women, lots of women, and babies, maybe, a car wreck, boat going down someday years forward. The cancer, God bless . . . Every big thing your life hold, that's what Mama see in some clear form or no. You I got nothing but this here one thing: the blood. Not blood but 'the blood.' Maybe you tell me why?"

He shook his head slowly. The scent of old blood in his dream, his sickness, if that's what it was. She couldn't know about that. Past her in the office Stephanie stood over the Lieutenant's desk, watching the two of them. The books and notes he'd given her were spread across the entire surface. He could smell the old paper like dust in his nose.

"You two are working together?" he asked. For some reason that made him uncomfortable.

"You gave me this material," Stephanie said. "No one knows it better than Mama Bouche. We're doing what we can to help."

"Avius, he find the oldest," Mama Bouche said. She set her hand atop one of the notebooks. Her nails were hooked and yellow. "Man got a nose for it, dig it out from wherever. Course the Church she sit on the best, he maybe got the inside line there." She surveyed the books. "Things in here Mama half-forget or never knew. We find you something."

"There are more—" Alain began.

"I know," Stephanie said. "I asked them to take them to the library at the university, but you need to release them as evidence or some ridiculous thing. The stacks open at seven. I need other resources to cross-reference what we're finding. I have a private study carrel. It's one of the perks of being a spinster scholar."

Mama Bouche snorted.

"I'll get someone to take you," Alain said. "I'd prefer if you spent most of your time somewhere other than home or at your office. He dug in his pockets for a pen to sign the evidence slip then noticed that the room had gone silent. Both women watched him.

"Sorry," he said, "I'm officially a shit. This case . . . I'm screwing this up. Dr. Bourbonnais, will you help us? Please." He kept his eyes on Stephanie. If he looked at Mama Bouche right now he might melt right through the floor. He felt ten, eleven years old, tops.

"I was just waiting for the magic word," Stephanie said.

Bob reappeared from the washroom, scrubbing his hands with a paper towel. He tucked the crumpled ball into a pocket when he realized he had an audience.

"Ladies," he said.

Mama Bouche looked him up and down. She nodded, seeming satisfied. Alain wished he could ask what she'd seen for him, but he knew without opening his mouth that he'd get nothing more than a withering look.

"You seen it," Mama Bouche said. She seemed certain.

Bob plucked at the side seam of his jeans. "Not this time, no, but once."

The old woman nodded.

"Mama," Alain said, "does this mean anything to you?" He grabbed a notepad from the desk and began to sketch the design he'd found carved into the wall at Leon's: the overlapping triangles, the vee at the bottom.

She snatched the pad from under his pen.

"*Merde*," she cried, "*Homme stupide*. Stupid, stupid man."

Mama Bouche peeled off the top sheet with the rough drawing, holding it by the edges. She produced a heavy silver lighter from her bosom and set the edge of the paper aflame, holding it until the last second before dropping the dying fire into the wastecan. She crossed herself, then spat into the can, eliciting a hiss from the hot ash. Her hands shook.

"The morning star," she said.

"I'm sorry, Mama—" Alain began.

His head snapped back as she reached up to slap him, a surprisingly heavy backhand that rocked him to his heels.

"Lucifer," Mama Bouche said. "He was called the morning star, the brightest light in heaven before he fell. That his symbol. You never draw it again. Not ever."

"It was carved into the wall of Leon's living room," Alain said slowly. His jaw hurt. "Why?"

Bob ushered them farther into the office and closed the door quietly. The four of them formed a circle in the light of the desk lamp. Alain felt like he was standing outside of his own body watching this conspiracy, their cabal of the impossible. Avius' handwriting on his notes looked thin and scratched in the yellow glow. It looked like a dead man's writing should.

"Tell it all," Bob said.

Alain sketched out his trip alone to Leon's, the encounter with the loup garou in the devil's soup bowl. Mama Bouche crossed herself as he described its emergence from the brush. Then the cabin, the wrecked furniture, the symbol carved into the wall. He ended with the three of them finding Leon in the woods, his growing certainty that his friend was one of them.

"Where is he now?" Stephanie asked.

"The hospital," Bob said.

Mama Bouche made a dismissive gesture. "Ain't no doctor fix him now. Your friend been cursed."

"Cursed?" Alain asked. "How? By who?"

"By whom," Stephanie said. She looked chagrined. "Sorry. Habit."

"Mama can't tell you who or whom," Mama said. "All I hear tell is some loups garou been cursed. It take one already made the deal with The Dark One, they get that power to throw on another. Man's wife been stepping out, maybe, she and her lover put the loup garou on the husband."

"So it's not Leon's fault?" Alain asked.

The old woman shrugged. "Maybe so, you right, but when he change under the full moon he not in control of himself. He a beast through and through. Hunt, kill, eat. Dead be dead, no never mind fault."

Bob met Alain's eye. Rabies. Alain felt a cold knot form near his spine. Leon could still be his killer.

"Someone been cursed, now that ain't so good," she went on. "That in this book." She tapped the cover of one of the tomes. "Those you got to draw blood without killing. You get you a knife and cut him, see, and catch five drops of blood on your blade. Bury dat. He change back, and you don't mention the loup garou for a year and a day. Say it to him, he go back again, but if you keep quiet that long the curse be gone."

Alain turned toward the door. Had he heard a footfall on the other side? He crossed and opened it in one motion.

Janet jumped, then quickly recovered. She stepped into the office.

"What's going on here?" she asked. She smelled spiky to Alain, angry with an undertone of lavender. Her dark hair fell in damp ringlets.

"You're in early," Alain said. "Your shift doesn't start—"

"Ernie and I have an understanding," Janet said. "Now what is all this?"

He made quick introductions. Her eyes passed over Mama Bouche to settle on Stephanie, who was matching her look with one of her own. The room felt small and hot.

Bob moved for the door a shade too quickly. "Well, I'm going home to bed while I can. Be back in a few hours."

Janet watched him go.

"The reports are on your desk: lab, financials, fingerprints," she said to Alain.

He took one step toward the door, hesitated. All three women were now looking at him. He got out. The door closed behind him. What was that about? He trusted Janet. This post was her life and she wouldn't do anything to hurt his case. Still, he had no idea why she'd be angry. He thought about knocking. No, he should definitely take a look at those files first, a few minutes to let the women get acquainted. It seemed safer.

He headed for the coffee.

His copy of the reports lay face-down on his desk. He sank into his chair, put his feet up and started to scan.

The scenes were each covered in detail. Nothing new in the first one: two victims identified at the rectory, claw marks, animal hair, wolf suggested by Detective Logan as suspected culprit. The report from the scene at his house outlined the damage and mentioned that Logan had fired a weapon while off-duty, defending himself from said wolf. That let him off the hook. Shooting a person meant automatic administrative leave, but for animal targets the official scrutiny would be minimal. The evidence log listed samples of blood taken from the upstairs hall, presumably from where he'd shot the thing. That would be an interesting result to see. He wondered if it would come back as human, wolf, or something in-between. If he had a suspect, they might be able to get at least a partial DNA match. It wouldn't hold up in court, but Alain figured he'd burn that bridge when he came to it. This didn't seem like a case that would make it to trial.

In the report from Leon's house the lead officer had picked up on the detail that had taken Alain hours: the destruction started indoors and moved outside rather than vice versa like the first two scenes. Deputy Gilhall had been admitted to Marquette General hospital, having been found at the side of the road by a motorist at the outskirts of town. His condition at the time of the report was stable.

Alain turned to the results that had come back from the state lab and the financial and computer wonks down in Lansing.

Once upon a time they'd been able to email autopsy reports. That was before the state's multi-million dollar internet security investment had proved itself to be completely useless. It only had taken two stolen autopsies hitting the web to bring a hands-only delivery policy down the wire from the politicians.

The autopsy folder held photos and notes from the pathologist and lab technicians. Alain skipped the photos. He already had the image of Aimee's body lying on the forest floor imprinted in his mind, along with Avius and his housekeeper Edna. Worse than the photos were the smells in his memory—the stink of ruptured organs, clotted blood, fear—the scents of death. That was enough to stoke the ball of hatred inside him.

Traces of lubricant deep in the vagina meant sexual activity in the last twenty-four hours. She'd bathed since. No other fibers or traces found. A spermicidal lube, which likely meant a condom. He could pull up a database of brands that used that type from the FBI. His notebook lay open at his right hand, and he wrote "male partner?" and underlined it. Stephanie had said she didn't have a boyfriend, which made this a new thing. Either that, or she had a secret from her professor and, according to Stephanie, her friend. What wouldn't she tell her advisor? He wrote "affair?" People killed over sex. Motive, underlined.

She was on the pill. A belt-and-suspenders type of guy, definitely, which fit the profile of a married man who didn't want to get caught, or one who planned to commit a murder and didn't want to leave evidence behind. Unfortunately, it also fit a college kid who didn't plan on having a family and made sure there could be no chance of it. That sparked a thought and he added "class lists?" to his notes. Alain felt the pressure starting to build in his chest. After almost two days of chasing his tail, he had some leads to follow.

The list of wounds went on for two full pages. She hadn't simply been killed; she'd been ravaged by a beast. No disembowelment like poor Avius suffered, but Aimee had huge bite wounds on nearly every part of her body. It wasn't scavengers. Flesh seemed to be missing from the legs. One weighed two pounds less than the other. He closed the file with the taste of iron filings in his mouth. Alain squeezed his eyes shut. He tried to see it. The attack had been wild, out of control. No sign of knives or human action, only the raging of the monster. Most of the wounds appeared to be pre-mortem, meaning it had gone on for a while. The killings at the rectory were more careful. The prey there had been chased down and killed quickly. He wouldn't know for certain until he got the other two autopsies, but the defilement of Avius looked post-mortem due to the placement of the body. Was the monster gaining skill at controlling his powerful new shape, or had Aimee's death been personal rather than the business-like killings of the priest and Edna?

The time of Aimee's death cleared Leon. He'd been with Alain at the site of the poachers' crash. So it was whoever had cursed Leon. Whomever. What about the priest, though?

Aimee's financial reports told him nothing. Regular deposits from what looked like a trust, neatly balanced by a graduate student's simple expenses. It would take weeks to pry the church's reports out of them but it didn't feel like a promising lead to Alain. Her cell records were just as boring: not many out of state calls and few repeated numbers.

The fingerprint evidence from the lens of Aimee's camera was marked inconclusive, with tech's notes indicating that it was too large to be real. That was Alain's case in a nutshell. It wouldn't be believable no matter how much evidence he gathered. He wondered who the print might match if he could shrink it, warp it back into a human size and shape.

The priest had to be the key. Alain believed that the housekeeper had simply been in the wrong place at the wrong time. This felt bigger than anything slow Edna could be a part of. That left Avius as the target of the attack, along with Aimee, and then Alain. Leon, too, although his curse revealed a far more insidious bent than the other straight murders. What had Avius given or told Aimee that tied the two of them to the loup garou? Why curse Leon?

He heard the door to the Lieutenant's office open. He'd stalled long enough. Maybe one more cup of coffee on the way.

All three women eyed his arrival. The air in the room had changed. The tense situation had morphed into something . . . he wanted to say satisfied, as if the women had joined forces. Alain hoped he wasn't the focus of their attention.

"I heard you met Horace," Janet said.

Alain burned his tongue on his coffee.

"Horfle?" he asked.

"The former owner of your house, Horace Ganderson. Stephanie told me that the two of you got acquainted with him last night."

Alain met Stephanie's eyes over the rim of his coffee cup. She gave a tiny shrug.

He cleared his throat.

"I'm not sure you if you're aware of this," he said to Janet, "but Mr. Ganderson's been dead for seventy years."

"I know," Janet said.

"I don't know if he's met anyone new recently," Alain continued, "what with being dead and all."

Mama Bouche sighed. She seemed disappointed in him.

Janet put her hands on her hips. "That house has stood empty for the better part of those fifty years. People bought it, sure, big old place like that, but they never stayed. It's been a summer home three times, a boarding house, a bed and breakfast at least twice . . ." Her husband, the slickest real estate agent in town, was a philanderer like Ganderson, which made him a fool with Janet at home. No locals would do business with him, but plenty of tourists appeared each season for fleecing.

"A girl's school, once, oh what a disaster." She kept going. "It's changed hands about every five years, although some didn't even make it that long. Why do you think you were able to pick it up for back taxes, and the attic full of antique furniture to boot?"

Alain stood speechless at her tirade. Stephanie answered for him. She'd sidled closer during Janet's recital.

"Why?"

"He's still there," Janet said. "Ganderson."

"His ghost?" Stephanie said.

134

Janet nodded. "Everyone sees the same thing: an old man who looks like the pictures of Horace. He'd appear to the women—wives, older daughters, grandmas, he didn't care—always when they were, you know . . ."

Stephanie and Alain and Mama waited.

"Naked," Janet said. "He shows up when there are naked women in his house. He's a dirty old ghost, an undead letch."

Mama Bouche winked at Alain. It unsettled him.

"And now I need to get to work," Janet said. She reached out and touched his cheek. She almost seemed sad. She shared a look with the other two women before brushing close by Alain on her way to the front desk.

"I work here," Mama announced. "I don't need no library to understand this here." She spread her brittle hands over the piled folklore on the desk. "We find you something that help good."

He considered telling her that the Lieutenant might eventually want his office back. Alain decided to let him tell her himself, if he ever showed up. He retreated to his own desk. Stephanie followed. He could catch her scent if he tried, even as she walked behind him.

"You really didn't know about this?" she asked.

Alain shook his head. "If you're talking about the fact that my house is supposedly haunted, then the answer is no. Nobody saw fit to tell me."

"Well, they were waiting for you to see him, but he only appears to women. Attractive women."

"He did have a reputation as a randy old goat," Alain said.

Stephanie seemed flattered by the phantom whistler. "Maybe the women you've been bringing home haven't appealed to Horace."

Alain tried to count how many women had been in his house after dark.

"I haven't given him many chances," he said.

"Hmm," Stephanie said. "And you're remodeling. The literature says that's a wonderful way to stir up spirits, by changing their home."

She perched on his desk.

"This is an excellent example of local folklore," she said, "It helps that it's true, but is perfect even without that. The rich old man dies but his peccadilloes live on."

"Whoa. I'm not ready for dirty talk at this hour. What do you mean by 'true?'"

"Sexual proclivities," Stephanie said. "Stories about sex always survive better than any other topic. Humans have almost as strong a need to talk about sex as to engage in it, especially about how much fun someone else is having."

That kicked something over in the dusty recesses of Alain's mind.

"Did you say that Aimee wasn't seeing anyone?"

Stephanie shook her head.

"Not that I know of," she said. "Why?"

She'd been having sex with someone, and Stephanie hadn't known.

"I'm missing something," he said.

"What?" she asked.

He rolled a pencil across the desktop from one hand to other.

"Ah, right," she said. "If you knew, it wouldn't be missing."

Alain flipped on his computer. "What was wrong with Janet?" he asked.

That surprised her. "You didn't know?"

"What?" Alain asked.

"Hmm. Well, if you're busy, I suppose I'll be heading home to change into some clothes with fewer miles on them," Stephanie said.

She didn't leave. "You said something about an escort to the library."

"I'll have a patrol take you both places," Alain said. "I want you to be safe. I'll come by to pick you up at the library. It might be a while."

"I might wait," she said, turning to leave. She came back, tugged his head back by his hair and kissed him hard. "Thanks for protecting me last night."

"That thing came after me, too," Alain pointed out.

"Not that, you Neanderthal. When we saw the coyote, you put your arm out in front of me. A girl likes that sort of thing."

With that she made her escape.

Alain called Janet on the intercom and requested an officer to take her home and to the library. He asked that the boxes of books from Avius' office be checked out in his name to go with her, and promised to drop by with the proper forms within the hour.

After hanging up he sat there with his hand on the phone receiver and thought about the pieces still missing. He wanted to go downstairs and pound the punching bag. It would accomplish as much as the rest of his work so far. Retrace the trail: Aimee, Stephanie, Aimee's house, Mama Bouche, the rectory, Alain's house then Leon's. What had he taken for granted? What hovered right in front of him, too close to see?

Alain took a deep breath, checked his cell phone contact list and called Violet, the Provost's secretary, at her private number.

Two hours later he drifted back to the coffee machine for another cup. Fruitless time on the state's crime system, VICAP, had convinced him that whatever he had going on here was localized. The only other murders currently under investigation within two hundred miles were drug- or marriage-related, the usual reasons. His wolf case had started in Marquette for a reason. The killer had to be a local or a regular visitor, someone close enough to know what Aimee asked questions about and who it involved. He knew how the murders were being done but not why or who was doing it. Two animals: Leon, and who? He added his own name to the list in his mind. If he knew what the loup garou was after, he could figure out who it was.

Alain set his coffee cup in the sink, feeling a tinge of guilt for not washing it. He gathered his gear for a trip to the hospital.

The cold outside made him want a jacket. No frost yet, but it couldn't be far away. They'd had two in September along with an early snow squall then a good stretch of Indian summer, fading now into the crackle of winter.

The heavy envelope was propped against his steering wheel. The truck had been locked. He always locked it because of the rifle inside. The same paper stock with his name in cursive, the wax fucking seal. Alain tore it open this time.

Disappointing. We hope that you can redeem yourself with a speedy conclusion.

—HMC

The second sheet of folded paper in the envelope was his birth certificate . . . his forged birth certificate. Under pressure from the state after Waagosh's death to come up with paperwork surrounding his birth, his uncles had one made by a counterfeiting, bootlegging Ojibwa from one of the Ottawa reservations and snuck it into the courthouse records. It was the document he'd used to get into the State Police Academy. Someone knew.

He crumpled the papers and threw them into the back seat. Alain rummaged angrily through the gear piled there and pulled out his Filson's hunting coat. It had belonged to Waagosh. The waxed cotton shone with a patina of age. While not as waterproof as the high-tech modern stuff, it was as tough and silent as the old man had been. He pulled it on and wrapped his arms around his body. "*We hope . . .*" Not a person but a group. Alain didn't know what more he could be doing about this case. Not that he'd cave to their pressure. He didn't think he would.

The truck seat froze his ass through his pants, and the engine turned over a couple of extra times before catching. He had to check the plugs and clean the throttle body before winter set in for good. A truck that wouldn't start was more than a nuisance in the north; it could be the difference between life and death when the cold became a predator. His eyes in the mirror looked bloodshot. He could smell himself.

Marquette's streets stretched out quiet and gray, another October morning like any other. The steel-sharp light made last night seem like a fairy tale. A town built on hard work—logging, mining and shipping—had no room for nonsense. It felt as though he lived in two places at once. One town paved and sane—a boring, safe place where nature served her master, duly shorn, shackled or dug out as required. The other place, the one he'd visited last night, was made of wood and mud, a tiny frightened outpost caught in the reach of a looming forest and inland sea. Alain had a good idea which Marquette he'd choose if he only got to live in one, but he hadn't been given a choice. Both existed right here and now as he pulled up to the modern steel and glass medical center and went in to visit his friend who was sick with a nightmare out of the past.

He stopped, holding the door handle. That was a good way to think of it, as a disease, Bob's rabies explanation, or the doctor's struggle with old plagues that still appeared here as though time stood still. There had to be some rational explanation for this loup garou mess. Leon was ill, and Alain had to find the cure. If it involved cutting a wolf's foot with a knife like Mama Bouche had said . . . well, didn't they chew willow bark for hundreds of years before discovering aspirin? That sounded weak even to Alain.

Beatty, the trooper from the L'Anse post, leaned against the wall in a chair outside Leon's room, the front legs off the ground, her head tipped back. She'd been reading a paperback when he got off the elevator, but when she noticed Alain she stood and tried to hide the cover.

"You here to relieve me?" she asked.

He craned his neck to read the spine of the book.

"Lonesome Prairie?" he asked.

"The only book in the damned gift shop that didn't have pictures to color," she said. "If I'd known I had been named the full-time babysitter I would have brought some Tolstoy."

Alain held his hands out in front of him. "Kidding, kidding," he said. "Why don't you get breakfast in the cafeteria while I talk to Deputy Gilhall and the docs. Maybe we can check him out of here and you can go home."

"Fine." Beatty stormed past him, eyes snapping with dark sparks.

Alain noticed that she took the book with her.

Leon straightened with a guilty look as Alain came through the door but as soon as he recognized his visitor he changed gears.

"Damn it, Alain, what took you so long? Let's get out of here." He threw back the covers to reveal himself already dressed.

"They locked up my clothes in the closet," he said, "bureaucrats who want to charge me for another day. You can't trust them. They've got cheap locks, too, real substandard hardware."

Alain stood by the bed as Leon tried to rise. He seemed weak, although better than last night.

"They give you good drugs?" Alain asked.

"Boy, did they. Put me out like a smelly cat. I haven't slept so well since I flatlined when that punk shot me last year."

Leon sat on the edge of the bed attempting to maneuver his feet into hospital slippers without bending over. His wife had apparently forgotten to bring shoes when she'd brought clothes from his house.

"Speaking of getting shot, any word on what happened out there?" Leon asked. His hand trembled on the blanket. The light tone seemed brittle. He had a sense that something bad had happened to him, Alain guessed, but could not remember it.

"Let's get out of here. We can talk about it somewhere else," Alain said. He offered his friend a hand and the two of them working together managed to get the deputy vertical.

Beatty popped the door open and stuck her head in. "I think the cafeteria is serving the leftovers from the operating rooms. What kind of place . . . I'm going out."

"We're leaving," Alain said, struggling to get Leon's arms lined up with his jacket sleeves.

"You got him released?"

"We're leaving."

"Oh."

Two nurses tried to stop them and failed in the face of Leon's desire and Beatty's anger. Mel Philemon stood waiting when the elevator door opened on the first floor. He didn't seem surprised to see Alain.

"Heard about your friend, thought I might stick my nose in and see how he's doing," he said.

Alain dropped back a few paces with the doctor, sending the trooper ahead to prop up Leon. "Deputy Gilhall is very uncomfortable away from home. I'm sure he'll be fine. We'll call right away if there are problems."

"You know," Mel said, "I can help if he's sick. Even if it's something uncommon."

139

"Trust me," Alain said, "you don't want him in your hospital tonight. He gets cranky when the sun goes down."

Mel cocked an eyebrow at him. Alain floundered ahead.

"Speaking of which, it seems like he needs rest," Alain said. "Is there a chance you could help him get some of the medication he had last night? He said it really put him under. It might be good if he spent another night, you know, out of the picture," Alain said.

Mel shook his head. "Are you asking me for narcotics, Alain? I'm disappointed. If you want him to be treated, he has to stay."

Leon and Beatty had made it out into the parking lot. Alain cut his losses. "Of course. Thank you for everything."

"And what about your little problem, Alain," Mel called after him. "How are you sleeping?"

Alain could feel Mel's eyes burning holes in his back as he caught up to the other two outside. The old doc was a meddler. Alain had been able to push the dreams out of his mind. He had to sleep sometime, but maybe he could wrap this business up first. They bundled Leon into the passenger seat. Leon breathed deeply, eyes closed to slits, out of it again.

Now the question: where to take him? Alain's trashed house did not seem like a good choice. Ditto Leon's. The post had too many people coming in and out, and one of them might be leaking information. The killer had known the identities of the lead investigators on the case, and it seemed he or she had learned within hours when Alain made his attempt to talk to Father Avius. It could be coincidence, but he didn't think so. He watched his friend sleep. The timeline didn't work for Aimee's death, but what about the priest? Was Leon capable of that kind of destruction? If so, how would he keep everyone safe after the sun went down? He drummed his fingers on the wheel for a minute before stopping. He knew where to take an unwanted mutt.

The preferred method of suicide on the Ashman farm is as follows: dig a small hole; place a half-stick of dynamite in the hole with a short fuse; light fuse; place head over hole. Mr. Ashman has secured the store of dynamite under lock and key after three such occurrences.
6 June, 1899. The Palladium Superior.

Chapter Sixteen

Rhee did not seem amused by their arrival for the second time in two days, but the dogs swarmed around Alain's legs like a joyful furry river.

"Are more of our guests under suspicion, Detective?" she asked. "Did you receive another anonymous tip, perhaps?"

"I need your help," he said simply. She looked in the truck window at the unconscious deputy.

"What's wrong with him?" she asked.

"He's sick."

Alain hesitated.

"And he got shot last night," he said.

"Sick with what? Shot by whom?" she asked.

"It's a very long story," he said. "If I told you the whole thing you might call the men in the white coats."

She watched him. He blundered ahead, trying to fill the icy silence. The dogs had calmed, but continued to circle and nose at his hands, coat, boots.

"He's fine now. Great. Good, anyway, until the sun goes down. I'll fetch him long before then."

Rhee put her gloved hands in her coat pockets and continued to watch him struggle.

"There's a leak at the department. At least, I think that's where it is, and it puts Leon in danger. I need to stash him somewhere out of sight until I get things figured out. You two are fairly new in town, so..."

"So you decided that we should hide your friend," Rhee finished for him.

"Something like that," he said. Said out loud it did sound like a hell of a favor. "I can find somewhere else to take him."

She held up a gloved hand.

"What's in it for us?" Rhee asked.

"What's—? I don't, I don't know. You seem like good people," Alain said.

"People aren't good. They're selfish. Rhonda and I have seen what humans are capable of, and we are firmly on the side of these dogs. So, how does taking in your friend who is fine-until-the-sun-goes-down help these dogs?" Rhee asked.

Alain wracked his brain. He hadn't considered a trade of any sort.

"Food? Maybe we could start a kitty at the post—a"

"Our donors take care of most of that, although we'll take what we can get. Here's what I want: contacts. Help me get those jackasses over at the county shelter to understand how we can work together. They won't talk to a dyke, and they're gassing dogs every week that we might be able to place in homes or keep here. I want to meet the local politicos, the ones who really get things done instead of the pole-sitters. Finally, I want your name as a collaborator on a state grant or two."

"Done," he said. They could sort this out later. Alain felt sure that Rhee would do just that: sort him into usable bits and wring every possible advantage out of this deal.

She turned on her heel and headed for the trailer.

"Bring him," she said.

Alain hurried to unload the deputy and half-drag him toward the trailer. As soon as Leon's feet touched the ground the dogs went crazy. Hackles went up on some while nearly half cowered on their bellies in the dirt. The few remaining dogs ran in manic circles barking. Rhee held the door for them. The canine tide came along. Dogs underfoot threatened to trip them more than once. He dropped Leon where Rhee pointed, on a low couch covered with a simple quilt in bright colors. The inside of the home looked tidy and stylish, even if the furnishings showed their age. Rhee covered him with a second quilt.

"Rhonda's going to flip out when she sees what's using her goddess quilts," she said. The two of them watched the sleeping man. He looked better than when Alain had broken him out of the hospital. It didn't make any sense. Being dragged across town should make you feel worse, not better.

"Is he on anything?" Rhee asked.

Alain shook his head. "I tried to get him something from the hospital but they apparently don't release the good stuff as take-out. I need to figure something out. It would be a very good idea if he stayed whacked out until the sun came up tomorrow."

Rhee laughed, a short, nasty little sound.

"Detective, you keep dropping these dark hints," she said. "Do you want to tell me what's wrong with him or possibly why he deserved to be shot?"

Alain considered it for a moment. "When it gets dark Leon might act strangely or do things that seem totally crazy." He'd begun to feel as though he spent his whole life explaining himself to women, usually skeptical women. "He might act like an animal," he said.

"You mean, get fresh, 'eek, a big strong man,' that sort of animal?"

Alain shook his head again. "A real one," he said.

"Any hints? Does he do a good baboon impersonation? Possibly an otter?"

Leon looked normal under the quilt, like a farmer taking a nap after lunch. He looked peaceful.

"He could act like a wolf," Alain said. "A big, bad wolf."

Alain closed the gate behind him and drove off, having promised to return before dark to retrieve Leon. Rhee had seemed bemused by his story up until the word "wolf." She'd cut Alain off and almost pushed him out the door.

"Let's not say anything about that to Rhonda, shall we?" Rhee said. "She has superstitions." She hustled him toward the truck.

He swung back by the station. Mama Bouche leaned against Janet's desk, whispering earnestly into her ear. Both women looked up as he approached.

"She's not here," Janet said. Her smile was brittle and tight.

His mouth was dry. "I know. I signed the order to take her—" He stopped. They knew this.

Mama Bouche seemed amused. "We tell her you looking for her."

"I'm not—" He hadn't realized he had been. Maybe he had. Time to cut his losses. "Good, good."

On the way to his desk he passed an empty interrogation room. No fancy two-way glass in here like on the television police shows. They made do with a video camera in the corner and a tape recorder on the table. If they needed a witness to identify a suspect's voice they cracked the door and had the witness stand in the hallway to hear the suspect talk. Strictly a low-tech operation. His gaze fell on the tape recorder on the table of the interview room. He felt a click as one piece fell into place in his head.

Alain gathered up the case files from his desk, stuffing his notebook away in a pocket. Janet looked up as he approached her desk. He handed her the paperwork.

"You're a genius," he told her.

"I know. What finally made you realize?"

"No time," he said, "can you get Trooper Vullonen on the phone? And I'll need the evidence list from the break-in at the Willow Lane residence, too."

She had it for him in three minutes. A quick double-check with the list and with Brett on the phone confirmed that the only tapes at Aimee's house had been blank cassettes still in the wrapper. He had it: the first piece of the puzzle, and it felt solid. He knew why the monster had killed Aimee and the others. Now that he had the why, all he had to do was figure out who had done it. Then there would be the small matter of how to catch him, or her. Alain checked his watch. Driving out to the dog farm and back had cost him valuable time, and he still had to get back there before dark and find a new place to hide Leon. Seven or eight hours left until the bad guy grew hair, and maybe one of the good guys, too.

Alain swung by Janet's desk one last time on his way out the door. At his request she started calling the college's administrators at their homes. She'd keep beating the bushes until she found someone to open the records office for him. He made a list in his head on the way out: the library to check in with Stephanie first, then the records, then hide Leon. He added one more thing to Janet's to-do pile, a sticky that read: "Have Bob call my cell." She waved frantically at him as he started to turn away. He paused while she wrapped up the call.

"I know it's Sunday, but this is an emergency," she said into the receiver. "Yes, I know the Packers kick off at one o' clock. This is more important. Yes, really." A pause. "Thank you. If you open the building I'll find someone to run the computer system and get what we need." She hung up and rolled her eyes. "Green Bay fans," she said.

Alain drummed his fingers on the counter top.

"Ah, yes. Your shotgun's processed out. You can take it home. Here." Janet thrust the key to the evidence room at him. She usually controlled the access tightly to preserve the chain of evidence. It also cut down on the temptation of the money and drugs stored there. The evidence locker had a video system, but it happened to be on the fritz and Janet hadn't handed the key to anyone for a month.

"Camera fixed?" he asked, taking it from her.

She looked to the office where Mama Bouche had holed up. She took a deep breath, set her jaw and dialed the next number on her list.

"I trust you," she said without looking up.

Alain stepped around the corner to the barred door and unlocked it. It felt odd. Janet never bent the rules. He picked up his Mossberg from the rack, stripped the plastic evidence bag from it and checked to be sure it had an empty chamber. He needed slugs for hunting the loup garou. He had some in the truck. Alain made it all the way to the door and had swung it partway closed before he stopped. He looked around the corner at Janet, but could barely see the top of her head over the high counter. After a moment of consideration he crept back into the evidence room and picked up a few more things that might come in handy. A ball of lead rested in the pit of his stomach. Pinpricks of sweat sprouted on his face.

The door clanged when he shut it and locked it. He sauntered around the corner and passed the key over the counter, keeping his stash low. Janet took it without looking. Her face was flushed.

"Get what you need?" she asked.

"I hope so."

"Good hunting," Janet said.

"We find the small metropolis of Marquette, queen city of the Upper Peninsula, to be the highest civilization in strange juxtaposition with the fiercest wilderness." -An early visitor to our fair city.
3 March, 1899. The Palladium Superior.

Chapter Seventeen

With his loot safely stashed behind the seat, Alain drove toward campus. He angled crudely into a handicapped spot outside the library, threw his POLICE sign on the dash, double-checked the locks on the truck and headed for the main doors, edging around a half-dozen scruffy students at the curb loading camping gear into an SUV. The sight of Bob's twins brought him up short.

"Ladies," he said. The girls made him nervous. They seemed to vacillate between innocent kids and dangerous women, often in the same breath.

"Alain." Sara said. He had never been able to tell them apart until Jenny had pointed out the tiny mole above her sister's upper lip. Since, he'd tried in vain not to watch it move.

Jenny squealed and threw her arms around his neck. Jenny never squealed. Alain suspected it had more to do with the scowling young man leaning against the SUV than with him. He was reminded of kittens trying out their claws.

"You're going camping?" he asked. He disengaged himself from the girl without much effort. It was definitely a show. "Where?"

The girls shared a look and slumped into disinterest.

"You know what happened two nights ago?" he asked.

"Yeah," Sara said. She looked toward the SUV to see if it was packed, looking for an escape from this crushing concern for her well-being. "We're probably heading over to Mosquito Beach in Pictured Rocks."

"Okay, well—" Alain felt invisible. Old. "Have a good trip. Be careful."

He got nods. They'd tuned him out like a radio.

Alain knew the private study carrels were on the third floor. He swept past the circulation desk and took the stairs two at a time. The floors lay out in a U with the stacks stretching down each long arm past an area with tables and computers in the center curve. Small offices lined the space between the arms. The offices got progressively smaller and more spartan as they neared the end, which is where he found Stephanie. He rapped at the window. She jumped.

She let him in. With barely enough room for the two of them alongside the desk, chair and stacks of boxes he'd sent over, they hovered awkwardly for a moment before she sat on the desktop and he took the chair.

He got straight to the point. "Would Aimee have told you if she was sleeping with a student? Someone she was teaching in one of her classes, I mean."

"Maybe. I would have recommended that she stop. It's not a good idea, and Northern has a policy against it. She could have lost her fellowship. Do you think that's what happened?"

He ignored the question and pressed forward. "What about married men in your department, or in a related area? Is there anyone with a wandering eye that would be attracted to Aimee?"

No hesitancy this time. "No. Ick. I mean, yes, there are plenty who would, but she wouldn't want to take them up on it. No one would."

"No one Aimee would know that you can think of?" Alain asked. "Not an administrator?"

"Not a chance," she said. "It sounds like you found something."

"I want to pull her class lists. How many did she have?"

"Three, this semester, I think. If I can get to the computer in my office I can pull up lists," Stephanie said. "She had two sections of English Comp, which everybody has to take, and she was the TA for my folklore lecture. I never saw her spend extra time with any of the guys in there. There are only two of them, and I know at least one of them wouldn't be interested in, um, someone like Aimee. Or anyone without a Y chromosome, for that matter."

"I've got someone waiting in the Records office," Alain said. "That's my next stop. I'll want you to look at them, see if any names jog your memory, something she might have said. Even something small, like if they were doing well in class."

"Or poorly," Stephanie murmured.

"What's that?"

"She said," Stephanie began slowly, "she said something about a big dumb guy in Comp. How he was a meathead, but one with big muscles she found intriguing."

"A jock? Hockey player? You got a name?"

She shook her head. "I never thought a student . . ."

147

Alain felt a thrill. Blood trail. "Let's go look at some lists. Now. You're helping."

"Wait, let me get—" Stephanie seemed excited. She pushed aside a stack of books and snatched a plastic bag from the desktop. "Okay."

They'd reached the stairs, moving fast, when she showed it to him. "Where did this come from?" she asked.

Alain stopped on the landing and took it from her. It held the corners of paper he'd salvaged from the fireplace in Avius' study, still sealed in the evidence bag.

"I found these at the rectory. It looked as though the good Father tried to burn them. How did you end up with them?" he asked, starting down the stairs again, more slowly this time.

"I found the bag in the side pocket on my coat when I went home to change. I pulled out my gloves, it fell on the floor."

"I had them in my hand when I got back in the truck," Alain said. You must have picked them up in the dark when you got out and grabbed your things." They'd reached the doors to the library and pushed through. The wind rose. It had a cold edge. "Do you know what they're from?"

"That's what I've been trying to figure out," she said, hurrying to keep up with his long strides. "The paper's old. I haven't matched it to any of those books yet, but I've only made it through half of them. It really is an amazing collection. I've never heard of some of those titles. Do you think that the church might consider—"

She caught his expression.

"Right. Sorry. If it's in there, I'll find it," she said.

They reached the Records office doors. The lights were off, but the second door he tried opened. He led the way down the dim hallway toward the rectangle of light that marked the entrance to the main records room. Alain entered the room first and saw who Janet had found to run the records system for him. Violet sat at the computer playing a game of solitaire. She brightened when she saw him.

"There you are," she said. "I've been trying to reach you since you called me."

Alain tried to interrupt, to give her the sign to shut up but she motored on. "I've checked with absolutely everyone, and I think you're wrong. There's no reason for your folklore trollop to be involved. It would seem she was far too lazy to apply for grants this fall. And she couldn't have had a conflict with the girl over a man; I can't see that happening." She let her cool gaze fall on Stephanie as she entered the room, the corner of her mouth crooked up in a smirk.

Alain turned to find Stephanie frozen in the doorway, her mouth moving silently, before she turned and fled back into the dark hall.

"Stephanie—" he said. He followed her to the front door.

She wheeled on him.

"Was our little excursion a part of it?" she asked. Her eyes snapped even in the dim hallway. "Was I a suspect then?"

"Stephanie, I have to—"

"Are there any other suspects you've slept with?" She turned away and headed for the door. "With whom you've slept . . . damn it."

"I have to look at everyone," he said. "Absolutely everyone. Even you."

She stopped with a grip on the door handle.

"I've known you for two days," Alain went on. He took a step closer. "I don't think you had anything to do with it, but I need more than a gut feeling to cross you off the list. I made one phone call to be sure there wasn't any motive, any research money or grievance—"

Stephanie looked at him over her shoulder, her hand still on the door.

"I'll be in the library while you get the rest of the information from your deep throat operative," she said.

The door banged against the stop so hard the glass shook in its frames.

As Aimee's class lists for the current and prior semesters printed Violet apologized innocently. She seemed disappointed that he accepted it. He scanned the lists as they came out. The names meant nothing to him.

"Can you match up ages with these?" he asked. "Just for the guys—addresses here and in hometowns would be good, too."

"It's not set up that way, but I can do it by hand if you need that information," she said. Violet did not seem to know how to take him now that he'd failed to rise to her bait. "It might take me an hour or so. It would be longer if that poor girl hadn't been stuck with the 8:00 a.m. Comp sections. Those are always the smallest."

He started toward the door, thumbing through the stack. "As fast as you can get it done I need it. This is important. Scan the sheets, and email them to the post." He stopped, dug out a business card and wrote Janet's email address on the back. He didn't look back as the door swung shut.

The walk back to the library seemed to take longer alone. Alain dialed Janet on his cell phone and filled her in on the information coming her way.

"I want these guys tracked down as soon as those lists come in. Call the city, ask for help," he said.

"They're going to bitch," Janet said.

"Tell the chief to call in his part-timers, reserves, everybody. Get the campus cops in on it, too. If we can get on top of this guy maybe we won't have another murder in the city limits. I'd be willing to bet the mayor will authorize overtime for that. We can't have the tourists getting scared, you know. They don't spend as much when they're running for their lives."

"Where are you? I can barely hear you over the wind," Janet said.

"I'm at Northern. I have a meeting with Stephanie to look over the class lists, see if anything jogs her memory." Alain looked for a place to duck out if the wind to finish his call, but he was in the middle of the quad. An emergency call box on a slender pole offered scant protection, even when he leaned close.

"I can use Harold," Janet said. "He keeps calling in and asking about the case."

"You mean Hell?" Alain asked. He supposed he was postponing facing Stephanie, but it felt good to banter for a minute with one of the few women he hadn't made angry today. The callbox had been scored with graffiti carved into the paint, including a neatly-done scrollwork beneath the blue panic button. It read: "Push for enlightenment." Alain resisted the urge.

Janet laughed. "Harold, Hell, whatever you want to call him. He's a nosy little guy. You know, Harold is his middle name. His given name's even worse."

Alain straightened. "What's he asking about?"

"Everything. Where you are, where Leon is . . . he asks if anyone's heard about Leon a lot. He even asked about your professor," Janet said.

The second piece fell into place. "Janet," Alain said.

"Yes, Alain?"

"What's his given name?"

"Marvis, if you can believe that. Marvis Harold Burke. His parents must have hated him right from the start."

Alain rifled through the class lists again, running his finger down the names. The wind threatened to tear them from his grasp, and he struggled to keep the papers from flapping. The phone slipped out from where he had it pinned between shoulder and ear. It hit the sidewalk. The battery shot off in one direction, shards of the handset in another. He managed to get a grip on the lists and smooth them against his thigh. He found it on the second sheet, English Comp at 8:00 a.m., near the top: Marvis H. Burke.

He struggled to repair his cell phone for a few endless seconds before he realized what he stood in front of. Alain reached for enlightenment. The blue strobe on top of the pole began to flash, blinding even in cloudy daylight. A keening wail rose from the box. Every student on the quad turned to look, including a lanky young man passing by on the sidewalk.

"You don't look like you gettin' raped, man," he said.

The siren stopped, replaced by the voice of an operator.

"911, What is your emergency."

"State police. Put me through to dispatch," Alain yelled into the speaker.

"Sir, please tell me the nature of the emergency."

Alain gripped the side of the callbox, knuckles white, and spoke slowly through gritted teeth. "This is Detective Alain Logan of the state police. ID number 92317. Put me through to Dispatch." He couldn't hold back the growl on the last word: "now!"

Janet came back on the line. "What happened? Dropped call?"

"Janet, listen, give Hell nothing. You hear me?" Alain said. "Not a peep, give him a snowjob."

"Alain," her voice dropped lower, "is he a suspect?"

"I don't know yet. Keep him in the dark until I can find out."

"Oh, Alain, I wish you'd called five minutes earlier," she said.

"Why?" his voice felt as though he'd swallowed a piece of glass.

"He asked where those books were going. I guess he saw them being loaded. He wanted to know who signed them out, and for how long, and—" she hesitated. "I told him about Stephanie and the library."

"Alain?" she asked. "Alain, are you there?"

The campus police arrived to find her talking to no one.

Chapter Eighteen

Alain blew through the library doors at a run, splitting a couple of girls in matching rugby shirts. He hit the stairs two at a time. A blob at the front desk yelled something authoritative at his retreating back. Sorority girls coming down the stairs four-wide slowed him up, and he crashed through the phalanx of miniskirts with a muttered apology.

"Asswipe," one future trophy wife yelled.

On the third floor, even more students. Today, of all days, they'd decided to study. Alain scanned the walls until he found what he was looking for and yanked the fire alarm. A purple dye pack broke under his hand to mark him as the perpetrator. More flashing lights and sirens, this one a whooping like a European ambulance. The day had a theme: barely half over and he'd already cried wolf twice.

As the students covered their ears and herded toward the stairs, joking and ass-grabbing along the way, Alain slid along the wall between the stacks and the windows. He drew his Sig and slipped the safety off. Stephanie's carrel lay at the end of the long row, perhaps fifty yards away. With a quick look he cleared each row of bookshelves as he passed, scanning the center aisle and the stacks on the other side. The siren wailed on and the flashing strobes floated blue balls across his vision every time he made the mistake of looking in their direction.

Could Hell know Stephanie's exact location in the building? Alain thought of how he would solve it if it were him. If Janet told him who had delivered her and the books to the library, he'd have called that officer. Those books likely didn't walk up to the third floor by themselves, and even with an elevator she would have needed help. Alain had to assume Hell knew right where to go.

Stephanie came out of her carrel looking pissed. She stopped when she saw him with gun in hand. Alain held a finger to his lips and mouthed "hide." She put her hand on the door to her carrel. He shook his head and motioned her further away. Stephanie watched him as she retreated, disappearing into a row farther toward the end.

Movement caught the corner of his eye. Alain froze. He resisted the urge to turn his head. The end of a shelf shielded him. He'd only had a glimpse of a figure passing. Alain eased forward to the next row in time to see the back of a long black trench coat with Hell's buzzcut riding atop it like a hedgehog on a Sherman tank. Alain strode down the row and into the center aisle, pistol coming up into a two-handed grip. His words froze on his lips when he found no one there. He took a step forward, then grunted when Hell hit him from the next row.

The little bastard had suckered him. Alain tried to turn, step back, get the sights on him, but Hell seemed faster than he'd been two days ago. He came up under the gun and drove his shoulder into Alain's ribcage with a perfect form tackle. They flew back, all four feet off the ground, until Alain hit the shelves on the other side of the aisle. The pistol took to the air. Hell tried to stay on top, riding him to the ground, while Alain fought to get his legs into play. Hell would kill him if he managed to pin him down.

Alain arched his back and drove his hips up, bouncing Hell into the air and giving Alain a split second to move without his crushing weight on top. He pulled his right knee up and to the side, freeing it. Hell landed on him again. His foul breath smeared across Alain's face.

"I smelled you," Hell said. "Like meat." His teeth were worse than his breath.

"Fight it, Hell," Alain said. He locked grips with the boy and tried to leverage him off. "You aren't gone yet."

Harold flowed across Hell's face. Alain saw it happen. The boy was there for a fleeting instant—eager and helpful and scared, Alain saw it in his eyes—before whatever had a hold on him clamped down again and he attacked.

Alain twisted his head, moving his eye sockets away from Hell's drilling thumbs. He threw a weak left-hand punch into his tormentor's ribs. It felt like hitting a tree, but it made Hell sit up the inch that Alain needed. He kicked his free right leg up and brought it across his body and between the two of them, the crook of his knee catching the front of Hell's neck. Alain scissored hard, throwing the right leg down and the left up, using the most powerful muscles in the body to flip his assailant off of him. He went for the lock, trying to cross his ankles and crush the bastard between his knees, but Hell got an elbow loose and brought it down into Alain's crotch. A glancing blow, but definitely enough to make him falter. Hell broke free and rolled away, scrambling to his feet as he dug at the small of his back. Gun, thought Alain. The details of the room snapped into focus and the flashing of the strobes seemed to slow. He got in between the nearest shelves as Hell opened up. Rounds tore into the floor, books twitching as they absorbed hits, getting closer as Hell approached the end of the aisle. Alain backpedaled toward the window aisle and dodged sideways as Hell appeared at the other end and continued firing.

The glass behind him silvered with cracks as Hell blew three holes in it. Alain loped into the next row, thanking the librarians in their infinite wisdom for purchasing shelving with solid backs. Hell couldn't see him. Unfortunately he couldn't see Hell. He stopped. No sound. Crept forward, trying to watch both ends of the row at once. He jumped as Hell fired through the steel shelves. The bullet fragmented, spraying the books in Alain's row. Down near the window; Hell must be almost at the opposite end. He reached the center aisle and placed his back against the endcap to take a deep breath. One quick look . . . now. The row was empty. Hell had gone around the corner.

Alain felt like he was playing hide and seek with a madman. Time to gamble. He swung into the row Hell had just left, grasped the steep shelves and began to climb, trying to make no noise. The stacks loomed above him, suddenly twenty feet high. Kept climbing, slow, quiet, one more reach and he managed to pull his legs up and roll on top. Flat on his back, the tops of the shelves and hanging fluorescent lights marching off in dusty rows in every direction. He eased to the other edge and peeked. The buzzcut bobbed in the row, undecided. Hell must think Alain had a back-up gun, otherwise he would have rushed him.

Alain slipped his knife from its sheath. The black tanto blade, seven inches long with a point designed for punching through armor, was sharp enough for shaving.

He took another look, located his target and rolled over the edge. His zipper rattled on the metal surface of the shelving as he swung his legs over to drop feet first. Hell looked up. The expression on his face in the instant before Alain's boots made contact was priceless.

Hell spun as Alain came down on top of him. It threw off Alain's aim. He still landed a meaty shot to the face with both feet, but had planned to drive Hell's head straight into the floor under his full weight, putting an end to this fight. It didn't work out as planned. Hell's flailing arm hit Alain's legs and they ended up in a heap. Fire shot up Alain's ankle as Hell rolled onto it, and Alain collapsed to his knees. One of those knees found Hell's head again on the way down, and pinned it to the floor. The knee blew up in pain, and Alain gritted his teeth. Hell's head felt like a boulder.

As Hell struggled to raise his Ruger automatic, Alain slashed at Hell's wrist with his knife. The carbon steel blade went straight through the trenchcoat Hell wore and split his forearm open. The gun dropped. Hell howled as he grabbed for his wounded limb. He kicked Alain off in a mad frenzy. Both regained their feet. Alain and Hell's eyes met, then fell to the gun. It lay in the center of the row, closer to Alain. Hell licked his split lips as he measured the distance. He eyed the knife in Alain's hand. Alain tried to put weight on his bad knee and ankle.

"You need to stop that bleeding," Alain said, his voice low and cold, the knife steady.

Hell looked down at his arm. Blood ran down his face and dripped from his broken nose. He licked the blood from his sleeve and showed Alain a mouthful of teeth painted in gore. "Where's my dear brother-in-law?"

"Out of your reach," Alain said.

"I doubt that. I'll see both of you after dark. I'm going to take my time doing you." Hell held up his arm and watched a trickle of drops fall from his elbow to the floor like dark rain.

The siren halted. Voices from the elevator announced the arrival of the fire department. Hell's eyes ran to the gun, the center aisle, back to Alain.

"Something wrong?" Alain said. He might be able to make one good lunge for the Ruger, but he would pay for it. The knee already felt hot and swollen.

Hell turned and ran for the center aisle. Alain hobbled forward and bent to snatch the gun from the floor, juggling it as he switched hands with the knife. He straightened as Hell disappeared, lurching after him as best he could. The leg wasn't as bad as he'd feared. It loosened with each step. When he turned the corner he saw Hell at the door of Stephanie's carrel. The Ruger came up.

Stephanie stepped out two rows in front of Alain, his Sig-Sauer pistol grasped in both hands, and began jerking off rounds at the hulking deputy, screaming obscenities as she emptied the gun. Hell dropped like an anvil and rolled into the row opposite the door as the wood around the frame exploded into splinters and pages flew from the bookshelves.

Alain yelled her name.

Stephanie let the Sig drop, action locked open on an empty chamber. He stepped past her and limped toward the door. The sharp smell of cordite swirled in the air. Holes riddled the frame and window of the door from the DPX he'd loaded into his Sig. It had punched straight through and into the room beyond. The door to the emergency stairs gaped wide and broken. Alain looked down three double flights. The ground floor door already stood open, wind blowing up the stairwell and washing over him. His knee opted to drop out of the chase and suggested he go it alone.

"Cell phone," he said to Stephanie.

"What?" She seemed to still be in shock from opening up on Hell.

"I need your cell phone, damn it." He held his open palm out toward her.

"Won't work," Stephanie said. She waved a hand at the ceiling. "Quiet floor. Jammers in the ceiling. Phones won't work. I need to sit." She pushed open the door to her battered carrel and slumped in a chair while Alain went looking for a fireman with a radio. Every cop within radio distance would be converging on this spot, fearful of another horrific campus shooting. Hell would slip right past them in the other direction if Alain couldn't turn things around. His blood pounded in his ears. The fucker was so close.

At the moment the entrance team came through the front door wearing body armor and bearing automatic weapons, Alain was holding the assistant fire chief off the ground, shaking him like a terrier with a rat. The burly deputy in the lead shouted for him to drop the man. So Alain did.

He identified himself and, after a little more yelling, got his hands on a cell phone. He ordered Janet to turn the responders around and set up a net for Hell's car. She pulled up the plate and vehicle description and had it out in thirty seconds. If Hell still had his radio he might hear the call and switch cars, so Alain asked her to give priority to stolen vehicle reports for the next few hours. He also asked her to get in touch with the judge and start the paperwork for an entry warrant on Hell's residence, then passed her off to the entry team. As soon as she gave them the address they packed up and headed off to prep near the site. Beatty arrived with her shotgun, and he took thirty seconds to fill her in on what she needed to know to pick up the warrant, track down the judge and get a signature. She left at a dead run.

Clutching a small leather book and his pistol, Stephanie came down the main stairs almost as slowly as Alain had. He relieved her of the weapon, reloading it and slipping it back into his holster, before giving Hell's gun to the campus police, placing them in the hands of the officer in charge of the scene at the library.

"I'll be taking Dr. Bourbonnais's statement," he said. He had his hand on her elbow. No one questioned him as they headed for his truck.

She remained quiet until they reached the parking lot. "I don't want to do this anymore."

Alain opened the passenger side the truck and stood waiting for her to get in with his hand on the edge of the door. The metal felt cold under his hand, and his finger found a rough spot on the weld to worry at.

"He's not going to stop," Alain said. "Even if he leaves town, he'll still be . . . what he is."

"He's a monster, isn't he—a loup garou." she said without much curiosity.

Alain nodded, letting her work through it. The rough metal stung under his fingertips. He might have drawn blood. He didn't want to look.

"I found the text he's looking for. The one from Avius' office," she climbed into the truck, and Alain let go of the door edge. His fingers burned.

"It's not going to help," she said.

He shut the door with great care, made himself walk to the driver's side, and when he was buckled in she continued, holding up the leather-bound book for emphasis. "It's a translation of the journal of an early missionary to this area. He collected occult knowledge. It's like a witches' codex. Among other things, he claims to know the secrets of the loup garou, the Latin phrases that release the power of the devil, and set it down so that his brethren would be able to watch for and recognize it. Avius must have discovered it in the archives of one of the old churches. He didn't believe in the legend, though, so when Aimee came to visit—"

"He read it to her," Alain said, "and she taped it."

Stephanie turned to him. "You knew?"

"I suspected," he said.

Alain started the truck and pulled out of the space. He stopped at the entrance to the main campus road, because he had no clear idea where to go. The ankle seemed better, but his twisted knee had begun to throb. "The tapes were the only things missing from Aimee's belongings."

"Then you didn't need me." Her voice had an edge to it. "You had this all figured out and you used me as some kind of bait—"

"No." He shook his head as he stared out over the dash, unable to look at her. "No."

A VW behind him honked. "But I would have, if I'd thought it would help." More honking. He powered the window down and waved with one finger for the Bug to drive around. "I'd have told you first, though."

She put the book on the seat, folded and unfolded her arms, adjusted the vent on her side. "He knows that you know his identity, so he's going to kill you," she said.

"He's going to try."

Alain started to drive again. The post—he'd figure it out at the post. And have more coffee. It would be dark soon. He still had to figure out what to do with Leon.

"Mama Bouche said if you knew the words you could become the loup garou by choice," he said, "but she also said you could be cursed with it. I think Hell chose to be one, made the deal with the devil or whatever." She seemed to hear the little "d" when he said devil, and fingered the cross she wore on a fine chain. "Then he put the curse on Leon so he would have a scapegoat."

"Why did he kill Aimee?" she asked.

Alain shrugged. "Maybe he didn't mean to, or perhaps she threatened to tell his fiancé they were having an affair. I don't know. He seemed like a nice kid yesterday."

"She was sleeping with him?" Stephanie's hands twisted on her lap.

158

"I don't know yet. I'm hoping to find some evidence when we take down his residence. That should happen any minute. Judge Hopkins would sign a warrant on UFO abductee testimony. I'm hoping they'll find those tapes."

She straightened in her seat. "The recordings might help. The text won't. There are pages razored out of the book, the phrases themselves. It says they are supposed to be in there, but that section is missing." She flipped through the book and showed him the neatly-cut stubs where a few pages had been removed.

"Avius burned them?" Alain asked.

"I'm no paper expert, but the corners you found only match this text."

"How did Avius know that the phrases were dangerous?" Alain wondered.

"It could have been cold feet. Aimee might have talked him into recording them even if he had doubts. The Catholic Church never releases a good secret unless they have to, but Aimee could make grown men do anything."

He made a mental note to pull the rectory phone records. If Avius had called Aimee after the recording, there might be something to what Stephanie said. Mental note, hell, he needed to write it down or it would be gone into the damp morass of his mind. He needed sleep, wanted to go back to the bear tree of his youth and climb inside and hibernate until spring.

And with that thought, he knew what to do with Leon.

Chapter Nineteen

Janet thrust a stack of message slips at Alain when he walked in. Stephanie went straight to the ladies' room, and after a look at Alain, Janet hurried after her. He shuffled through the pile of pink paper, shredding the ones from reporters, then commandeered the closest phone. The ranger answered on the first ring.

"Bob Androtti."

"Alain."

"Son, where the hell have you been? I called twice." Bob didn't sound as though it had hurt his feelings terribly. Alain wondered if Bob had felt the same sense of the loose reality at daybreak, the queasy feeling that the events of last night were only a bad dream. He didn't ask. Bob remained as solid as Upper Peninsula bedrock. If he had doubts Alain didn't want to know.

"You decided what we're going to do with your friend?" Bob asked.

"As a matter of fact, I have," Alain answered. He sketched out his plan as Bob listened silently. After he finished, a pause stretched out between them on the line.

"Might work," Bob finally said. High praise, coming from him. "I'll get Chris to liberate what we'll need. He is a larcenous young fellow. Apparently the military supply system is the same as my day and theft is still necessary to speed distribution. It'll take time to get it all."

Alain started to give him directions to the dog farm, but Bob cut him off by the second turn.

"Know it," he said. Taciturn Bob, back to normal. "Meet you there at four." With that, he hung up.

Janet returned to her desk and gave him a status report: warrant signed, entry team about to hit Hell's house, Stephanie okay. Alain didn't think Hell would be home. He had to know they'd look there first. Alain would also bet that he hadn't decided to run, so the airport check and roadblocks would come up empty. He would go to ground somewhere in the million acres of forest surrounding Marquette, or hole up in an abandoned mine shaft like a wounded animal. At dark, he'd come out to hunt. That's what Alain would do. It meant that he would be almost impossible to find. Alain had no idea where to look next. All he could do was wait. And eat. It felt like he hadn't eaten in days.

He shuffled through the file of dog-eared delivery menus and coupons Janet kept at her desk. Greek—hadn't had that in a while. Alain held the menu up so Stephanie could see it as she came out of the bathroom. She shook her head at first, then stopped.

"I'll take a gyro," she said. She pronounced it correctly, like "hero" with a hard "h."

"Sacrificial lamb it is," Alain said. He dialed and placed her order, then piled one up for himself: lemon potatoes, skordalia, pita bread and lamb kebabs.

"You're going to reek of garlic. Anyone will be able to find you from a mile away," Janet told him. She'd declined an invitation to join them after another shared look with Stephanie. These women . . . The plastic jack o' lantern on her counter mocked Alain.

"I'll be safe from vampires, at least. Besides that, maybe I want to be found."

Alain led the way to the break room and cleared gun and car magazines off the table. Stephanie sat opposite him.

"I'm almost too tired to eat," she said. "You must be dead."

He nodded, toying with the plastic salt and pepper shakers some enterprising law enforcement officer had lifted from a fast food place. "As long as I keep going, it's not a problem. It's when things slow down that I start to crash."

"Adrenaline junkie," she said.

He shrugged. She reached across the table and took hold of his hands. Alain sat stiffly for a moment, then put his head down on the smooth backs of her hands held in his.

"Alain," she said.

He opened his eyes.

"Alain, the food's here. Janet's calling over the intercom."

He sat up and blinked. "But, I—" He looked at his watch.

"You were out for twenty minutes," she said. "My hands fell asleep."

"I'm sorry," he said.

"Now they're going to be up all night."

He laughed. She snorted, deep and loud and sudden. It sent both of them over the edge. When Janet showed up with a ticked-off teenage delivery boy in tow they had tears in their eyes, gasping for breath.

It helped. Alain sat opposite Stephanie for the third time in a day and a half. He could still feel the aftereffects of their laughter in his stomach muscles, a sagging quiver preferable to the cold-metal fear he'd been carrying around since Hell had opened fire at the library. The books in his memory still jumped as they took the rounds meant for him.

Stephanie pitched in on the dip and the potatoes and before long the greasy cardboard containers were empty.

"Amazing," she said. She wiped her lips with a paper napkin as she eyed him over the remains. "You really do look like rough."

"Thank you, Ms. Bourbonnais, you are looking lovely your own self." Alain felt a little drunk after the big meal.

She stood up and came around the table to take him by the hand.

"Come on."

He stood up and followed her without question. She led him to the Lieutenant's office and opened the door. Stephanie installed him on the couch despite his protests. She pushed him back into the soft leather.

"Sleep," she said.

"I need to leave at three-thirty," he said. The pull of the couch seemed irresistible.

"I'll wake you in time."

"Listen to the tapes if they come in," he said.

"Alain, shut up and go to sleep."

The room fell away as he closed his eyes. Maybe five minutes.

He has a front door on his house again, standing wide open to the night. In the front hall the grandfather clock chimes. It shrinks down to his alarm clock, then stops and falls on its side. He hopes his gun isn't hidden in there because he'll never get it out. He opens the closet under the stairs to search for the thing he needs to find.

"Hurry up, ass-clown," Leon says. He wears his full uniform with a Smokey the Bear hat and even a patrol coat.

A peppy whistling floats down from the top of the stairs. Alain knows if he looks up there he'll see Horace Ganderson winking at him. Stephanie must be in the shower. He has to warn her to put on a towel before she comes out so Ganderson won't see her naked again. Leon pushes him out of the way to look through the closet shelves himself.

"Damn government employee, can't be trusted . . . ah-ha." He pulls out Alain's deer rifle, the 30-30 that had belonged to Waagosh. Nothing fancy: a gun to put meat on the table. "Got you, little darling," he says.

He thrusts the weapon into Alain's hands. They stand in the upstairs hall now. Ganderson lolls against the banister, happy as the devil in a whorehouse, and tips his bowler to Alain with the same glint in his eye he has in the portrait. The picture hadn't done justice to the fact that he's barely five feet tall. Leon pays him no mind. He drops to all fours in the center of the hall.

"Ready?" he asks.

The shower stops and Horace straightens his ascot and admires his whiskers in an antique hall mirror Alain doesn't own.

"Let's get the lead out, son," Leon says, "in a manner of speaking." His Smokey hat moves, twitches on Leon's head like the hair underneath might still be alive.

When Alain presses the muzzle of the rifle against Leon's neck he can feel it against the back of his own, the cool circle of metal between the nobs of his spine. Off. Back on. He leans into Leon with the rifle and the pressure on his own neck increases.

Leon looks up at him. "In the mouth?" he asks. "Hemingway style?"

Alain does not want Leon to open his mouth for fear of what he might see. He can taste the gun oil himself. That stuff is a carcinogen. Put a gun barrel in his mouth enough times and the cancer will get him.

"The main question," Leon says, "is what are we going to do about that hole?"

The door opens and the moist heat of the shower falls into the hallway.

Standing out behind his house, he and Leon study the hole. It is obviously the den of a large creature, something living under his house. Flat and barely wide enough for a skinny man, the dirt is trampled and tamped down by years of use, hardened by weather.

"One of us needs to go in there," Leon says.

"Why?" Alain asks.

Leon runs his fingers along the sharp brim of his hat. "Don't you want to know what really lives under your home?"

The opening elongates and slides to Alain's feet. It closes over him like a grave.

Dirt under his hands and knees, not loose but earth packed by the weight of generations. The darkness presses down on him, fills his eyes, ears, his lungs. Smells, too, powerful as physical contact: wet fur, milk, hints of carrion and an undertone of old blood. He wants to plunge his hands into the dark, find the walls of this place and locate the way back out. The growling freezes him. It echoes thick and low off the walls of the den. He can feel the vibrations in his chest. Some live thing was in here with him. Some angry animal. He lets his hands fall to his sides. They touch his gun, his cuffs . . . his detective tools. His flashlight. He holds it in his hand for a moment before twisting the switch.

The space is tight, womblike. His light bounces from the ceiling to illuminate every fold and crevice. He kneels in the center, alone, fingers and toes dug into the dirt, the heavy growl emerging from his own throat.

Alain jerked upright in the Lieutenant's office on the old couch that smelled vaguely of sweat. His brain ran at a hundred miles an hour as it decided what to believe. Desk, plaques on the wall, not in his house or underneath it. His heart took a minute to catch up, then Alain stood and left the dim room, as wide awake as if he'd been dropped in Lake Superior.

Stephanie and Janet conversed in low tones at the front desk. They turned at his approach.

"You have another fifteen minutes to sleep, if you want it," Stephanie said.

He shook his head. Alain flexed his leg, where he could still feel soreness in his knee and ankle from landing on Hell at the library. He had to end this tonight. The fear of what might happen to him if he couldn't was like a blade in his chest.

"Tapes?" he asked.

"Seized contents are on the way," Janet said, "the warrant served nice and easy. No one home—" She held up one manicured finger as a call came in. "One moment, please," she said into her headset and tapped two buttons on the console. The phone on the closest desk began to ring.

"Trooper Vullonen wishes to speak with you," she told Alain.

He grabbed the handset.

"Alain here."

"Detective," said Brett Vullonen.

He paused so long that Alain wondered if they'd been cut off.

"Lot of strange things happening around town the last few days," Brett continued. He didn't seem inclined to go further.

"Yes," Alain said.

"Yep. Lots of strangeness. Everybody's on the lookout."

More silence.

"Is there a reason you called, Trooper?"

"Well, I wanted to check in and see if the detective in charge of the case knew anything about a chromed-out Dodge pickup pulling a trailer with state plates," Brett said. "I ran the truck license number, and it comes back to a Chris Angell, late of the Marine Corp. Isn't that the name of the young guy taking over for Bob with the Department of Natural Resources?"

"I believe it is, Brett, yes," Alain said.

"Thought it might be. I wonder if you might know why Mr. Angell passed me doing ninety on Highway 41 a few minutes ago," Brett said.

"Heading which way?" Alain asked.

"North-ish. Weaving a bit, though. The trailer looked empty, maybe a little light on its axles. I don't think those live bear traps are set up to cruise at that kind of speed," Brett said.

"I'll be sure to mention it to Chris if I run into him," Alain said.

"That's a good idea. I'll tag along and make sure no one else on the team stops him to tell him first. Best if he hears it from you."

"I would appreciate that Brett," Alain said. The line went dead. He replaced the receiver with care.

Janet's eyebrows were raised when he returned to the desk.

"Status report," Alain said. "Any other news?"

"The team has shot three coyotes on or near roads," she said. "I've got two extra officers on the day shift and the mayor's office has graciously agreed to supply four of their personnel for patrols inside the city limits so we can push father out."

"Good," he said. "Drop them into circulation now and rest some of our folks. Double-shifts tonight."

Janet nodded and began calling unit numbers almost before he finished speaking.

They met at the turnoff to Hope Pines Farm: Alain in his truck, Chris standing beside his Dodge with the state bear trap hitched to the back, Bob at the side of the road. The old ranger leaned against Brett's cruiser to talk through the window. All three nodded to Alain as he pulled up and got out. He joined Bob on the shoulder.

"Trooper," Alain said to Brett, "thank you for the escort."

Brett shrugged. Bob watched.

"The folks who run the farm here have been having trouble with an old sow bear—" Alain began.

Brett held up one hand to stop him. "Don't want to know," he said. He shifted the cruiser into drive and began to roll. "You gentlemen be careful," he added.

"That's a bright young man," Bob said.

"Where's your truck?" Alain asked.

"Wife dropped me off. She wanted the truck for something or other. Figured I'd get a ride back with you or Chris."

Both men watched Chris adjust the safety chains on the bear trailer. The trap consisted of a thick steel cylinder a yard across, ten feet long, with heavy metal grates covering each end. Either or both grates could be lifted up and locked in position. A pressure plate in the center would be baited with smelly food like tuna casserole or trout guts, and when the bear took the snack the gates fell shut. The whole contraption had been mounted on a heavy-duty axle and truck tires to tow it from place to place. It saw use primarily to relocate campground raiders who had lost their fear of humans and begun to associate them with easy meals. The state would trap the trouble-makers and haul them far out into the wilderness to drop them off. In lean budget years, or when the University of Wisconsin Badgers beat the Northern Michigan Huskies in hockey, the drop-off point always happened to be close to the state line.

"You explained to your friend yet that we're sticking him in a trap for his own good?" Bob asked.

Alain shook his head. Leon was going into the trap whether he felt like it or not. When he changed, one of them could do Mama Bouche's knife ceremony, and then all Alain would have to do is catch Hell without knowing where to look. Easy as pie.

"We need to get him out and away from these folks and their dogs first," Alain said. "Any ideas about where to go?"

Bob scratched at his chin, his whiskers making a sound like a hedgehog being scrubbed.

"We got the county garage past Big Bay," he said. "We could hole up there. It's the last post this side of the Club, and nothing beyond for forty miles to L'Anse. Not too far from where we found that girl."

"The Club" meant the Huron Mountain Club, property owned by the descendants of wealthy industrialists who had recognized the value and beauty of the Upper Peninsula early. They controlled tens of thousands of acres northwest of Marquette in near-sylvan condition: protected, never logged and un-mined since the nineteenth century. The group was so selective that they'd kept Henry Ford waiting for nearly a decade before allowing him to purchase membership at a mark-up. Guarded by private armed security and with enough political clout to re-route federal highways around their playground, the Club was a force with which to be reckoned. Of course if he'd been in their shoes, with the money and timing to buy a chunk of paradise, he'd have done the same thing.

HMC: Huron Mountain Club. He understood the cryptic notes now. It was nice to be threatened on such expensive paper. Alain had had no idea they'd even known his name.

"Let's leave Chris out here and you come with me to pick up Leon. Has he got the rest of the stuff we need? The call-blasting equipment?" he asked.

Bob grunted an affirmative and headed for Alain's truck, adjusting his jacket to hang straight as he walked. He looked, to Alain's eye, like a man not used to carrying a gun.

If Hell needed Leon to fulfill his plans, they might be able to draw him in once Leon was changed and in the trap. The DNR's call-blaster was basically a stereo system that could pump out animal calls over wide swaths of forest: wolf calls to challenge, the sounds of wounded prey to pull in the hungry ones.

Alain took the wheel of his truck and they bumped off the gravel onto the rough dirt track in silence. Scrub pine branches seemed to reach for the cab. Undergrowth trailed claws along the rocker panels. Alain gunned them through a boggy spot, picking up speed before the surface turned to mush and then backing off. They reached the steel gate. When Bob got out to open it he left the passenger door ajar. A keening wail hung in the air. At first he'd thought it might be a loose belt or a bad bearing on the fan motor, but with the door opened he could hear it in the distance. Moaning. Howling.

Bob hopped back in spryly for a man who qualified for senior discounts.

"I believe your friend may be causing some difficulties," he said.

Alain hit the gas. The Ford began to buck along the bumps of the forest two-track road.

The howling grew as they approached the trailer until clearly audible with the windows up, over the engine and the increasing wind. They topped a rise and entered the open area where Rhonda and Rhee's trailer lay with the barn beyond. Alain braked to a stop.

The trailer sagged a little on its foundations, tired but not yet broken by winter. The ground around it had been worn to bare dirt, no attempt to maintain a yard aside from a few planters with straggling flowers.

A ring of dogs encircled the trailer, scores of them, perhaps a hundred total. They sat on their haunches facing the house and howled. Not all at once, but in twos and threes or a half dozen at a time. As one dog tapered off another would lift his muzzle to take up the cry. Big dogs, little, medium, brown, white, mottled—they focused on the trailer and gave voice to their displeasure. A few patrolled the perimeter, keeping their charges tight in formation and occasionally skipping closer to the house before curving away and releasing another bell-tone bawl. One yellow dog who looked to have some German shepherd in her blood snarled constant anger at the windows of the house as she approached closer than any other before returning to the ring.

The door to the trailer swung open. The dogs surged to their feet to take a few steps closer. They fretted. More began to circle the edges.

A figure appeared in the doorway. Alain recognized Rhonda's work shirt and short hair. She backed out, shouting and gesticulating at someone inside. At the sight of her the dogs went wild.

Rhonda turned and saw Alain's truck. She shook both fists at them.

"That young lady desires our company," Bob said.

Alain doubted that, but he took his foot off the brake and let the truck roll slowly toward the line of dogs. Rhonda came off the porch and the dogs swarmed to her, touching her with their noses and head-butting her legs.

Alain cracked his truck door and hesitated for a moment. When he saw the dogs ignoring him he swung it open completely and stepped out, but stayed close enough to leap back in if anyone showed fangs. Bob climbed out the passenger side.

Rhee eyed Alain and Bob with distaste as she took a few steps forward and settled her hands in the pockets of her chore coat.

"Haven't you bothered us enough?" she asked.

Alain spread his hands and tried to ignore the yellow shepherd at Rhee's knee who seemed to be deciding what flavor he might be.

"We're here to pick up Leon, and we'll be on our way," he said. "We don't want to cause you any more trouble."

Rhee stared at him. Bob offered no help. He scratched one of the more forgiving mutts behind the ears.

"Is he inside?" Alain prompted.

"You people should try talking to one another," she said. "It would save taxpayers the cost of some gasoline."

He tried again. "Ma'am?" Mistake.

"Mister," she said. Her eyes had narrowed to dark points. "Your henchman picked him up half an hour ago."

Alain's chest tightened.

"Excuse me. An officer picked him up?" he asked.

Her Bryn Mawr influence had disappeared entirely. "Squatty little prick who thought he was the goddess's gift to women. I thought Rhonda might deck him before he left. The animals started to go berserk right then, though, and we've had our hands full ever since." She jerked her head, indicating the barn as well as the dogs at her feet.

"Did he give you a name?" Alain asked. He already knew.

"He suggested we call him Hell," Rhee said.

Rhonda hurried around the corner of the house trailer, her breath coming in sobbing gasps. Bob straightened from the dog he was petting.

"Gone," she said, "he's gone. I seen him when that rat drove off, but now he's gone." Tears traced lines down her dirty cheeks to the corners of her mouth.

"Who's gone, honey," Rhee said. She caught hold of Rhonda's gloved hands. "Tell me."

"Daisy," Rhonda said. "He's run away."

Chapter Twenty

The men's heads bobbed and snapped in unison as the truck charged over the rough road. Alain's teeth came together with an audible clack on one particularly vicious jolt.

"The ladies said we were only thirty minutes behind," Bob said.

Alain gripped the wheel tighter.

"If we hit one of these hard enough, maybe we can get this rig up in the air and fly after him," the ranger continued, gripping the oh-shit handle over the window. "Course we also might break a strut and be out of the chase for good."

Alain slowed the truck. Some.

"I took too long," Alain said.

The snorting sound Bob made sounded like a pissed-off whitetail deer.

"Did this young man—" Bob said.

"Hell," Alain said.

"Hell . . ." again the snort, "did this fellow know your friend was out here?"

Alain shook his head.

"He knew about the place, knew Leon and I came out here earlier, but that's all."

"So, he got lucky," Bob said. "Luck don't last. You can count on that."

Alain nursed the vehicle back onto the gravel drive and accelerated. The pines dipped and whirled in the passenger window when he glanced over.

"Rhonda doesn't seem like the type to get that upset," he said.

Bob studied the vibrating dash, fiddled with the air vent.

"Her world got turned upside down," he said after a bit. "She thought she knew those dogs inside and out, and all of a sudden they start acting strange. Alien. Bottom dropped out on what she knew and it tossed her around a bit. Happens with people, just like animals. You think you know somebody, they up and become someone else right in front of you."

They neared the pavement. Chris had jockeyed his Dodge and the bear trap around to point out toward the road, ready for a fast exit.

"Leon's not going to hurt anyone," Alain said.

Bob nodded slowly. "I know that," he said. "I know."

Alain dropped Bob off with Chris and sped toward town. The sweeping curves of the road seemed to take longer than usual, elongating and multiplying despite his attempts to fast forward them with the throttle. The rangers would follow at a more sedate pace. Until he knew Leon's location there was nothing they could do but wait.

Digging around in the pocket that usually held his cell phone, Alain realized that pieces of it still lay strewn across campus where he'd dropped it. He slowed and pulled to the side as he yanked the radio from its charger mount on the dash and keyed the mike.

"Base, this is 3-17," he said.

Janet's voice filled the cab, the same throaty purr whether things were calm seas or sinking.

"3-17, this is Base," she said.

"I need the cell phone number for Deputy Burke."

He scribbled it in his notebook and signed off abruptly after giving Janet specific instructions. The little shit might have heard that and he might not. If he had Leon along and was feeding him a line of bull, he couldn't afford to have the radio blurt out his name as a suspect. Alain needed to figure out how he'd slipped through the net they had set up around the county. He jumped out of the truck and waved Chris to a stop when he came into sight. Radio still clutched in hand, he asked Bob for the loan of his cell phone.

In fifteen seconds he rolled out again, leading their pointless little parade toward town. The first call, to Leon's phone, he made without much hope. A mechanical voice informed him that the cellular customer he'd tried to reach was unavailable. No shit.

His second call reached Hell. It rang once, twice, three times before being answered by its owner.

"Took you long enough," Hell said.

"Cut to the chase. Where's Leon?" Alain asked.

"Yeah I could go for some fishing. I've got time off coming. I could use the rest."

Alain forced himself to relax his grip on the phone when its plastic case began to creak. Leon sat three feet away from Hell, but Alain couldn't talk to him.

"Where are you, you little bag of dirt?" he asked.

"Yes, sir," Hell said. "That sounds fine."

He was enjoying himself. Alain could hear it in his voice.

"You want to know what I think?" Alain asked.

"Can't say that I do," replied Hell.

"I think it started with an accident. Or at least you figured out you'd made a mistake pretty damned fast. I think you went to Aimee's campsite to ask for help, to ask for her to save you."

The silence at the other end of the phone seemed as dark and dead as an abandoned mine.

171

"She'd played the tapes for you. Maybe you stole it, the verse or formula or whatever, you took it from her and learned it well enough to make it work. You performed the ceremony and traded your soul in exchange for the power of the loup garou. Maybe you didn't think it was real. But it was."

Alain had climbed far out on a limb with this, but it felt solid. Aimee's wounds at the campsite were too scattered to be an attempted murder. Hell had tortured the girl, trying to extract something.

"Don't you want to know why?" Hell asked.

"Not interested anymore."

"She said I could never say it out loud," Hell whined. "Not the verse, or what we were to each other. Nothing. We had to keep living a lie."

"I'm not your shrink. I'm just the man who's going to kill you. What's it like to meet the devil, Harold? What did he call you? Is that what changed your mind?"

"You have no idea what you're talking about," Hell said.

His voice sounded quiet and deep, so far buried in hopelessness that Alain drew back from the speaker a fraction of an inch.

"Let me pull over for a second," Hell went on, "it's not safe to drive and talk, you know. You want to chat with Leon? He's right here."

Alain sat speechless for a second, shocked by the sudden change in gears. Then he heard Leon's voice in the background and started to shout a warning over the rustle of sound as the phone changed hands.

"Hey, buddy, where's the fire?" Leon asked.

"It's Hell, he killed the girl—" Alain managed to get out before Leon began to scream.

Alain recognized the rhythmic crackling sounds accompanying Leon's agony: a Taser putting fifty thousand volts of electricity into his friend, spasming every muscle in his body many times a second.

"Stop it! Stop, asshole," Alain yelled into the phone.

He flipped on his lights and siren, then shut them off and pounded the dash in frustration. The plastic cracked under his fists. He couldn't chase someone if he didn't know where they were.

The sound stretched out for an eternity, Hell holding down the trigger long past the safe limit. The crackling cut off, but the cries only dropped in volume and intensity. The phone must have fallen to the floor of the car. He could hear muffled thumps and what sounded like Hell's voice in the distance, followed by a second short burst of the Taser. After a minute a car door slammed, another. Someone picked up the phone again.

"He sure didn't see that coming," Hell said. "Thanks for providing the distraction. Took me a minute to get him cuffed and shackled."

Alain couldn't put together the right words before Hell butted in again, gleeful as a kid with a balloon.

"Still there, Detective?"

"I'm going to hunt you down," Alain said, "and when you're dead or close enough to it I'll skin your hide for a rug. For the rest of our days Leon and I are going to wipe our boots on your ass."

Hell's return laughter rang cold and empty.

"Tell me about the girl," Alain said.

Hell fell quiet. Alain heard a police radio in the background.

"I know you went looking for her. Did you change after you got there?" Alain asked. "Lose control maybe?"

"Shut up."

"Not able to stop yourself once you got started, Harold? Was she tender, Harold? How did Aimee taste?"

"Shut the fuck up!"

"Do you even remember what you did? You erased the photos, but the next day you stood ten feet from the body at the scene without so much as a whimper. How much of that night did you lose, Harold? When did the memories return? You having nightmares, maybe? Did you see your friend you made the deal with, Harold? Does he come at night to show you what you've done?"

Alain heard sobbing. Hell balanced on a knife edge, confident and cocky one second and a shattered wreck the next. He had to be either the finest actor Alain had ever heard, or he stood on the brink of madness. Alain had a good guess about which one was correct.

"There was no counter-spell on the tapes, so you tried the priest next," he continued, "and the same thing happened. Hell, you can't control when you change, can you? You get worked up and the next thing you know the only people who might help are gone. After the priest the next thought in your mangy head was me, so off you trotted to my house. Surprised to find me ready for you? How did you like that buckshot? I've got more if the first course didn't take."

"Is it in the book?" Hell asked. His voice rang like breaking glass, the sobbing swallowed and put away. Rational Hell had made it back, if only for a moment. "There's something in the book that can help me, right? Has your college slut got it? Maybe I should ask her in person."

Alain held the truck in his lane with some effort.

"I've got the book, and the tapes," he said. "You looking to trade?"

Hell laughed. It sounded like he choked on it.

"Bring them to me," he said, "and somebody might survive tonight."

"Tell me where you are," Alain said. "I'll be right over."

Again, Hell's nasty laugh came out of the speaker.

"So, the great detective doesn't know everything, huh?" Hell said. "I've found the perfect place. It's almost like it was made for something like me. Maybe you can follow the sound of the screams."

Hell hung up.

Alain punched in Janet's number. She answered on the first ring.

"Did you get him?" he asked.

"Sorry, Alain. He's got the GPS locator turned off," she said. Modern cell phones all broadcast their location unless the user disabled the feature. It had been a long shot.

"We got it narrowed down to two cells, but they cover a big area. I can tell you he's heading west," she said. "He passed from one cell into another, heading that direction. The phone guys are working on it for me, but without a helicopter and a scanner that's the best they can do."

He pulled to the side of the road and stopped. If Hell was headed west Alain needed to pull a one-eighty. "Well, get—" he began.

"It's on the way up from Traverse City," she said, "along with a Coast Guard chopper to help search. The feds are starting to smell blood. They might be delayed, though, because there's a front coming in. Rain or maybe snow."

"It had to happen sooner or later," he said. The weather and the federal involvement were equally inevitable. "Does Stephanie have the tapes?"

"Locked in the interview room with them as we speak. Where are you?"

"Coming into town. I'm going to mix in with the patrols, and put another pair of eyes on the street. Call me if you hear anything," he said.

174

Alain closed the phone and dropped it on the seat, not wanting to lie to Janet any more than he had to. He leaned his head back on the headrest and slowly banged his aching skull against the padding. There had to be a way to find out where they were and separate Leon from Hell's grasp without using the rest of the department. Bob and Chris were his solution. With Leon safely out of the way Alain could call in the troops to nuke Hell.

His stomach tangled. He made it out of the truck, fell to his hands and knees in the weeds and began to retch. He shuddered and thrashed. It felt like it all came up, but the mess of front of his eyes told him differently. Bread, vegetables, nothing that looked like meat. He'd only kept the lamb and beef down. He hawked and spat, trying to clear the bile from his throat, as well as the remembered tang of gun oil.

Chris nosed his Dodge up behind Alain's truck and honked. The men disembarked and politely waited for Alain to struggle to his feet for a meeting at the side of the road. Dust devils flattened their clothes to their bodies and forced them to turn their heads to avoid mouthfuls of grit. The whirling breezes passed on into the treetops to thrash the branches and turn the birch leaves over to show their pale undersides. The air had the snapping taste of snow in it. Alain could smell it like wet iron. His skin felt too tight. When he turned his head too fast his vision blurred at the edges. He closed his eyes and took a few deep breaths. Get through the night.

"Storm," Chris said.

Bob nodded. No one mentioned Alain's troubles.

"Janet says there's a big front coming in. Our quarry is heading west," Alain said, raising his voice over another gust.

"I would have thought he'd head to town," Bob said. "More targets."

"Would he go back to Aimee's campsite?" Alain asked.

"The girl?" The ranger scratched at the gray stubble on his chin. "Why?"

"Where else would he go," Alain wondered out loud, "the Huron Mountain Club? Those people might hush up anything that happened on their land. They hate the press more than we do. I don't think that's what he's looking for, though. He wants a way out, a path back to normal."

"Where's that going to come from?" Chris asked.

"From me, he thinks. Hell wants to believe that the source of the loup garou spell also has a counter-spell. Stephanie, the folklore professor, is working on the books and some interview tapes, but I'm not holding out much hope."

175

"So he thinks you have something he wants," Bob said, shielding his eyes from the wind, which now carried a few random, fat drops of water. Not real rain yet, only moisture blown ahead of the storm by the driving wind. "It's getting dark, and he's got your friend."

Even if a spell existed and he could change back, there were still the murders. Hell couldn't make them disappear. They would be a bitch to prove, but Alain would keep them open forever if need be.

"Shit."

Alain had figured it out.

"He wants a patsy for the killings. He sets up Leon in a place near victims, right as he's about to . . . change. Then he sits back in the woods and waits for me to show with the counter-spell. He uses it, the crimes get blamed on Leon, and he's scot-free."

Bob nodded.

"He's in his element and it's nighttime so everything is on his side," the old ranger said. "Of course, he'll have to kill you to keep you from blabbing."

"Of course," Alain said.

"He might even get the credit for solving his own killings," Chris added.

"Maybe he's not as smart as he thinks," Alain said. "He obviously doesn't know about you two."

Bob checked his Colt again without seeming to know it.

"Victims," Chris offered. The quiet young man made Bob seem gregarious. "Where's he going to find them?"

Alain buttoned his coat against the cold creeping under it. "There's not much out there," he said.

"Tavern, maybe, or a church," Bob said.

Alain shook his head. "I don't think he'd want to be indoors any more. Last time I nearly had him."

"Not hunters, not yet," Bob said, "unless he knows where somebody is scouting out land."

"Would he go after grown men with guns?" Alain asked. "Or look for somebody easier?"

"You got an idea?"

"There were kids at Northern packing up for a camping trip when I stopped by there this morning," Alain said. "Your girls . . . they said they were headed to Pictured Rocks. That's east, but the cell phone track had him moving west. Maybe another group of college kids?"

"Shit," Bob said.

"Might need a permit if they're in the backcountry, or they may have rented gear with the outdoors club at the university," Chris said.

Bob nodded. The young ranger moved back to his truck.

"He'll call it in?" Alain asked.

"Quietly," Bob said. "Chris can get in touch with folks at home. If they got permits or information or gear from one of the offices, he'll find them."

"You all right?" Alain asked him.

"The girls told you they were going to the Rocks?" Bob asked. "They said that to you directly?"

Alain nodded. "Why?"

"I love them to the end of the world," Bob said, "but as soon as they learned to talk they learned to lie if they think someone is going to get in their way. You would have stopped them if they'd said they were headed this way?"

Alain didn't answer the question because it seemed obvious. Bob's face was twisted into something Alain had never seen before. It might be fear.

"I need to call the wife," Bob said.

Alain stepped away to give him space. He had three missed calls from Janet. When he called her back her voice sounded clipped, a sign of high tension in her.

"Where the hell is Leon?" she asked. "His wife is driving me insane. You checked him out of the hospital, Alain, but you didn't take him home."

"He's resting up in a safe place, Janet."

Alain hated to lie to her.

"Is he in trouble?"

He hesitated a moment too long before answering, and she pounced.

"If Leon gets hurt because you're screwing around with this case, I'm going to take it out of your ass, Detective." Janet the momma bear.

"He's fine, Janet—"

"Don't 'fine' me. That's not why I called. Your professor needs to talk to you," Janet said.

The phone changed hands.

"Alain?" Stephanie said.

"Have you finished with the tapes?" he asked.

"Yes," she said, "and you need to hear them. Where are you?"

"On Big Bay Road a few miles out of town, but you can't—"

"I'm on my way," she said.

"Stephanie, no."

"He called me," she said.

Alain's throat tightened.

"Burke called me," she went on, "Hell, or whatever his name is. He called me on my cell phone to give me a message for you."

"Tell me."

"He's going after the students in the woods. If you don't bring the book and the tapes, he'll kill them. He said to come alone."

"Where?" Alain asked.

"I'll tell you when I get there," she said.

"Stephanie, no. You can't. I need you to stay away. Something is happening to me. I might be dangerous."

"I know. If you go without me you'll die," Stephanie said.

The line clicked in his ear, empty, and the answer came not from the phone, but from behind him. He heard footsteps and the whistling breath of a man in pain.

Bob's skin had drawn tight over his skull. Alain knew what he would see on the day he looked into the old ranger's coffin.

"They went out to the McCormick Tract, Alain," the ranger said. "And my daughters are with them."

Chapter Twenty-One

Alain pressed his foot harder into an imaginary brake pedal on the passenger-side of his truck as Bob took them over a hundred miles an hour. The old man's hands locked at ten and two on the wheel, knobby masses of bone and purple veins. He stared straight ahead and took the curves smoothly. Twenty miles of forest highway without so much as a stop sign unrolled in fast forward.

The McCormick Tract was state wilderness that had been a rich man's playground. Cyrus McCormick made a fortune in farm equipment and bought twenty-seven square miles of the U.P. as a hunting retreat in the late 1800s. The land was covered in rugged stone outcrops, cedar swamps and towering white pines that might be three hundred years old. He never enjoyed it. Tragedies befell his extended family there, seemingly every year: drownings, disease, murders, a final deadly fire. After the death of his only son Cyrus deeded the property to the state and retreated a broken man.

A place with a history of death, a cursed land . . . a place made for something like Hell.

Five o'clock. The shadows had begun to lengthen and grow. They rocketed past the sign for the dog farm. If only they'd known where to go, they wouldn't have lost an hour of time chasing their tails.

"The girls told their mother. I would've made them stay home this weekend. Dad don't know nothing about the woods, of course, so don't ask him," Bob said.

Alain kept quiet. Bob and Ellen had had the girls late in life, he knew, and they were the only things they loved more than each other. A year ago a drunk driver had run one of the girls, Sara, off highway 41 late at night. Her car had been totaled when it had snapped off two pines like broom straws. She'd been shaken rather than hurt, but it could have been much worse. The offender, a tourist, got a suspended sentence as a first-timer. Bob hadn't shown any reaction, but he didn't seem surprised when the driver's million-dollar cabin got broken into the next time the man drove down to Chicago for the week. Hundreds of dead fish had been scattered throughout every room, and the doors and windows left standing open. By the time the man returned, half the scavengers in the forest and about ten million maggots occupied his retreat.

Chris had been left behind to intercept Stephanie and turn her around. Alain wanted the book, but she had no business being there.

"You, me, and the young man," Bob said. "We finish it tonight like we planned. I'm not going in there looking to arrest anybody. I don't want to be tripping over a bunch of Dudley Do-rights. If this Hell wants to act like an animal we treat him like one."

Bob had distributed hunting radios to all three of them, short range devices that couldn't be heard on the police bands.

"As far as we know it's a hostage situation," Alain began.

"As far as we know, there are two werewolves out there with my little girls," Bob finished. "You got a chapter in your book on that?"

Alain unbuckled his seat belt and began digging in the back seat.

"You got an answer back there?" Bob asked.

Alain turned back around with his arms full of guns. He didn't say a word but popped the top on the ammo box and began to feed slugs into his shotgun.

Bob slowed to a merely insane speed as the roads narrowed, turned to dirt. He slung them through the curves, navigating the unmarked intersections without glancing at a map.

"Some kind of dare," he said. "Go out in the woods for Halloween, never mind that the girl got killed not ten miles away as the crow flies."

"Not real bright," Alain agreed.

"They think they're immortal. All of them, the deputy included."

"You mean Hell," Alain said. He toyed with a spare slug that wouldn't fit in the shotgun's magazine or the side saddle carrier.

Bob stared straight ahead into the wipers blurring across the windshield. Alain waited until the old man nodded.

"We'll get your buddy out of there, too," Bob said.

Sleet pecked among the raindrops.

"Nice night for a camp-out," Alain said. "Maybe the kids will pack it up and head home."

"Not my girls," Bob said. "They've slept outside in every month of the year. A little ice won't stop them."

The acknowledgement that he had not raised any shrinking violets seemed to release something in Bob's carriage. He wasn't relaxed by any means, but the coiled spring of his emotions seemed to have eased a half-turn. He grunted and swerved to miss a rabbit in the road, at least the fourth they had seen. The double-thump on the undercarriage told them he didn't make it.

"Animals are moving," Bob said.

No reply necessary. Ordinarily when a storm sets in the forest goes quiet as the animals bed down to wait it out. Now something stirred them. Bob slowed the truck further, touching the brakes for the first time since they'd left the pavement behind. They were close.

He pulled off in a turn-around short of the spot where most people parked to hike into the McCormick. If Bob or Alain were the ones being followed they would have set an ambush. They climbed out of the truck, silently gathering gear. Alain adjusted his uncle's hunting coat and slipped into the straps of his rucksack. Tonight it rode heavy and off-center with the extras he'd lifted from the evidence room. He filled two coat pockets with spare ammunition. Bob carried Alain's rifle with the ammo pouch from the back seat and dug a flashlight out of the door pocket.

They closed the doors gently and moved into the woods to work their way along either side of the road. Twilight filled the forest—the mix of dark shadow under the trees and brighter sky interfering with their vision. The rain swirled and gusted on the wind, fine droplets alternately water or ice as the temperature rode the freeze line. The trees shook themselves as though trying to stay awake and smothered all other sounds.

Alain rolled the collar of his coat up to block the wind and wished he'd thought to bring a hat. The chill and the rain thrilled him, got up in his nose and made the hairs on the back of his neck bristle. He felt guilty for enjoying this part of the hunt. He tried to focus on Bob's girls.

Around a final kink in the forest road they found the tiny trailhead parking area. The SUV he'd seen on campus, a brand-new Jeep Cherokee that looked as though it had never been off the pavement, sat nosed in next to a pick-up truck with a cap on the back. Alain looked for Bob but couldn't find him in the shadows. He stepped out onto the shoulder of the road and waved. A particularly dark spot waved back but did not join him.

Alain approached the cars at a slow walk, shotgun held ready at his shoulder, muzzle low. He could feel Bob covering him with the rifle from the woods. Twenty yards, ten, a buzzing in his head as his senses tried to reach out in every direction. He reached the truck bed and chanced a quick look under the cap over the bed. He saw scattered gear, a boot, but no one hiding. Alain crouched between the Jeep and the truck and took a glance underneath. No monsters, no feet on the other side as best he could tell in the last of the light.

He stood and moved to the front of the vehicles. Both hoods were cold to the touch. Bob stepped out from the cover of the underbrush into the road and knelt. He played the beam of the flashlight across the dirt two-track.

"Alain," he said. "Look here."

The top layer of dirt had been softened by the precipitation. Alain could see wide tire tracks leading past the trailhead lot. The two men didn't have to say a word. They melted into the woods again, bracketing the road, and moved forward.

Not fifty yards beyond the lot Alain almost stumbled into Leon's cruiser run straight into the woods between two pines. Another piece of the puzzle clicked. Alain felt stupid. This was how the bastard had been getting around without being spotted. He chirruped like a spring peeper, which brought Bob hustling, and the two of them gave the police car a quick once over. The hood felt still warm. Bob tapped on the window to get Alain's attention and pointed to Leon's shotgun, still locked in its rack next to the radio.

"I don't think he needs it after dark," Alain said.

Bob leaned the rifle against his shoulder and put his hand on his bony hip. "You think he's planning on getting away with this?" Bob asked.

"I do," said Alain. "I think he's planning on it."

"Well then, he'll need a getaway vehicle, won't he?"

Alain's knife punched through the sidewalls of the rear tire like it was cardboard. Bob straightened from slashing the tire on the other side.

The ranger said, "Let's go kill a wolf."

Most of the ground looked too hard to hold tracks, but Bob stooped at the base of the trailhead sign and illuminated a muddy spot with his light.

"Your boy Leon got big feet?" he asked.

"Huge," Alain answered, "like canoes with toes."

"Well, then, Mr. Hell is wearing little tactical boots."

Alain leaned over Bob's shoulder to look. A small print in the mud had 5.11, a popular paramilitary cop brand, stamped dead center. He burned the tread pattern into his memory before Bob killed the light.

Bob moved through the deepening dark in long steady strides that ate up trail. No attempt to hide—they relied on speed and quiet to allow them to come upon their quarry unaware. Alain had his doubts. In the fight at the library, Hell claimed to have smelled him before he saw him, which meant that he had the senses of a wolf even when in human form. He loped faster to close the gap between himself and Bob and began to whisper as loudly as he dared.

"When Leon is a . . . a wolf," he said, feeling stupid despite what he'd seen, "he's black with a broad silver streak on his chest. You can't miss him. He's as big as a pony."

Bob said nothing. He continued his stalk up the trail.

"I don't know what Hell looks like," Alain continued. "It was pitch black in my upstairs hallway. All I saw were the eyes. His eyes reflect orange, and Leon's are green."

Still nothing.

"Bob?"

The old man slowed his killing pace and turned. In the last light of day Alain saw his face. Behind his eyes, nothing—holes opened onto blank sky. No tension, no fear, nothing there to interfere with the hunt.

"I've got it, son," he said.

His voice had that same metal calm to it. Alain shivered as a cold wet gust of wind curled over the collar of his coat and found a slice of bare skin.

"Hell is orange," Bob continued. "Thank you for the information. Now shut up and let me listen."

Alain said nothing, and finally Bob started up the trail once more.

The trail seemed longer than Alain remembered, stretched out by the dark and the urgency of their chase. He checked their backtrail every few moments for movement. Bob didn't slacken his stride. Alain felt a trickle of sweat run between his shoulder blades.

The ranger stopped so suddenly that Alain almost plowed into him.

"No tracks," Bob said.

The trail had joined an old carriage road. Over the decades it had evolved to a jeep track, then a footpath, still hard-packed. The two men spread out, sliding from one shadow to the next with Bob in the lead. Only spots of light remained in the woods, a few small windows of daylight. Until the moon rose they would be running blind aside from the puny beams of their flashlights.

A shadow appeared out of the gloom, and Alain swung the barrel of his shotgun toward it before his reflexes told him it posed no threat. Another reared up, then a gap, followed by a third stone: the ruined remains of a row of markers. Bob hunkered in the middle of the lane and waited until Alain caught up.

"This fence," Bob nodded at the stones, "runs the last mile up to the site of the old lodge. You been here before?"

"Handful of times, but not since high school."

The old ranger leaned in close so he could be heard over the rising wind. He bit each word off like a man whose time ran short. "One end of the place is still standing, along with the fish shack on the big island, but the stables and boathouse and all the other outbuildings burned when the big place went up. I'm going straight in—"

Bob froze, staring into the dark over Alain's shoulder. Alain tried to control his breathing. In the woods behind him, something took one crunching step, then another. Anything more was lost in the thrashing trees. He felt rather than heard the tiny click as Bob released the safety on the M14 rifle.

His back felt exposed and vulnerable: the tender kidneys and spine, the hamstring muscles that wolves severed so their prey couldn't escape, all his juicy targets pumping blood at a steadily rising rate. He fought the desire to spin around. He tightened his grip on the shotgun.

The muzzle of the M14 started to drop, smooth and steady, the stock rotating up. Bob had welded his gaze on one spot. The weapon glided into place, no rush, like the second hand on a Swiss watch. His opposite arm came up to cradle the forearm of the rifle, his head bowed over the sights as the stock reached his shoulder and became a part of it.

Alain didn't want to move his feet, so he sank slowly into a crouch as Bob aimed past his shoulder. His hearing would be gone if he couldn't get his head farther from the muzzle. The storm paused to take a breath, and for a suspended instant the trees rested and the mist hung in mid-air and Bob's finger took up the slack of the trigger and Alain could almost feel it: the smooth pull, neat and crisp, leading to the instant where it all rested on a single additional pound of pressure and the final breath of the hunted.

The shot never came.

A massive weight crashed into his back and pitched Alain face-first on the road.

The Mossberg skipped and slid on the rocks as it flew out of his hands. He covered his head with one arm and rolled, trying to get out from under the body pinning him to the ground. Fetid breath poured down over his neck. Alain groped for the hilt of his knife. Where was Bob? What the hell did he think he was doing? A strong hand caught his wrist before he could draw the blade.

"I think this one knows you," Bob said.

Alain peeked up at the shape panting on him. A gobbet of drool fell on his ear.

"Daisy, get off me," he said.

The mastiff took a pair of mincing steps back and settled on his wide haunches, mouth split in a smile that framed his steam-bellows breathing.

"Any chance this is one of your wolves?" Bob asked, peering into the dark from which the dog had appeared.

"I wish."

"Then we've got to move." He looked back at Alain, who had scrambled to his feet and retrieved his shotgun. "Your buddy's not going to be much help. A wolf will tear his throat out in a half-sec. Might give us a chance to get a shot off, though."

He set off at his loping pace. Alain hesitated, looking from the ranger advancing into the dark to the dog sitting at his feet. Daisy watched him, and when Alain followed Bob the dog trailed along.

Shifting his backpack so it didn't bounce so accurately on his kidneys, Alain attempted to match his pace to his partner's. The knee he'd smashed on Hell's head in the library felt swollen, but it had loosened up enough to allow him to run. The dog shifted around him in a far-ranging circle: bounding ahead, ears flapping, but not past their leader, then swinging off to the sides to vanish in the dark, or falling back to canter and snort at Alain's heels. Scents filled his head: the bite of the coming storm, Daisy's musk, the tin underside of Bob's fear.

A mile through the woods was still a mile. At each sloping curve of the path, winding around and under the granite outcrops of the land, he expected to see the road widen out into the drive that ran up to the McCormick lodge. Every time the curve arrived only to reveal more woods and another stretch of road. He sweated under his coat and pack despite the gusts and drizzle. Daisy limped. Bob's pace seemed to be flagging, too, as the adrenaline wore off and fatigue sank its poison into him.

Bob pulled up, panting as hard as Daisy. Alain took the opportunity to swing off his backpack and dig into the contraband he'd stolen. With the help of a piece of duct tape from his first aid kit, he made an addition to the leather collar encircling Daisy's thick neck and then tucked everything back into the sack. Bob watched with his hands on his knees, trying to control his rattling breath.

"I'm not," he said, "even gonna." Bob straightened up. "Ask."

"Best that you don't know," Alain replied. He slung the backpack over his shoulders and tightened the straps. "How much time do you think we've got before the moon rises?"

Bob looked at his watch then studied the sky. "Twenty or thirty minutes, maybe." He looked around at the forest. The ranger seemed to consult the map in his head. "Half-mile to the lodge— we'll make it, but it's going to be close."

Alain's eyes had adjusted to the dark by this time, and the road seemed to glow at his feet. The mist shifted to rain again, interspersed with stinging pellets of ice that bounced off his cheeks and gathered in his eyelashes. A good sign: they headed into the wind. Their scent would be hard to detect for anyone or anything ahead of them. Alain's knees buckled as Daisy crashed into and past him to gallop into the dark. He gave one low whistle, but the dog disappeared without looking back. Damn. Alain couldn't worry about the goofy mastiff. He unclenched the numb fist he'd made of his free hand and shook it. He tried to concentrate on the trail.

Night had taken complete hold by now, but the clouds above flew limned in silver from the full moon just below the horizon. The glow they cast outlined the shapes of a few scattered pines leading to his left, following a spur ridge. From the fresh scent carried on the wind, he assumed the lake lay beyond that. The road curved to the right and continued out of sight. At the limit of his vision, the extensive ruins of what had been the largest summer home in the area, McCormick's Castle. Rubble and a few waist-high pieces of granite wall were all that had survived a devastating fire at this end of the house long after it had been abandoned. The burned skeleton of the house extended for sixty rooms into the darkness.

Bob appeared beside him without a sound and knelt. He pointed left. "Boathouse, what's left of it," he said, "and beach," indicating a dirt path that left the road directly ahead of them. "That's where the kids will be."

A scream rose on the wind. Both men left their crouches like sprinters out of the blocks.

Chapter Twenty-Two

Alain stepped into empty air, came down hard and off-balance when his foot finally encountered the ground. His knee twinged. He bit into his tongue. The taste of blood filled his mouth. Pain flooded through him to mix with the adrenaline. He ran on, hot and wide awake, but even that small stumble on his part allowed Bob to surge into the lead. The lake stretched along a beach of perhaps fifty yards, the water luminescent. Moonrise couldn't be more than five minutes away.

A cluster of small backpacking tents faced toward the lake's edge. A handful of figures milled around a bonfire that whipped and spat in the wind of the approaching storm. Ten yards remaining, five, and the two men pulled up at the edge of the firelight, panting. Their sudden appearance elicited another shriek from one of the girls.

"Dad?"

"Let's go," the ranger's voice rapped out like the sergeant he had been. "Flashlights only, stick together. We're all leaving. Now."

The other kids stood shocked into silence. Three of them started for their tents, but Bob's twin girls had seen this act for years.

"No way. We just got here—" Jenny began.

"You aren't in charge of the woods, Dad," Sara finished.

Bob took a breath to yell, and Alain intervened with his badge in his hand. "We have reason to believe there is a dangerous animal in this area, and we need you to leave for your own safety."

"Oh my god," a skinny blond boy with a weak beard said.

"We saw it," another student said.

"When?" "Where?" Bob and Alain overlapped.

"About half a minute before you came galloping up to save us," Jenny said. "Something ran past. Lissa screamed."

The brunette she indicated had her arms wrapped tightly around herself. The girl's eyes remained locked on Alain's badge.

"What did you see?" he asked the girl.

She shook her head, and her long hair fell over her eyes. She opened her mouth and Alain strained to hear her over the wind. "I don't know. Something huge on four legs."

He waited. She shrugged. No more details.

Alain triggered the light on the foregrip of his shotgun. He played the powerful beam into the dark, searching for eyeshine and finding nothing. He looked to Bob and realized he could see the ranger's face clearly even though both of them faced away from the fire. The clouds had rolled back to reveal the moon rising over the lake.

Fat and peach-colored, the hunter's moon looked like it hung from the pines on the far shore of the lake. The surface of the water bore a long reflection running to the beach at their feet.

The moonlight fell on the crag that topped the ridge. On the very edge, Leon stood. Alain would have known his gangly frame from a mile away. Alain began to shout, well aware of Bob leveling his rifle at the figure on the cliff, but neither of them got any further.

Leon wavered. He didn't stumble or fall. He wasn't indecisive. Instead, he shimmered like a heat mirage or an image viewed through the edge of a lens. The outline of the man stretched out of normal then rebounded. He jerked and spasmed, but kept his feet until his shape twisted again, his stomach protruding. Something inside Leon needed to get out. He fell to his knees, raised his arms to the moon and threw back his head to howl.

It sounded human at first. Then a deep bell-tone joined his wail, a second voice that shaped and reverberated through a long muzzle, with a timbre like black lake water. Leon and the wolf howled together from the same mouth. He bowed his head to take a deep breath. When he opened his mouth again, it gaped wide and kept on opening as the nose of a wolf emerged from his throat to call once again. His jaw fell away to his chest, his skull became a hump sliding down the back of the wolf. Thick paws appeared from his guts, clawing to get out, and the skin that had been Leon split and fell to the ground as the monster struggled its way free of the man.

The girl that had screamed earlier managed a leaking whimper, the rest shocked to silence. The muzzle Bob's rifle remained steady on the beast but his trigger finger seemed to have turned to stone.

The wolf sniffed at the remains of the body it had discarded, then seized the loose sack of skin and began to eat it. Sliding down his own gullet in pieces, the outline of Leon made the wolf retch and gag before he got it all in. The sight of an empty foot being vomited and eaten twice broke the spell over the spectators. Skinny Lissa let out a shriek like a 747 coming in for a landing. Seven students broke in seven directions as the wolf's head turned to find the source of the scream. Leon's wolf-eyes gleamed green from the top of the cliff, then winked out as he leapt into the cover of the trees.

"Stay here," Alain yelled at the retreating students. Four of them still disappeared into the darkness.

Bob lowered the rifle with shaking hands. "Dammit," he said. He collared one of his girls trying to get into a tent and yanked her upright. "The other end of the house," he said. "Get everyone into the part that's still standing."

Jenny pulled her arm free and moved, gathering the crumpled, sobbing Lissa and another coed, dragging them up the slope toward the ruins. Sara, having already reached the same conclusion as her father, re-appeared in the firelight with the skinny guy dogging her footsteps. Alain handed her the Mossberg. He dug loose shells out of his pockets and dumped them into her free hand.

"Seven slugs in the magazine, one in the chamber. Got it?" he asked.

Sara had taken a deer with a slug-gun every year since she'd turned twelve. She coolly checked the safety, gave the spare ammo to her bearded shadow and broke into a run after her sister. The wind came back with a vengeance, nearly extinguishing the fire, covering the moon with a ghostly blanket. Bob pulled at Alain's sleeve.

"You can't be out here with a popgun." He gestured to Alain's holstered pistol and hefted the M14 rifle as if to hand it over.

"I'm set," Alain said. He knelt, unzipped the backpack at his feet and reached inside. The walnut stock of the poacher's elephant gun he'd stolen from the evidence room fitted itself to his hand. The wood felt warm to the touch.

"Well, that might work," the ranger said. "If the second floor of that tower is still sound, I'll be up there with a good view. You get either one of those bastards out in the open with some light, you raise your hand and I'll take them out," Bob said. "That first time, I couldn't bring myself to . . . I knew he's your friend . . ."

"You get those five holed up," Alain said. "I'll send the other two students your way as I find them."

Bob stopped trying to explain and ran.

Alain duct-taped his flashlight under the dual barrels of the elephant gun, close enough that he could work the switch to turn on the light with his left hand. He opened the action to feed it two weighty cartridges, then snapped it shut. The loaded gun lay across his arm like a viper while he stuffed extra rounds into his pockets. In his hurry to escape the evidence room, Alain had only grabbed two boxes of ammunition: ten rounds total.

The clouds shut tight. The storm had arrived in force. Sheets of rain and ice blew across the lake to batter at the shore. Alain ducked his head to avoid the worst of it. He headed for the spot where he'd last seen the students, up the slope and into the dark.

189

The base of the cliff ran from the water's edge to the road, picking up a straggling cover of pines as it climbed. He triggered his light. Tennis shoe tracks in the mud proved he'd chosen the right direction. A clump of light-colored material resolved itself into a girl tucked into a ball at the base of a tree.

He reached out to shake her, and she flinched away from his hand with a gasp. She didn't look up. The girl was in shock. He dropped the gun to be able to use both hands, and rolled her head up far enough to look at him.

"You need to go to that way," he said, pointing the direction of the ruins. "Run for the tower and Officer Androtti will take care of you."

The girl shook her head. She tried to pull away.

Alain didn't have time for this. He seized her earlobe between his thumb and forefinger, pinching so hard his nails met, and lifted. The girl rose like she rode an elevator, giving off a high-pitched squeak. By the time she stood on her own two feet, her eyes snapped with pain and anger.

"You fucking prick, my dad's going to—"

"I'd love to meet him, if you survive," Alain said. "Move!" He gave the girl a shove, and she stumbled off in the direction of the others. One down, one to find. He reclaimed his trophy gun before striding up the slope through the whipping branches.

At the top, the wall of granite that made up the ridge curled to his right. In front of him lay the road. The clouds fragmented under the onslaught of the wind. Stray beams of light illuminated the drama in front of him.

The Leon-wolf crouched in the drive, the same black monster Alain had seen in the devil's soupbowl. The student in front of the wolf had broad shoulders and looked as if he might be an athlete. He held a dead branch out in front of him with both hands like a wooden sword, keeping it between the wolf and himself and shouting a babble of half profanity. The kid had balls, if not brains.

Alain slid his finger into the trigger guard, finding the heavy first trigger for the left barrel. He brought the gun to his shoulder. Leon toyed with the boy, feinting and dodging, growling like an oversized puppy. Alain had seen the same behavior in coyote pups as they practiced how to kill a deer that had been crippled by the pack. Eventually blood would flow. Where was Hell? He had to be somewhere close, hiding and watching. Alain stepped out of the cover of the trees.

"Leon, you mangy, neutered cur," he yelled.

The beast's ears pricked up and swiveled to find the new threat. Those green eyes settled on Alain. He felt their cold glare to the depths of his bowels. A growl issued from the huge throat. The ears laid back against the massive skull.

190

"No!" Alain got out. Too late.

The kid swung his improvised club like a baseball bat. The thunk as he made contact would have been impressive if it had had a noticeable effect. The stick flew from his hands. Leon moved so fast that he didn't seem to occupy the space between where he was struck and when he stood over the fallen young man, teeth bared to rip out the student's throat. Alain's brain sent the message to pull the trigger but he was too slow. Too slow by far.

Froth dripped from Leon's mouth as he lunged for the killing blow, the stink of fear hit the air when the kid's sphincter let go at the sight of his own death, and two hundred and sixty pounds of mastiff came out of the dark to hit Leon in the side.

Daisy had entered the fight.

Leon rocked to his haunches, twisting to take the impact from the big dog. Big for a dog, at least. Next to the loup garou, Daisy looked like a puppy. Daisy's jaws spasmed and clenched at the shoulder of the wolf, trying to get a grip with his fangs. The Leon-wolf stood on his hind legs, hauling Daisy off his feet. The dog's rear legs dangled and kicked for purchase. The monster swung from side to side until the dog lost its grip and flew twenty feet through the air. Daisy skidded to a stop before charging back into the battle.

Alain leapt forward to snag the kid by the collar. The kid rolled over and scrabbled to his feet, then barreled directly into Alain as he fled. Alain's ankle folded under their combined weight. A spear of pain shoved up his leg.

Alain struggled up to one knee, the bad leg tucked behind him. He leveled the elephant gun at the ground short of the ball of canine fury and pulled the trigger.

He'd had no time to consider what it might be like to fire the big gun. Alain had shot slugs from a twelve-gauge all his life, absorbing the wicked kick as a matter of course. The flaw in his logic became apparent as soon as the thick walnut stock hit him and his shoulder blades attempted to meet behind his back. The barrel jerked up to the level of the trees with the recoil. A geyser of dirt and tiny rock fragments cascaded over the dog-wolf-deputy fight, and everything stopped.

The thunderclap of the shot seemed to stun the combatants for a second. They looked around, dazed. It felt to Alain as if he'd sprained his neck trying to hold onto the shoulder-cannon.

Daisy recovered first, taking advantage of the pause to strike under the head of the wolf, locking his jaws into the soft folds of flesh at the base of Leon's throat. Leon roared and surged to his hind feet again. He pulled the dog off the ground again but Daisy refused to let go, clinging to Leon like a leech. Leon thrashed and clawed at him. Alain found the trigger for the second barrel by feel and waited for a clear shot. He rose to his feet, testing the twisted ankle. It bore the weight. If he could take out one of Leon's legs, then move in with the knife and cut him to remove the curse, they all might make it out of here tonight.

Leon swung his shaggy head from side to side, attempting to dislodge Daisy's grip. The dog weakened, scrabbling at the monster less by the moment, his growls fading. The Leon-wolf swung him like a pendulum. Daisy tore free. An arc of Leon's blood followed the dog as he came loose to fly into the shadows at the edge of the road out of sight. A pine tree shook with the impact. Leon lunged after the dog.

Shit. Alain staggered forward, the ankle burning each time his weight came down on it. He switched on the flashlight and trained the beam into the trees. It illuminated the hind legs of the loup garou on all fours, tearing at something on the ground. Alain fired from the hip this time, bracing against the recoil with his entire weight, shooting the monster directly in the hind quarters.

The blast still shook Alain. The impact of the round spun the loup garou halfway around, one leg crumpling. His rumbling growl rose to a yowl of pain. The light from the flashlight set the wolf's green eyes ablaze. White powder coated his jaws, tongue and nose. He took an unsteady step toward Alain, who dropped the empty hunting rifle to pull his knife.

"Come on, asshole," Alain said, sinking into a crouch, knife held low before him. "Time to fix you up." He reached across his body to clumsily draw his pistol with his off-hand.

The loup garou shook its head, seeming to try and focus on the man before him. Alain backed away onto the roadway. The loup garou followed, weaving from side to side. Without his light, Alain had to rely on the slashes of moon. He tightened his grip on the knife.

The loup garou limped out into the lane with his right rear leg curled protectively into his body. Alain feinted a lunge. The monster bared its fangs, but did not yield ground.

"I need five drops," Alain said as he circled slowly, keeping ten feet between himself and the animal. "You in there, buddy? You listening? Five little drops, and we can put an end to this. Stick out your paw and make it easy on me."

The loup garou lunged and snapped at the hand holding the knife. Alain jerked back. He'd felt its hot breath on his knuckles.

"Maybe not," Alain said.

He fired two shots into the ground next to the wolf. It cringed away from the flash and noise. Alain charged, slashing with the blade.

Snarling, stumbling and whining, the loup garou retreated from him, and then turned tail to run. Even on three legs it outstripped him to disappear into the night. His own injured ankle throbbed. The knee he'd bashed in the library had woken with burning pain. Alain managed two running strides before pulling up in a cloud of swearing. He scuttled back to where he'd dropped the elephant gun, snatched it up and hit the switch for the flashlight. He juggled the armload of weapons for a moment until he managed to sheath the knife and holster his side-arm. Digging in a cargo pocket for rifle shells to reload the big gun, he almost missed the groan.

The low, wet sound floated from under the pines. Daisy. Alain slid two fresh cartridges into the chambers and snapped the breech shut before moving cautiously under the trees.

The mastiff lay stretched on his side, ribs heaving as he panted. Again, he let loose with the groan that sounded almost human. Alain took one look back at the loup garou's trail before dropping to his knees beside the dog. With Leon playing for the other team, Daisy was the closest thing he had to a partner.

The light revealed deep scratches along Daisy's flanks. They had already clotted with pine needles and dirt. The bleeding didn't seem severe. He shifted the light further up the dog's body. White powder covered the ground around Daisy's head, the same stuff that the loup garou had all over its face. Alain unbuckled the remains of the dog's thick leather collar, with bits of plastic still held in place by Alain's duct tape job, and then dug into his pack for the first aid kit. The loup garou had gone straight for the throat. At least one fang had sunk in, causing deep puncture wound on Daisy's neck. Alain placed a gauze pad over it and applied pressure to stop the bleeding.

He brushed the powder off the dog, and blew gently to clear it away from Daisy's head. Daisy had likely inhaled some of it, but not nearly as much as the loup garou had gotten when it had grabbed the plastic bag taped to the dog's collar. The monster may have expected to get a mouthful of Daisy's throat, but what he got instead was a healthy dose of the nearly-pure heroin Alain had stolen from the evidence room. It might slow the beast down a little.

Alain attempted to roll the dog to check for wounds, but that made Daisy groan again, louder this time, so he settled for sliding his hands under the big body to check for open wounds. He couldn't be sure, but he thought that the dog might have broken ribs or other bones when he landed against the tree trunk. Daisy lifted his head and tried to lick Alain's hand.

"Stay here and keep quiet," Alain said. "You don't want Hell coming across you like this. We'll get you out of here after I go collect a pelt."

Great. Now he talked to a dog as if it might understand. Of course, he'd been talking to Leon the same way a few minutes ago. Daisy settled back down, his panting slower as Alain packed a fresh pad atop the first bandage and secured the dressing in place with more duct tape—messy, but effective.

He crossed the road in a crouching run, counting fifty paces before stopping. The ankle still hurt. He could manage the knee.

A rifle shot split the night, coming from the ruins. Had Hell set a trap in the tower? *Shit.* Too much ground to cover. He took two steps toward the sound of the shot and then stopped. If there had been an ambush, Alain bet that he would have heard more shooting from Bob and his girls. Shots again: the heavy thack-thack-thack of a .308 firing on full automatic. Bob must have found the selector switch.

A long, belling howl rose above the wind. It tapered to scattered barks and whines, then rolled up again into one sustained alpha note. The recording looped and began again. Chris must have reached the end of the 4x4 trail into the far side of the property and begun call-blasting. That meant he had the trap in place.

Alain headed for the ascent leading up to where they'd first seen Leon change shape, skirting Daisy's hiding spot as he went. The sleet began to mix with falling snow now, fat flakes that blocked the little light available, absorbing the sound of the storm and laying a thin calm across the forest as it caught in pine branches and accumulated on the low spots in the ground. Not enough yet for tracks, but soon . . . He held the rifle low, the stock snug to his hip, ready to fire. The gun had been designed for following wounded lions and elephants into the brush, never intended for any serious use on this continent, but its weight felt solid and at home here in Alain's hands tonight.

His breath began to come faster as the grade increased. Close to the top now but he couldn't see it. In only a few minutes the snow had intensified, the orderly slanting rows devolving into a swirling mess. Soon visibility would be down to nothing. Alain concentrated on controlling his respiration, visualizing his heart pumping smoothly, silencing the demands of his body so that he could absorb the sound of the woods. Sticks cracked under his feet, muffled in the snow but like gunshots in his hearing.

Movement to his left—he fired without thinking, all reflex, the recoil rocking him before the shape had fully registered in his forebrain. Alain took three strides uphill to change his position, his ankle still radiating pain but from a distance as if it belonged to someone else. He waited, gun barrel aimed down the slope where he'd seen the shadow. Had it been big enough to be one of the loup garou?

Only one round left in the big gun. He fumbled another cartridge out of his pocket with numb fingers and broke open the breech. Alain pulled the spent brass out and slipped the new shell in place by feel. His eyes dropped automatically to try and see what he was doing in the dark. He looked back to see nothing down the hill where he'd fired, and then glanced upslope over his shoulder, and into the teeth of Hell.

Chapter Twenty-Three

Alain flung himself backwards down the slope, twisting to face the monster. The loup garou leapt. Time seemed to slow for him as it had during the gunfight in the library. With a detached interest he noted that his obedient hands closed the breech of the elephant gun. The meticulous German craftsmanship of hardened steel and walnut slid into place like a work of mobile art, engaging and locking with a snap that he felt in the bones of his numb fingers. Rotating in mid-air now, controlled by those same smart hands of his, the stock coming back and the barrel swinging toward the monster falling down the hill toward him. His fingers slid into the trigger guard and found both curved, cool pieces and then the gun was between them like a connecting rod, the tip of the barrel nearly brushing the fur of the giant wolf's belly and the stock inches from his own abdomen and it would be a very bad idea to pull both triggers at once but his fingers did not get the message.

The recoil drove the stock so deeply into Alain's gut that he felt the wood touch his spine. The rifle flew out of his grasp, his nerveless fingers unable to hold it. His right wrist had snapped like a bundle of sticks when both barrels went off, but that barely registered before the loup garou came down and sank its teeth into his shoulder and covered him in the blood and stink of a gut shot.

They tumbled down the hill, Alain crushed then carried along over the top like a paper doll. He could feel his flesh tear around the wolf's fangs. His knife came to his hand and he punched the short blade repeatedly into the Hell-wolf's side as they slid to a stop. He pulled free of its slack jaws and scrambled back up the slope away from where the loup garou lay crumpled. Rifle, rifle . . . *Where the hell was it?*

The Hell-wolf tried to get to its feet.

Alain's shoulder radiated heat that spread down his side. He put his hand down for balance, lost the knife. Droplets of blood hit the snow and spread out into black buttons in his sight. His right hand wouldn't obey; it only flailed at his belt as he tried to draw his pistol.

The loup garou screamed in pain and rage. It began to drag itself up the slope with its front legs.

Alain ran. Up, higher, take the high ground. He forgot about the rifle and the rest of it and ran.

Chris's recorded howl rang out again. It sounded flat and dead to Alain. No wolf would mistake that for a real animal.

The last twenty feet of the cliff narrowed to a point that hung out over the lake. The drop disappeared into the swirling snow. Alain stared into the storm for too long. Nausea roiled his stomach. He rolled away from the edge with vertigo pulling at him, then slumped to his knees and dropped the pack, worked his left hand across his body to grasp his pistol and slide it from the holster. He tried to ignore the blood running down his arm from his left shoulder, but he could feel it coating the grip of the Sig. The dizziness yanked him to the ground.

A tearing cough came out of the darkness down the hill, as if the loup garou were retching up its guts whole. Alain rolled onto his back, knees bent, steadying the Sig between them. He aimed in the general direction of the hacking and let off two rounds. White-blue sparks and the scream of a ricochet told him that he'd hit rock instead of monster, so he closed his eyes and waited for another sound to guide his aim. The time stretched. He struggled to stay focused. He had to kill the thing. Maybe he could drag it off the cliff and solve two problems at once.

"Alain." Hell's voice. He'd changed back to human form. Unless the wolf talked with his voice like in a cartoon.

Alain tracked and fired.

"Not even close," Hell yelled over the wind.

A double-tap this time—two quick shots. The little shit probably lay behind cover.

"That was good, with the big gun," Hell went on as if they were having a conversation over the back fence. "I didn't expect that. You ever been gut shot, Alain? Hurts like a mother. Damn, I can still feel it."

Alain's shoulder pulsed now. Each individual snowflake burned like a spark of pain as it landed on the jagged puncture wounds. He focused on the gun's front sight, tried to keep it steady as it wandered over the few trees he could see through the storm. Alain fought back the desire to yell out, to answer the challenge. Hell had to know he was on the point, but not exactly where.

The crack of metal on rock surprised him. He let off another round in reflex. Lower, he thought, perhaps fifteen yards down the slope. Again the sound came, like someone swinging an axe. The noise ended in a sharp splintering. Alain rolled onto his side and tried to sit up. The shoulder had frozen stiff, as if rods of frigid metal ran through it and into his back. A thin shape came flying through the air, end over end, to slide to a stop short of his feet—the stock and receiver of the elephant gun, smashed and broken. He heard something else hit off to one side, bounce off the rocks with the tick of metal and disappear over the edge. Perhaps the barrels.

"All we need to do now is wait for your girlfriend," Hell said.

She's not coming.

Alain watched the snow ripple and coalesce into solid forms. It covered the ground with a trace of white now and collected on his clothes. Struggling, he managed to get to his knees. He put the gun down and tucked his broken right arm into his coat pocket. The edges of bone rubbed against each other for a moment and the cliff spun underneath him. *Crepitus.* He'd learned the word in first aid training and carried it in a corner of his mind ever since. The sound of broken bones grinding together.

The Sig lay on the ground. How many rounds left now? Using his relatively good left hand, Alain pulled a spare magazine from the carrier at his belt. He stood it upright on the ground, picked up the gun, ejected the mag from it, and then placed gun down over the fresh magazine until it locked in place. Twelve, plus one in the chamber. Lucky number.

Hell groaned, a sound so like Daisy's that Alain looked around for the big dog. This time, the sound climbed into a scream. The little bastard must be changing again, turning back to the loup garou. He'd gained control of the process. Alain wondered if Hell really wanted the counter-spell after all, or if he liked what he'd become. Regardless, Alain knew that when he'd finished with the shape-shift Hell would come up and kill him. Alain struggled to his feet and took a single step toward the agonized sounds before crashing to his knees again. If he could get there mid-change and shoot Hell ten or thirteen times in the head that would be good. Rest a second and then stand up. Do something. Oh, yes, shoot the wolfman.

Help. He should call for help. Alain set the gun down, which seemed wrong because he was supposed to do something with it. He hauled out the hunting radio, smearing blood across it in the process, and twisted the slippery knob until he'd managed to turn it on. Static. Squelch. He pushed at the buttons. Chris. Needed Chris.

He tried to say, "Hello," but a gurgle came out instead.

"Alain?"

Stephanie.

"Alain, can you hear me?"

More static. He heard the edges of words in the white noise, floating like branches in a maelstrom. Could not make them out. Why was he talking to Stephanie?

The sounds downslope had stopped, which Alain thought might be a problem. He concentrated on speaking clearly into the radio.

"Hep," he said. One more time. "Help."

"Are you hurt?" She had a nice voice. "Listen to me. Are you paying attention?"

Alain managed to grunt an affirmative. A huge black dog appeared out of the snow, taking slow steps toward him as if it could sneak up on him even while he watched it. Biggest one he'd ever seen, the size of a cow.

Nothing but the white noise on the radio now, as if Alain could hear the snow fall.

Hell. The thought came to him that he should pick up the gun again. It lay next to him, dusted with snow sticking to the blood on the grip. If he did that, though, he'd have to put the radio handset down, and Stephanie had told him in her teacher-voice to listen.

"Alain!" Now she sounded angry with him. And loud. Her voice came out of the sky, from the same place as the recorded wolf howls, using the microphone on the call-blast system. Stephanie must be with Chris. That seemed impossible. Chris had been told to send her back. She always followed directions. Something seemed wrong with that idea, but Alain couldn't work it out. "The tapes had more than the loup garou verses on them," she said, "other lore from the same time period, and you need to hear it. Alain, there were people who could become wolves without making a deal with Lucifer."

The wolf's ears swiveled forward at that name then lay back against its skull. Its lip curled up to reveal canines the size of railroad spikes. It growled.

"You are a part of this story for a reason," she said. "Listen to Father Avius."

The click of the tape recorder echoed above the trees, followed by a hiss of background noise. The wind had calmed. The storm seemed to take a breath.

"*Le Sang du Loup.*" The dead man's voice was soft and deep. "The blood of the wolf, or the wolf's heir; it translates both ways."

Mama Bouche had called Alain 'the blood.'

"Every hundred years or so," the priest went on, "a human baby is born to a wolf mother. The origin of the story varies: it's supposedly because of the human flesh they eat, or their ability for domestication to man. Regardless. *Le Sang* is a balance to the evil of the loup garou: an animal who has become a man."

A young woman spoke. "But they can change back?" Aimee.

At the sound of her voice the giant wolf's growl became a whine, and its advance halted. Hell cocked his head at the sky.

"Once they accept their birthright, yes, with the agency of the Church. Once they are named as the heir," Avius said.

Alain could hear the crackle of the fire in the background of the recording. He could see the den in the rectory: the worn rug, stacks of books.

"The baby would be left as an orphan for a human to find, to raise it," Father Avius said.

Alain remembered the dust shifting down from the boards of the attic where his mother must have kept watch until Waagosh entered the cabin. Avius' voice had unlocked something. He remembered now, being carried in powerful jaws, the smell of her fur.

"*Alain Logan, vestri nomen est...*" Stephanie spoke over the recording. "Say it."

Alain mouthed the words. He almost had it.

"*Alain Logan, vestri nomen est...*" She repeated. "You have to say your name. I can't help you with this part." She sounded like she was about to start sobbing.

He struggled up onto his good elbow. The pain flowed down his wounded shoulder like water.

Alain said it.

Avius continued, the priest's voice assuming the authority of ages as he began the investiture of *Le Sang du Loup*. The ancient words fell out of the sky like bars of light. Latin: not the dry language he'd learned in the drafty pine chapel on the reservation, but living, breathing words, the sound of eons of life in Rome, blazing like fire and drifting down toward him.

Hell whirled in place and bounded away from the terrible noise.

Alain recognized one more word—*cruor,* blood—before Avius' voice landed on his skin and passed through. He seized like a body immersed in freezing water, his spine bowing into an arc. The words entered the bridge of his vertebrae and traveled up, each one falling off in turn, the feeling in his lower body dropping away like the expended stages of a rocket until the fiery language reached the level of his shoulders and split in two. It washed through his torn shoulder and traveled the length of his shattered arm. He unraveled, his soul following his body into a senseless void. Then he felt it stop. Or pause. The verse outlined his shape as a man, the way he saw himself. It flexed and contracted, the core of who he was flowing, changing into an animal curled tightly into itself . . . his self. Suspended over a plain as vast and featureless as Superior, he hung, incorporeal, as the final phrase walked up the bones of his neck and entered his mind in a flare of all colors.

The shooting woke him. Consciousness returned in a slow tide of senses. His legs felt bound, tied. Alain kicked free of the cloth and rose to an onslaught of scent. It was staggering, overwhelming, like colors painted on his mind: a familiar smell on the clothes he'd struggled out of, the copper taste of blood on the rock, a thick fetid odor of decay that hung in the air.

The night was planes of gray screened in silver snow. Even the snowflakes had a scent, a smell like dizzying heights.

Steady shots came from the direction of the ruins.

He sneezed and shook his head. The smell of death was so strong he could see it. Follow it. He knew instinctively it was the hell-wolf, and it had to die. Alain leapt forward, claws digging into the rock, and tracked it into the trees. Something hung at the edge of thought, a sense of wonder, surprise, but the desire to kill the source of that scent overrode all else and he loped on, powerful and limber and lean, as he had always been.

The snow fell straight down in a marching wall. He bounded down the slope. The land was alive in his muzzle; he could smell the trees shutting down for winter, the loam under his paws, the voles buried in the leaf litter that froze in terror as he passed.

At the bottom of the slope he turned onto the unnatural hard surface and dropped his pace to a trot, nose held high to follow the rank scent trail. He paused in front of a large pine. The animal lying flat beneath the lowest boughs smelled like a canine but not one of his pack. It was wounded. The canine was larger than Alain, but he knew he could easily finish it if he wanted to. He stood over the animal. It seemed familiar, again that nagging sense of something at the edge of sight. Powder scattered on the ground smelled alien and poisonous. The canine inhaled deeply to catch Alain's scent. His brow furrowed. He looked confused, but wagged his tail slowly against the ground in a gesture of friendly submission. Alain snarled and bounded back into the storm to find his real prey.

The pack was close. He caught trails crisscrossing the road, all strange wolves but he knew they were his pack the same way he knew how to breathe.

The ground lay scorched and dead between the rubble of the fallen walls. He passed through the skeleton of a house, no roof but still holding the shapes of rooms and halls. Alain advanced by short rushes from shadow to shadow. Scrubby brush, catbrier and hackberry, had forced its way up through the ground alongside the remains of the house.

The gun blasted again, the muzzle flash splitting the falling snow to his left, perhaps sixty yards away. He reached a partial wall running along the edge of a long, narrow open area. Metal framework, twisted from the heat of the inferno, lay scattered around.

The object of his hunt faced off in the center of the clearing. Two of them: the hell-wolf that smelled like death, and another. The storm had torn apart the piled clouds for a moment, allowing the moon to backlight the snow and slime their fur in silver. The whipping flurries revealed and hid them in fits and bursts, shuttered scenes.

The second beast confused Alain. It was almost the same height but lankier than the hell-wolf. Its green eyes were dull. It staggered and swayed. Even from this distance Alain could smell the alien powder on it, a spiking rasp that made Alain want to rub his muzzle. Its shape was wrong. Not broken, but wrong, forced. For a second in the moonlight Alain thought he could see a man-shape inside the thing, straining at its outline and attempting to break free.

The hell-wolf snapped at the second monster's hindquarters, driving him toward the north end of the conservatory where the walls of the house still stood. Each time the guns opened fire. He limped, but still the hell-wolf drove him on, perhaps trying for a rush where he could follow and overwhelm the defenders. The green-eyed monster spun and snapped at the heavier wolf, trying to keep his distance from the bite of the bullets. Leon. Where had that word come from? It was right, though. He felt it. The second one was Leon, or at least the man inside was.

They circled and then both charged, rising onto their hind legs at the moment of impact. The crash as they came together seemed to shake the earth. The monsters clawed at each other with their forepaws, wrestling for control, each attempting to throw the other down on his back. Their muzzles bashed, fangs smashing and clacking against fangs over the sound of the storm as they sought an opening to reach the opposing throat.

Leon threw one arm under the jaw of hell-wolf and drove it back. Then Leon snared his feet a piece of metal and both of them went down. The hell-wolf tore at Leon's underbelly with his fangs. He rose to his feet again as Leon scrambled back and away, kicking weakly at the metal that trapped his bloody legs.

Alain struck from the shadows: a lightning attack to the hamstrings.

Hell-wolf spun faster than Alain could follow and caught him mid-leap. Its claws dug into Alain's side and found purchase to throw Alain through a wall. The rotted brick gave way in a cloud of rubble and dust. Alain slid to a stop in the snow.

Pain. Ribs, his front leg. Alain groaned and whimpered. He tried to roll to his feet.

The hell-wolf stepped over the ruined wall. Its heavy growl cut the wind. The monster gathered itself to leap upon him.

The pack came.

It attacked from behind. Timber wolves—gray and black and brown, slender and lithe females—struck at the devil-wolf, slashing at its hamstrings with their fangs. The beast roared in pain. A shadow flowed past Alain to bite at the devil-wolf's front legs and then was gone.

Individually, it outweighed the bitches by a factor of ten and could have killed any one of them easily. This was not a one-on-one fight. They came in waves, streaks of darkness coming out of the ruins to strike and then disappear, or taunt it from barely out of reach to allow another wolf to circle and attack from the rear. It charged and rolled and snapped at them, jaws closing on air more often than not.

Leon fled with a pair of wolves at his heels.

Alain charged the hell-wolf, his wounds forgotten. He wanted blood. He wanted to kill it. Tear at the eyes, claw for the heart. Sink his fangs into the underbelly. Strike and retreat, feint and stab. Other males joined him, young heavy-chested brutes and scarred veterans. The circle of death tightened around the hell-wolf. A black she-wolf overreached, darted in too boldly alone to sever the tendons at the back of the hind leg. It buckled, but the beast still turned in time to catch her in his jaws and crush her. As if at a signal the pack came in a rush, and before the dead one hit the ground he staggered under the weight of a dozen bodies. The wolves flowed up his bulk, leaping lightly from ground to flank to head, sinking teeth into whatever flesh they could find. It made an attempt to stand on its hind legs and got up for an instant, animals hanging off it like a second skin. It crashed to the ground. They tore into it. Alain buried his fangs in its throat, slowly crushing the windpipe as the rest of the pack slashed at the unprotected underbelly, spine, legs, ears, eyes.

It began to scream like a man as best it could in Alain's jaws. The blood in his mouth tasted like rot. The pack tore it to pieces. The struggling slowed and finally stopped after a full minute of snarling and ripping. The pack dissolved, slipping into the shadows of the ruins and melting away as quickly as it had appeared. Following Leon.

Alain ran with them.

A howling rose like a tower of sound in the direction he'd fled.

The run seemed to take only an instant. Alain remembered bounding over piles of stone and weaving through snowy brush to reach the road. The call of the pack pulled him a hundred yards past the last remains of the house and back into the woods. Wolves, everywhere—his pack and many more—arrayed in a circle around a truck and trailer on the narrow two-track.

The headlights and off-road lights of the truck cut lines into the falling snow, the fallen tree that had stopped its forward progress clearly visible. Outdoor speakers, the call-blasting unit, collected snow on the hood. The animals sitting between Alain and the truck were lit as well, and he knew by scent that their numbers extended all the way around. Likewise, he felt the presence of more pacing through the woods surrounding the road and its occupants, circling, circling. Hundreds of them. More wolves than the experts said lived here. Wolves up from Wisconsin, and down from Minnesota, and maybe wolves climbing out of the den of years past, from the time when they ran free over these lands.

The howl cut off as if choked by his arrival.

The final ring of wolves around the truck opened, one female with a streak of yellow down her flank standing aside and regarding him with ancient eyes. He stepped forward and she sat again to close the ranks.

As he moved to the side of the truck he could see past the blinding lights to the man and woman inside. They sat quietly, as people might do when they reached the end of reality and looked around the edge to find that it had been nothing more than painted scenery the entire time.

The truck rocked on its suspension, and a clanging broke out from the trailer. Alain kept walking past the cab, his paws leaving tracks in the new snow.

The bear trap shook again, and a growl emerged from it to be answered by the surrounding guardians and Alain himself. He could still feel the edge of his bloodlust. Through the steel mesh Alain could see the outline of a huge nose. The beast was crammed into a bear trap made to hold an animal half as long.

Leon's eyes were unfocused and vague, drool dripping from his black lips, but he still thrashed against his captivity and bent the mesh out away from its moorings. He'd hidden in the first safe spot he'd found. Coward. Better to face the justice of the pack.

Something wasn't right about that. It was right in the way that snow falls down rather than up, but the same nagging sense that had distracted him earlier made him wonder. He thought about what he'd seen earlier, the man-shape trying to break free from its animal prison. Alain shook his muzzle. More things crowded into his head. The name: Leon. Where had that come from? What was a Wisconsin, and how did he know this was a truck, that other thing a gun? His head felt full of things without scents, which should have been a clue that they were false, but he couldn't let them go.

Two bitches entered the circle and dropped items in front of Alain. He recognized the cloth bindings he'd been tied in when he woke. They had a familiar scent, not a pack member but close. He realized he could smell the man and woman inside the truck. Alain walked to the door and looked at her through the window. She met his gaze and her mouth fell open. The man smelled like guns and leather. Her scent was harder to pinpoint. Worry. A hint of estrus that burned in his mind like a hot coal. Something else, too, clean and natural and sweet. Vanilla. Stephanie smelled like vanilla and he knew what vanilla was and Alain was his name and these things in the snow were clothes and boots. He was a man.

The twisting inside his head blinded him with pain. It cleared long enough for him to grab some of the clothes and bound into the trees before the world flared white behind his eyes.

Alain staggered to the back of the trailer, holding his breath against the fetid musk of the loup garou mixed with the smell of the rotten meat Chris must have used to bait the trap. It seemed he'd only been out for a minute or two. The scene was the same: wolves, trailer, Leon. He felt like a hollow tin can. He could still taste Hell's rotted blood. The snow burned his bare feet. Until he'd managed to shove them into his boots and struggle into Waagosh's worn jacket he ignored the wolves.

"No socks?" he asked them.

Someone whined. This must be what insanity felt like. It wasn't bad.

Chris and Stephanie were watching him through the back window. He still had work to do.

Leon's hind legs smashed against the retaining mesh in back. Alain reached for his belt knife first, but found only an empty sheath. He vaguely remembered losing it in the fight on the ridgetop. He dug into a buttoned pocket and miraculously found his Swiss Army knife. He opened the biggest blade and reached through the mesh to cut deeply into the loup garou's exposed toe. Leon fought and kicked, but the trap held him. Alan managed to catch a gush of blood on the steel of the blade. It spilled, hot and greasy, over his hand. He fought the desire to drop it.

When he turned away from the kicking beast the wolves shifted out of his way. Most of them melted off into the dark, returning to dens and hunting grounds and long sleeps. A cadre of four, led by the yellow female, surrounded him in a shifting cloud as he walked into the woods with the fouled knife held out before him. He concentrated on keeping as much of the blood balanced on the blade as possible, and also ignoring his fleet, silent companions.

Alain couldn't say how long they hiked—a minute or an hour—nor could he describe exactly where they stopped, where the wolves allowed him to stop and dig. Even if he'd wanted to find it again, he couldn't. And he didn't want to. The ground felt soft, the loam warm under the snow from countless cycles of gently rotting leaves. He dug deeply with his hands. When he paused to rest, the yellow wolf shouldered him aside and made the dirt fly from the hole. Each animal took turns until the final resting place for his favorite pocket knife was half the depth of a grave. Alain placed the knife into the hole and pushed the dirt back over it, ending by rolling the largest rocks he could move over the top of the disturbed earth.

When Alain looked up, he was alone. The wolves had disappeared as if they'd never existed. He dug his flashlight out with shaking, filthy hands and began to retrace his steps to the truck.

When asked about his future plans, one citizen, broken and ruined by financial setbacks one after another—closed mines, a poor harvest, an inability to get logs to the river due to a lack of ice—indicated his desire to return to the area of Marquette. When asked why, after all that has happened, he would wish to do so, his answer: "Because there is no other place quite like it."

12 May, 1899. The Palladium Superior.

Chapter Twenty-Four

Wolf prints surrounded his tracks in the snow. They flowed around the edges and overlay his own, paws and boots atop one another. He wove around and through the pines, staggering with exhaustion more than once. Alain felt as if his head had been packed with cotton. He followed the beam from his flashlight numbly, with no sense of time or what lay at the end of the trail. When the truck's lights appeared from the darkness it came as a surprise.

Stephanie and Chris stood at the rear of the bear trap. Chris had raised the gate. Alain could see bare feet inside the pipe.

Stephanie turned at his approach.

"Is he—" she began.

Alain held a finger to his lips. She nodded. Mama Bouche had said that the curse would be broken if they didn't mentioned it to Leon for a year and a day. No matter how much it sounded like something from a fairy tale, it seemed no more ridiculous than anything else. He owed that old woman a kiss. Maybe a shrimp dinner.

"I feel so funky," Leon said from inside the trap.

"Come on out," Chris said.

"No, you guys come in here," Leon said.

Alain stooped to peer into the trap. Leon lay curled on his side, naked, with his face against the metal, examining the surface of the pipe at a distance of a half-inch. He looked up.

"It goes all the way around," he told Alain solemnly.

"What's wrong with him?" Chris asked.

"He may still be a little high," Alain said. "I drugged him."

"Aren't you cold, buddy?" Alain asked.

"No way," Leon said. "I feel . . . I feel . . ." He squeezed his nose. "Holy shit, I can't feel my tongue."

"You need to come out and put some clothes on," Alain said. "There's a lady present."

Stephanie moved up behind him and rested a hand on the back of Alain's neck. The touch seemed to clear some of the cobwebs from his head.

"We should all get naked," Leon said. "It will be beautiful." His teeth began to chatter.

The three of them managed to coax him from the trap with promises of cheeseburgers. They tucked him into the truck with the heater running, wrapped in a wool blanket and happily humming along to some of Chris's heavy metal music.

"Do you have another blanket?" Alain asked Chris. They stood in a tight knot next to the truck as if not wanting to stray into the dark. No one said a word about wolves. "I have a second patient for you, but I think we'll need a stretcher."

"I have a tarp," Chris said.

"That'll work. I'd like to get the other one loaded as quick as possible, then you can get out of here," Alain said. "There are going to be enough questions as it is."

Bob had herded the kids out of the tower and back to the road near the beach by the time Alain reached it. His girls led the rest of the students back out to the trailhead, where the reinforcements had likely arrived. Alain made no attempt to influence what they might say if interviewed. At this point, it didn't seem to make a difference what might go into the official report. No one would believe it anyway.

He and Bob fashioned a stretcher for Daisy, who groaned when they rolled him onto it but wagged his tail weakly in appreciation. He sniffed at Alain's hand with great concern. Chris and Bob pronounced that the dog would live. They loaded him into Chris's truck and unhooked the trailer so the young ranger could get turned around on the narrow road.

"Give this to the veterinarian," Alain said. He dug out a credit card and gave it to Chris. "Tell them whatever he needs."

Chris examined the card before sliding it into his pocket.

"Who do I put down as the owner?" Chris asked.

Alain considered the sheer size of the beast.

"It's me," he said. "I'm responsible for him."

"Got something to show you," Bob said. He led Alain and Stephanie back to the site of the fight with Hell.

"I couldn't see it real clear," the old ranger said, "but it looked to me as if he fell near here, right?"

"Where's the body?" Stephanie asked. She glanced around into the dark and rubbed her arms.

The corpse of the wolf that had been Hell was missing. Alain distinctly remembered the feel of the throat under his fangs, the leg torn completely off. Those memories were fading though. It felt like something he'd seen in a movie, or that had happened to someone else.

"It didn't walk away," Alain said. "He couldn't have."

Bob knelt to illuminate with his flashlight a granite flagstone still set in place in what had been the floor of the hall.

The shape in the surface of the rock looked familiar. It had to be a natural phenomenon. Erosion, maybe, or something a kid had chipped or carved in an idle moment. It only resembled a cloven hoof-print sunk into the stone.

Alain wanted to say that it was coincidence. He held his tongue.

Stephanie poked Alain in the arm. "So where did all the other wolves come from?" she asked.

"I didn't see a single one," said Bob. "Aren't enough around here to make up what you saw, not from what Chris said."

"The call-blasting . . ." Alain said. It sounded stupid even to him. He'd seen hundreds of the animals. They way they'd swirled in their concentric circle, keeping the loup garou in the trap at their center, as if they'd come to take care of something. To right a wrong.

He had questions about what came next. What if it happened to him again? What if it didn't?

Stephanie caught his hand and twined her fingers through his.

As they hiked out to the trailhead, Alain ran through the list of things he still needed to do. Everyday stuff. He was walking back to normal, back to electric lights and warmth and video games. Back to Marquette, and paperwork, including one very long and mostly fictional case report. Back to his house, which needed a front door and maybe an exorcism if he ever wanted Stephanie to take her clothes off again.

It would be daylight soon, when old stories lost some of their power and evil was run-of-the-mill. Tomorrow would bring more crimes, more idiots. He still had a job to do, protecting Marquette, his own strange little town. These were his woods, his land, his people. His pack.